Rosamunde Pilcher h[...] [...]
career as a novelist an[...] [...] was her
phenomenally successful novel, *The Shell Seekers*, that
captured the hearts of all who read it, and won her
international recognition as one of the best-loved story-
tellers of our time. She now lives with her husband near
Dundee. They have four children and nine grandchildren. Her bestselling novels, *September* and *Coming
Home*, were made into television films. *Winter Solstice*,
her most recent bestseller, was also made into a television
film. She was awarded an O.B.E for services to literature
in 2002.

### Praise for Winter Solstice

'Rosamunde Pilcher's warm spell is charming and utterly
convincing'  *Daily Mail*

'An entrancing tale of middle-aged love, broken hearts
and teenage angst'  *Daily Express*

'Britain's most under-rated novelist'  *Sunday Times*

'Pilcher's strength is knowing what she can do well and
writing about what she knows. She has a way of tapping
into the emotional life of her readers and making them
care about characters not unlike themselves'
*Daily Telegraph*

# ROSAMUNDE PILCHER

# FLOWERS IN THE RAIN AND OTHER STORIES

HODDER

*In this second collection we have tried to select stories which present the same varied relationships and aspects of love which were incorporated in* The Blue Bedroom. *Emotions experienced not only by the very young and the young, but also by the older members of this extraordinary society in which we find ourselves.*

*For me, personally, each story has its own private significance.*
*For readers, I would like to think that they will not only follow honourably in the steps of* The Blue Bedroom, *but open new ground on their own account.*

Rosamunde Pilcher

# Contents

# FLOWERS IN THE RAIN
## and Other Stories

# ❧ *The Doll's House* ❧

Opening his eyes, William recognised the feel of Saturday morning in the lightness of the atmosphere, the ambience of freedom. From downstairs came the smell of frying bacon and, outside in the garden, Loden, the pet spaniel, began to bark. William stirred and reached for his wristwatch. It was eight o'clock.

Because there was no pressing urgency to be up and about he lay for a little, considering the day ahead. It was April, and a lozenge of sunlight lay across his carpet. The sky beyond the window was a pale, pellucid blue, traversed by slow-moving clouds. It was a day to be spent out of doors; the sort of day when his father would have collected the family together with a shout and an impetuous plan, piling them all into the car and driving them to the seaside, or up on to the moors for a long hike.

Most of the time William tried not to think too much about his father, but every now and then memories would come surging back like pictures, clean-cut and with very sharp edges. He would see his father striding up a bracken-covered slope, with Miranda on his shoulders because the climb was too steep for her short, fat legs; or hear his deep voice reading to them on winter evenings; or see his clever hands mending a bicycle or doing intricate things with electric plugs and fuse boxes.

He bit his lip and turned his head on the pillow, as though to turn from some unimaginable pain, but that was even

1

worse, because now he was confronted by the object which stood, accusing, on his work table at the other side of the room. Last night, when he had finished his homework, he had laboured upon this thing for an hour or more, and had finally climbed into bed knowing that it had defeated him.

Now, it seemed to his imagination, it openly sneered at him.

"You haven't a hope of enjoying yourself today," it whispered maliciously. "You're going to spend this Saturday wrestling with me. And you'll probably lose."

It was enough to make him despair. Twenty pounds it had cost him, and all he had to show for it was something that looked more like an orange box than anything else.

After a bit, he got out of bed and went across the room to examine it more closely, hoping that it would look better than he remembered. It didn't. A floor, a back, two sides; a pile of small pieces of wood about the size of nail-files, and a page of baffling instructions.

*Glue scotia angle to the top front edge of the front panel. Glue window jambs to inner head sills.*

It was meant to be a doll's house, a present for Miranda's seventh birthday, two weeks away. It was a secret, even from his mother. And he couldn't finish it because he was too clumsy or too stupid, or possibly both.

Miranda had always wanted a doll's house. Their father had promised that she would get it for her seventh birthday, and the fact that he was no longer there had made no difference to Miranda, who was too young to understand, too young to be told that she must learn to go without.

"I'm going to get a doll's house for my birthday," she boasted to her friends while they dressed up in tattered party clothes and old ostrich feathers and shoes sizes too big for them. "They promised."

2

William, worried by this, had a conference with his mother. This took place when they were alone, eating supper. Before his father died, William used to have high tea with Miranda and then watch television, but now, at twelve years old, he had been promoted. So, over the chops and broccoli and mashed potatoes, William said, "She thinks she's getting that doll's house. We must give her one. Daddy promised."

"I know. And he'd have bought her a beauty, no expense spared. But now we don't have that sort of money to spend on presents."

"What about a second-hand one?"

"Well, I'll look."

She looked. She found one in the local antique shop but it cost more than a hundred pounds. A second-hand dealer produced another, but it was so shabby that the thought of actually giving it to Miranda for her birthday was somehow an insult to the child's intelligence. Together, William and his mother cased the toy shops, but the doll's houses there were horrible plastic things with pretend doors and windows that didn't open.

"Perhaps we should wait for another year," his mother suggested. "It would give us more time to save up."

But William knew that it had to be this year. If they let Miranda down now, he knew that she would probably never trust an adult again. Besides, they owed it to his father.

And then the answer came. By chance he saw the advertisement on the back page of the Sunday newspaper.

*Build your own traditional doll's house from one of our kits. Full instructions so simple a child could follow them. Special*

3

*offer, open for only two weeks. £19.50 including post and packing.*

He read this and then, more carefully, read it again. There were snags. For one thing, woodwork was not his strong point. Top of his class in English and History, he nevertheless found it well-nigh impossible to hammer a nail home straight. For another, there was the question of money. He was saving his pocket money to buy a calculator.

But needs must when the devil drives. The instructions were so simple a child could follow them. And he could probably manage for a little longer without the calculator. He made up his mind; wrote out the order form; bought a postal order and sent away for the doll's house kit.

He didn't tell his mother what he had done. Each morning he got up early and went downstairs to intercept the postman before she should see the parcel. When at last it came, he carried it straight up to his bedroom and hid it under the wardrobe. That evening he took a deep breath, found a hammer and set to work.

To begin with it wasn't too bad, and he got the main part of the house together. But then the problems started; there was a diagram for fitting the windows into their apertures, but the instructions might have been written in double Dutch.

William turned from the maddening object, got dressed and went downstairs to find something to eat.

As he crossed the hall the telephone rang, and he picked up the receiver.

"Hello."

"William?"

"Yes." He made a private face. It was Arnold Ridgeway, and Arnold, he knew, rather fancied William's mother.

Although William could understand this, he found Arnold's company fairly heavy weather. Arnold was a widower and very cheerful and noisy in a hail-fellow-well-met sort of way. Lately, William had begun to suspect that Arnold had private plans to marry his mother, but he hoped very much that this wouldn't happen. His mother did not love Arnold. There was a certain look about her that only happened every now and then – a secret radiance – and William hadn't seen this since his father died. It was certainly never evident when she was in Arnold's company.

There was, however, always the possibility that Arnold might wear her down with the sheer force of his personality, and she would marry him for the comfort and security of his worldly goods. She would do such a thing for his sake and for Miranda's, he knew. For her children she would be prepared to make any sacrifice.

"Arnold here! How's your mother this morning?"

"I haven't seen her yet."

"Such a lovely day. Thought I might take you all out for lunch. Drive you over to Cottescombe, have lunch at the Three Bells. We could go and look at the Game Park. How does that sound to you?"

"It sounds great, but I think I'd better get my mother." Then he remembered the doll's house. "But I don't think I can come. It's very kind of you, but I've got, well, lots of homework to do, and things like that."

"That's a pity. Never mind. Another time. Fetch your mother, there's a good boy."

He put down the receiver and went into the kitchen. "That's Arnold on the phone . . ."

She was sitting at the table, drinking coffee and reading the morning paper. She wore her old turquoise wool dressing-gown and her beautiful red hair lay like silk down to her shoulders.

"Oh, thank you, darling." She stood up, laying aside the

paper, and brushed his head with her hand as she went out of the room.

Miranda was eating her boiled egg.

"Hello, Bootface," William greeted her and went to the hot drawer to find his breakfast. It was bacon and sausage and egg.

"What does Arnold want?" Miranda asked.

"Inviting us all out for lunch."

She was immediately interested. "To a restaurant?" She was a sociable child, and loved eating out.

"That's the idea."

"Oh, good." When their mother returned: "Are we going?" she asked at once.

"If you'd like to, Miranda. Arnold thought Cottescombe would be fun."

William said, shortly, "I can't come."

"Oh, darling, do. It's such a lovely day."

"I've got things I have to do. I'll be all right."

She didn't argue. She knew, of course, that there was a secret up in his bedroom, but it was always carefully dust-sheeted when she went up to make his bed, and he knew that she was too highly principled ever to peep.

She sighed. "All right. We'll leave you behind. You can have a peaceful day on your own." She picked up the newspaper again. "The Manor House has been sold."

"How do you know?"

"It's here in the paper. It's been bought by a man called Geoffrey Wray. He's the new manager of that electronics factory in Tryford. See for yourself . . ."

She handed the newspaper over to him and William read the item with some interest. The Manor House used to belong to Miss Pritchett, and this house, the one in which

William and his mother and Miranda lived, had once been the gate lodge of the Manor, so whoever bought the big house would be their nearest neighbour.

Old Miss Pritchett had been an excellent neighbour, allowing them to use her garden as a short-cut to the common and the hills beyond, and letting the children pick apples and plums in her orchard. But old Miss Pritchett had died three months ago and since then the house had stood empty.

But now ... the manager of the electronics factory! William made a face.

His mother laughed. "What's that for?"

"Bet he looks like an adding machine."

"We'd better not go through the garden any longer. Not until we're invited to."

"He probably won't ever invite us!"

"You mustn't have preconceived ideas. He might have a wife and a lot of children for you to make friends with."

William worked all morning on the doll's house. At twelve, his mother tapped at his door and he went out on to the landing, carefully closing the door behind him.

"We're just off, William. There's a shepherd's pie in the oven for your lunch. And take Loden for a walk if you've time."

"I will."

"But don't go through the Manor House garden."

The front door closed and he was alone. Reluctantly he went back to his task. He had made the staircase, gluing each little tread carefully into place, but for some reason it was a fraction too wide to fit into place.

He went back, for the thousandth time, to the instruction sheet.

*Glue stair treads to base. Glue second mid wall to base.*

He had done all that. And still the stairs wouldn't fit. If only he had someone to ask, but the only person he could think of was his woodwork teacher whom he didn't much like.

Suddenly, he longed for his father. His father would have known exactly what to do, would have taken over, reassured, explained, eased the little staircase into place.

Horrified, unable to do anything about it, he felt the lump grow in his throat and the half-finished doll's house and all its attendant bits-and-pieces were dissolved, lost, in a flood of tears. He hadn't cried for years, and was appalled at his own childishness.

He found a handkerchief and blew his nose, wiped away the shameful tears. Beyond the open window he saw the warm spring day beckoning to him. He thought, 'Oh, to blazes with the doll's house,' and was out of the room and down the stairs before he had even thought about it, whistling for Loden.

When he could run no further, and was panting and gasping, and had a stitch, it was better. He felt refreshed. He bent double to relieve the stitch, to embrace Loden and bury his face in the dog's thick dark coat.

When he had got his breath back he straightened up, and it was only then that he realised he had forgotten his mother's stricture and his feet, in their headlong escape, had carried him quite naturally through the gates of the Manor House and halfway up the drive. For a moment he hesitated, but the prospect of retracing his steps and going around by the road was too tedious for words. Besides, the house had only just been sold. There would be nobody there. Not yet.

He was wrong. As he came round the last curve of the

lane, he saw the car parked in front of the house. The front door was open and a tall man on the point of emerging, with a dog at his side. Immediately, all was lost. Miss Pritchett had not owned a dog, and Loden considered this his garden.

Dark mutterings sounded in Loden's throat, but the other dog was already bounding towards them, a friendly-looking Labrador, ready and waiting for a game.

Loden growled again. "Loden!" William jerked his collar. The growl changed to a whine. The Labrador approached and the dogs tentatively sniffed at each other. Loden's hackles subsided, his tail began to wag. Cautiously, William released him, and the two dogs began to romp. So that was all right. Now he had to deal with the Labrador's owner. He looked up. The man was coming towards him. A tall man, with a pleasantly weather-beaten look, as though he spent much time out of doors. The wind ruffled his greying hair. He wore spectacles and a blue sweater and carried a clipboard.

William said, "Good morning."

The man looked at his watch. "Actually, it's good afternoon. Half past one. What are you doing?"

"I'm taking my dog for a walk over the common and up on to the hill. I always used to come this way when Miss Pritchett was alive." He enlarged on this. "I live in the lodge at the bottom of the road."

"What's your name?"

"William Radlett. I saw in the paper this morning that this house had been sold, but I didn't think there'd be anybody here."

"Just looking around," said the man. "Taking a few measurements. My name's Geoffrey Wray."

"Oh, so you . . . ?" He felt himself grow red in the face. "But you . . ." He had almost said, 'you don't look like an adding machine.' "I'm afraid I'm trespassing," he mumbled.

"No matter," said Mr Wray. "I'm not living here yet. As I said, just taking a few measurements." He turned to look back at the worn fabric of the face of the house. As though seeing it for the first time, William noticed the rotting trellis which supported the upper balcony, the blistered paintwork and broken guttering.

He said, "I suppose it will need a lot done to it. It's a bit old-fashioned."

"Yes, but charming. And most of it I can do myself. It'll take time, but that's half the fun." The two dogs were by now quite at ease with each other, chasing around the rhododendron bushes, searching for rabbits. "They've made friends," observed Mr Wray. "How about you? I was just going to have a picnic. Like to share it?"

William remembered the shepherd's pie uneaten, and realised that he was ravenously hungry. "Have you got enough?"

"I imagine so. Let's go and look."

He took a basket from the back seat of his car and carried this to the wrought-iron garden seat which stood by the front door. In the sun and out of the wind, it was quite warm. William accepted a ham sandwich.

"There's a fruit cake too. My mother makes excellent fruit cake."

"Do you live with her?"

"For the moment. Until I come to live here."

"Are you going to live here alone?"

"I'm not married, if that's what you mean."

"My mother thought you might have a wife and children for us to make friends with."

He smiled. "Who's us?"

"Miranda and me. She's nearly seven."

"Where is she today?"

"She and my mother have gone out for lunch."

"Does your father work in the town?"

"I haven't got a father. He died nearly a year ago."

"I am sorry." He sounded genuinely sympathetic but, blessedly, not in the least embarrassed by William's revelation. "I lost my father when I was about your age. Nothing's ever quite the same again, is it?"

"No, it's not the same."

"How about a chocolate biscuit?" He held out a packet. William took one and looked up, straight into Mr Wray's eyes, and suddenly smiled, for no particular reason except that he felt comforted and at ease, and – last, but not least – not hungry any longer.

❧

When they had finished the picnic they went indoors and explored the house. Without furniture, smelling chill and slightly damp, it could have been depressing, but it wasn't. On the contrary, it was rather exciting and flattering to be discussing plans as though he was a grown-up.

"I thought I'd take this wall down, make a big open-plan kitchen. Fit an Aga in here, and build pine fitments around that corner."

Mr Wray's enthusiasm dispelled the gloom even of the kitchen, which smelt of cold and mice.

"And this old scullery I'll turn into a workshop, with the work-bench here under the window, and plenty of space for hanging tools and storing stuff."

"My father had a workshop, but it was in a shed in the garden."

"I expect you use it now."

"No. I'm not very good with my hands."

"It's amazing what you can do if you have to."

"That's what I thought," said William impulsively, and then stopped.

"What did you think?" Mr Wray prompted gently.

"I thought I could do something because I had to. But I can't. It's too difficult."

"What would you be trying to do?"

"Build a doll's house from a kit. For my sister's birthday."

"What's gone wrong?"

"Everything. I'm stuck. I can't get the staircase to fit, and I can't work out how to put the window frames together."

"I hope you don't mind me asking," said Mr Wray politely, "but if woodwork isn't your particular scene, why did you embark on this in the first place?"

"Miranda was promised a doll's house by my father. And they're too expensive to buy. I really thought I could do it," he added, making a clean breast of his own stupidity. "And it cost twenty pounds!"

"Couldn't your mother help you?"

"I want it to be a surprise."

"Isn't there anyone you could ask?"

"Not really."

Mr Wray turned and leaned against the old sink, his arms folded. "How about me?" he asked.

William looked up at him, frowning. "You'd help me?"

"Why not?"

"This afternoon? Now?"

"Good a time as any."

William was flooded with gratitude. "Would you really? It won't take long. No more than half-an-hour . . ."

*~≫⌇≪~*

But it took a great deal longer than half-an-hour. The instructions had to be carefully studied, the little staircase sandpapered down and fitted into place. Then, on a clean sheet of newspaper, Mr Wray placed all the little pieces of wood in order, arranged into five small window surrounds, ready to be glued.

"You fit the glass in first, and then the frames fit round it, and keep it in place. Just like an ordinary window."

"Oh, I see."

Like all things, once explained, it became marvellously simple.

They worked on, companionably, and so preoccupied was William, so involved, that he didn't hear the car coming up the road and stopping at the gate. The first inkling that he had of his mother's return was the sound of the front door opening and her voice calling to him.

"William!"

He looked at his watch and was astonished to see that it was nearly five.

He sprang to his feet. "That's my mother."

Mr Wray smiled. "So I guessed."

"We'd better go down. And, Mr Wray, don't say anything."

"I won't."

"And thank you so much for helping me."

He went from the room, and hung over the landing banister. Mother and sister stood below in the hall, their faces turned up towards him. His mother carried an enormous bunch of daffodils, wrapped in pale blue tissue paper, and Miranda clutched a new doll.

"Did you have a good time?" he asked.

"Lovely. William, there's a car outside with a dog in it."

"It's Mr Wray's. He's here." He turned as Geoffrey Wray emerged from the bedroom, closing the door behind him, and came to stand beside William. "You know," William went on. "He's bought the Manor House."

His mother's smile became a little fixed as she gazed in

some astonishment at the tall stranger who had so unexpectedly appeared. William hastily filled in the ensuing silence with explanations. "We met this afternoon, and he came home with me to give me a hand with ... well, with something."

"Oh ..." With a visible effort, she collected herself. "Mr Wray, how very kind."

"Not at all, it's been a pleasure," he told her in his deep voice, and went down the stairs to meet her. "After all, we're going to be neighbours."

His hand was outstretched. "Yes. Yes, of course." Confused still, she juggled the daffodils into her left arm and took the proffered hand.

"And this must be Miranda?"

"Arnold bought me a new doll," Miranda told him. "She's called Priscilla."

"But ..." William's mother had still not quite got the hang of the situation. "How did you meet William?"

Before Mr Wray had time to answer this, William began to explain. "I forgot about not going through the garden, and Mr Wray was there. We ate his picnic lunch together."

"What happened to the shepherd's pie?"

"I forgot that, too."

For some reason this broke the ice, and suddenly they were all smiling.

"Well, have you had tea?" his mother asked. "No? Neither have we and I'm longing for a cup. Come into the sitting-room, Mr Wray, and I'll go and put the kettle on."

"I'll do it," said William, running down the stairs. "I'll get the tea."

In the kitchen he laid a tray, found some biscuits in a tin, filled the kettle. Waiting for this to boil, he went, with some satisfaction, over the events of the day. The problem of the doll's house was now solved; he knew what he had to do, and he would finish it in good time for Miranda's birthday. And Mr Wray was coming to live at the Manor House, and he was not the walking adding machine that William feared, but the nicest person he had met in years. He was willing to bet they would be allowed to walk through the garden, just as they had done in Miss Pritchett's day.

And so, with one thing and another, he felt better about life than he had for a long time. The kettle boiled and he filled the teapot, set it on the tray and carried it through to the sitting-room. From the back room came the sound of the television which Miranda was watching, and from the sitting-room a steady, comforting murmur of voices.

"When will you move in?"

"As soon as possible."

"You'll have a lot to do."

"There's a lot of time. All the time in the world."

He pushed the door open with his foot. The room was filled with evening sunlight and there was something in the air so tangible it could almost be touched. Friendship, maybe. Ease. But excitement, too.

All the time in the world.

They stood by the fireplace, half-turned towards the newly kindled flames, but he could see his mother's face reflected in the mirror which hung over the mantelpiece. Suddenly she laughed, though at what he could not guess, and tossed back her lovely red hair, and there was that look about her . . . the old glowing look that he hadn't seen since his father died.

His imagination bolted ahead like a runaway horse, only to be reined firmly in and brought to a halt. It wasn't any good making plans. Things had to happen at their own speed, in their own time.

"Tea's ready," he told them and set down the tray. As he

straightened up he caught sight of the daffodils, lying on the window-seat where his mother had tossed them down. The tissue paper was crushed and the delicate petals beginning to wilt, and William thought of Arnold, and had it in his heart to be very sorry for him.

# Endings and Beginnings

Tom said, without much hope, "You could come with me this weekend."

Elaine gave a derisory laugh. "Darling, can you see me freezing in a castle in Northumberland?"

"Not really," he admitted, with honesty.

"Besides, I haven't been invited."

"That wouldn't matter. Aunt Mabel would love a new face around the place. Particularly one as attractive as yours."

Elaine tried hard not to look pleased. She adored compliments and absorbed them as blotting paper absorbs ink. "Flattery will get you nowhere," she told him. "And I'm very cross. You were meant to be coming down to the Stainforths' with me this weekend. What am I going to tell them?"

"Tell them the truth. That I've got to go north for my Aunt Mabel's seventy-fifth birthday party."

"But why do you have to go?"

He explained again, patiently. "Because somebody's got to put in an appearance, and my parents are in Majorca, and my married sister's living in Hong Kong. I've told you that three times."

"I still don't see why you have to leave me in the lurch like this. I don't like it." She gave him one of her most persuasive smiles. "I'm not used to it."

"I wouldn't leave you in the lurch," he assured her, "for

anyone in the world but Aunt Mabel. But she's a very special old girl. Her husband, Ned, died some years ago and she doesn't have any children of her own. She was always so marvellous to us when we were young, and she must have had to go to a lot of effort to organise any sort of shindig. I think it's very plucky of her. It would be churlish if I didn't turn up. Besides," he finished in truth, "I want to be there." He said again, "You could come with me."

"I shouldn't know anybody."

"You would, after you'd been there for five minutes."

"Anyway, I hate being cold."

He stopped trying to persuade her. It was always fun taking Elaine to places and introducing her around to his awestruck acquaintances. She was so sensational to look at that Tom's own self-esteem took a welcome boost. On the other hand, if she was not having a good time, she would make no effort to hide the fact.

Staying with Aunt Mabel was always a bit dicey. One's well-being and comfort depended heavily on the state of the weather, and if the coming weekend turned chilly or damp then Elaine, hothouse London flower, might turn out to be the worst possible companion.

Tom put his hand over hers. "All right," he said. "You don't have to come. I'll ring you when I get back and tell you all about it. And you'll just have to say I'm sorry to the Stainforths."

The next day was Friday. Tom, who had already squared things with his boss, left the office at lunchtime and headed north up the motorway. As he drove he was able to allow his thoughts a free rein. Inevitably they chose to chew over the problem of Elaine.

He had known her now for three months and, despite the fact that she frequently exasperated him, she was nevertheless the most engaging person he had met in years. Her very unpredictability he found delightfully stimulating, and she never failed to make him laugh. Because of this, he had taken her home once or twice for long weekends, not anticipating that his mother would find Elaine just as attractive as he did.

"She's perfectly charming," she kept saying, but she was a model mother and managed, with obvious effort, not to say more.

Tom, however, knew very well what she was thinking. He was, after all, nearly thirty. It was time that he settled down, got himself married, provided his mother with the grandchildren that she craved. But did he want to marry Elaine? It was a dilemma that had been teasing him for some time. Perhaps getting away from her for a little while would be the best thing that could happen. He could view the problem at a distance, as though he were studying some complicated painting; get the details of their relationship into a true perspective. The best way to start doing this was to stop thinking about her, so he put visions of Elaine firmly out of his mind, and concentrated instead on the weekend which lay ahead.

Northumberland. Kinton. Aunt Mabel's party. Who would be there? Tom was the sole representative of his side of the family, but what about all the other cousins? All Ned's young relations, who had formed the larger part of that gang of children who had run wild at Kinton when they were all young? He ran a mental finger down an imaginary list. Roger was a soldier. Anne married and with a family. Young Ned was in Australia. Kitty ... Putting on speed to overtake a thundering lorry, Tom found himself smiling. Kitty was Ned's great-niece. Kitty the rebel, the one who led the way. Kitty, who fell out of the tree-house. Kitty, who organised the skating party the night the lake was frozen. Kitty, who slept out on the battlements because one of the others had dared her, and because she thought she might see a ghost.

The rest of them over the years had, more or less, conformed. Taken typing courses and become secretaries. Been articled to chartered accountants or solicitors and finally qualified. Joined the Services. Kitty had conformed to nothing. In desperation her parents had sent her to a French family in Paris as an *au pair*, but after Madame had found her being passionately embraced by Monsieur, she was given – unfairly, everybody agreed – the sack.

"Come home," her frantic mother had cabled her, but Kitty didn't come home. She hitched a lift to the South of France where she met up with a most unsuitable – everybody agreed again – man.

He was called Terence, a wild Irishman from County Cork, and he ran a yacht charter service out of St Tropez. For a while Kitty had chartered yachts with him, and then brought him back to England to meet her parents. The opposition to him had been so deadly and so absolute that the inevitable happened and Kitty married him.

"But why?" Tom had asked his mother when he heard this incredible news.

"I've no idea," said his mother. "You know Kitty better than I do."

"She was the sort of person," Tom had told her, "that you could lead with a carrot, but who wouldn't respond to the spur."

Once, on the way back to London after a weekend in Sussex, he had gone to see Kitty and her husband; they lived on a houseboat and Kitty was pregnant. The boat, and Kitty, had both been in such a state of shambles that Tom, without having meant to, asked Kitty and her husband out for dinner. It had been a disastrous evening. Terence had got drunk; Kitty had talked, non-stop, as though she had been wound up; and Tom had said scarcely anything at all. He simply listened, paid the bill, and helped Kitty get Terence back on board. Then he had left her and driven back to

London. Later he heard that the baby had been a boy.

Once, when he was in his teens, Mabel had told Tom that he should marry Kitty. He had bucked from the very idea, partly because she was like a sister to him, and partly because he was embarrassed, at nineteen, even to be talking about such things.

"Why do you say that?" he had asked Mabel.

"You're the only person she's ever taken any notice of. If you told her to do something, or not to do it, then she'd behave herself. Of course those parents of hers have never known how to deal with her."

"She's so bouncy, she'd wear me out," Tom had said. He was just going to Cambridge and bouncy sixteen-year-olds like Kitty had no place in his plans.

"She won't always be bouncy," Aunt Mabel had pointed out. "One day she'll be beautiful."

The road unrolled like a great grey ribbon behind him. He was through Newcastle and now deep into Northumberland. He left the motorway and headed into the country, through hilly moorland and small stone villages, and down steep avenues of beech. By now it was late afternoon. The sun was setting in a blaze of pink, casting rosy shadows on the undersides of large, wet-looking clouds.

He came at last to Kinton, rounded the squat, square-towered church and the main street of the village stretched before him. It was an unremarkable street: two rows of small houses, little shops, a pub. It could have been anywhere. Except that, at the far end of this street, a cobbled ramp climbed a grassy slope and passed beneath the arch of a magnificent gatehouse. Beyond the gatehouse was a high-walled courtyard as big as a rugger pitch and on the far side of this stood the castle. Four storeys high, square and turreted with pepper-pot towers; romantic, unexpected, incongruous.

This was the home of Tom's redoubtable Aunt Mabel.

The older sister of Tom's father, horse-mad, leathery and down-to-earth, Mabel had never been expected to find a husband. But when she was approaching thirty, love – or something very like it – had struck. She had met Ned Kinnerton, and was married to him within the month.

The members of her family had been, by all accounts, torn between delight and horror.

"Isn't it marvellous that she's found a husband at last?"

"He's twice her age."

"She's going to have to go and live in an enormous, unheated castle in Northumberland."

But Mabel loved Kinton as much as Ned did. Their union had not been blessed with children but, as though to make up for this slip of nature, a selection of nephews and nieces descended upon Mabel and Ned for their school holidays. Mabel never minded what anybody did, provided no one was ever unkind to an animal. So, unchecked, they climbed battlements, slept out in a make-shift tent beneath the cedar tree, poured make-believe boiling oil from the slit window over the massive front door, swam in the reedy lake, contrived bows and arrows, fell out of trees.

After Ned died, everyone imagined that Mabel would move out of Kinton. But the only male relation who might have been capable of shouldering the massive responsibility of the castle had already taken off for Australia and was making a good life for himself there, and so Mabel remained. "Don't need to heat all the rooms," she pointed out and shut off the attics by means of draping thick, woolly blankets across the tops of the circular stairs.

Apart from that, life carried on as before. Still castlefuls of children – now in their teens and fast growing up. Still immense meals at the long mahogany dining-table. Still dogs everywhere, smouldering log fires, tattered snapshots stuck into the frames of mirrors.

Kinton. Tom had arrived. He eased the car gently up the cobbled ramp, passed beneath the shadowed arch of the gatehouse.

On the far side was an immense, ragged lawn. The road separated, and ran around this on both sides, to meet again in front of the massive door. The encircling walls were part of the most ancient remains of the castle, and the crevices between their stones sprouted with wild valerian and wall-flowers.

Tom parked the car and got out. The evening air smelt sweet and fresh but was cold after London. He went up the steps and grappled with the huge wrought-iron latch of the front door, and it swung slowly inwards, creaking slightly like a door in a horror film. Inside, the high, unheated hallway struck with a damp chill. The floors were stone, an immense fireplace stood flanked by dusty armour and crowned with a ring of ancient swords. He crossed this hallway and went through another set of doors, and now it was as though he had left the Middle Ages behind him, and was stepping into the Italian Renaissance.

When he had first come to Kinton as a small boy, expecting only spiral staircases and secret passages and small, darkly-panelled rooms, he had been flummoxed by all this opulence. He had looked forward to living in a medieval castle and felt slightly cheated. But when questioned, Ned had explained to him that one of Ned's Victorian forebears had taken as his wife a lady of great wealth, and one of her conditions for marrying him was that she should be allowed a free hand with the interior of the castle.

She had subsequently spent five years and a great deal of money in transforming Kinton into a showpiece of pseudo-Renaissance splendour. Interior walls, as much as possible, were ripped away. Architects devised the enormous curving stairway, the wide, panelled passageways, the delicately arched and pillared windows.

An Italian was imported from Florence to design and paint the highly decorated ceilings and to transform the walls of the heiress's boudoir, by means of a *trompe l'oeil* mural, into a Mediterranean terrace, complete with plaster troughs of scarlet geraniums.

After all this structural work had been completed, it was still another six months before the young couple were able to take up residence. Wallpapers were chosen, curtains hung, new carpets laid in all the rooms. The Kinnerton portraits were hung on the dining-room walls, family mementoes were displayed in glass-fronted cabinets.

But since those days of mad extravagance, nothing very much had been done to Kinton. Nothing had been changed or renewed, although from time to time various articles might be glued or nailed together, mended, repainted, or patched.

Fires smouldered in the grates of sitting-rooms, but the passages and bedrooms at Kinton were apt to be piercingly cold.

There was a smell: musty, familiar, dear. Tom ran up the curve of the staircase, taking the steps two at a time, his hand brushing lightly against the mahogany rail that had been polished to a sheen by generations of hands. At the top, he paused on the wide landing and listened. There was no definite sound, but he knew that Mabel would be somewhere around.

He found her in the library, wearing an apron and a hat, surrounded by the usual army of old and faithful dogs, as well as a litter of newspaper and flower stalks. She was constructing, in a priceless Chinese bowl, an elaborate arrangement of flowers.

"Oh, my dear."

She laid down her secateurs and enfolded him in her embrace, which was something of an experience as she was as tall as Tom and twice as wide. Then she stood back, holding him at arm's length.

Her face, he had always thought, was a man's face: strong-featured, large-nosed, square-chinned. This masculinity was emphasised by her uncompromising coiffure, her grey hair drawn tightly back and screwed into a straggling bun.

She said, "You're looking marvellous. Did you have a good journey? How splendid of you to come. Look at me, trying to make the place look presentable for tomorrow night. Can't describe to you what it has been like. Eustace – you remember my old gardener – he's been in, shoving furniture around, and his wife's polished everything in sight, including the dogs' bowls, and the kitchen's full of caterers. Hardly know my own house. How's your mother and father?"

She picked up her secateurs and went on with her task while Tom, leaning up against a table, with his hands in his pockets, told her.

"Wretched creatures," she remarked, "going off to Majorca at a time like this. I really wanted them to be here. There!" She inserted the last flower and stood back to admire the finished result.

"Aunt Mabel, isn't all this a frightful lot of work for you?"

"No, not really. I just tell people to do things and they do them. It's called delegating. And we're not having a proper orchestra. Nobody knows how to waltz these days, so I've ordered a disco."

"Where's it going to be?"

"In the old nursery. We emptied it of all the old toys and the doll's house and the books, and Kitty's decorating it to look like a jungle."

After a bit, Tom said, "Kitty?"

"Yes. Kitty. Our Kitty."

"She's here?"

"Of course she's here."

"But the last time I saw her — she was living on a houseboat."

"Oh, dear, you're very out of date. That marriage broke up. She got a divorce."

"What happened to Terence?"

"I think he went back to the South of France."

"And the little boy?"

"He's with Kitty."

"Is she staying here?"

"No, she lives at Caxford." Caxford was a village out on the moor, a few miles from Kinton. "She came to stay with me after the divorce, and then she bought this derelict cottage. Heaven knows what with, she doesn't appear to have two brass farthings to rub together. Anyway, she bought it and told us all that she was going to do it up and live there. With that, the council slapped a preservation order on it. I thought that would be the end of it, but she managed to get quite a good grant, and she's been there ever since, living in a caravan with Crispin."

"Crispin?"

"The boy. Nice little chap."

"But what is she going to do with herself?" Tom asked.

"Oh, goodness knows. You remember what Kitty was like, once she'd got the bit between her teeth, you could never get a word of sense out of her. Do you want tea?"

"No, I'm fine."

"I'll give you a drink later on." She began to clear up the

litter of her flower arrangement, but as she did this, a knock came at the door, and an unknown head appeared.

"Mrs Kinnerton, it's the man with the glasses. Where do you want them to go?"

"Oh, dear life, if it isn't one thing it's another! Tidy this up for me, would you, Tom, and put a log on the fire . . ."

And she took herself off.

Tom was left in the empty room. He dutifully threw a few dead flower stalks into the fire, added some logs and then went off to find Kitty.

The old nursery at Kinton was situated at some distance from the main rooms, and shut off from them by a swinging door studded in red baize. It was contained within the walls of one of the many towers and so was round, with two low-arched windows, and this in itself had made it fascinatingly attractive to small children. Now it stood empty. The ceiling and the walls, however, had been draped with garden netting suspended from a central fixture in the roof, and this netting was woven with long strands of trailing ivy and sprays of evergreen.

As well, there was a tall pair of steps and on the top of these, with pliers gripped between her teeth and a ball of green string in her hands, was a tall and slender girl, her blonde hair scraped back into a ponytail and a look of agonised concentration on her face as she struggled with a recalcitrant branch of spruce.

As he came into the room, she took the pliers from her mouth and, without looking at him, said, "If somebody would just get this ivy out of my face . . ."

"Hello, Kitty," said Tom.

She turned, at some peril to her own safety, and looked down at him. The spruce branch fell to the floor and the ivy wound itself around her neck like some pagan wreath. After a few seconds she said, "Tom."

"You seem to be having a good time up there."

"I'm having a miserable time. I can't get anything to stay in place."

"It looks fine to me."

Cautiously, she disentangled herself from the ivy, tucked it away in the folds of the netting and then turned around and sat on the top step, facing him.

She said, "I knew you would be coming. Aunt Mabel told me."

"I didn't know you were here."

"Nice surprise for you."

"You're thin. It suits you."

"That's all my hard work. Have you heard about my house?"

"Mabel just told me. She told me about the divorce too. I'm sorry."

"I'm not. The whole thing was a ghastly mistake and one that I should never have made." She shrugged. "But you know me, Tom. If ever there was a stupid thing to do, then I did it."

"Where's your little boy?"

"Around the place somewhere."

She was wearing a dirty old pair of jeans and blue canvas sneakers. Her sweater was so old as to be ragged. There was a hole in one sleeve, and Kitty's elbow protruded from this. Looking up at her, he realised how much she had changed. Where once cheeks had curved above that stubborn chin, bones and planes and angles now showed. There were lines about her mouth, but the shape of that mouth was the same, with laughter hovering, and a dimple which appeared when she smiled.

She smiled now. Her eyes were intensely blue. He dragged his gaze away from her and searched for other things to talk about. He saw the complicated contrivance of garden net and greenery. "Did you do all this yourself?"

"Most of it. Eustace helped me get the netting up. It's going to be a disco. Isn't Mabel a marvel? Imagine having a disco at your seventy-fifth birthday party!"

"You've made a good job of it. It looks very night-clubby."

She said, rather wistfully, "How's London nowadays?"

"Same as ever."

"Have you still got the same job? With the insurance people?"

"So far."

"So far so good. And how's your love life? Isn't it time you were getting married? Not that I'm much of an example to follow."

"My love life is doing very nicely, thank you."

"I'm glad to hear it. Here!"

He caught the pliers that she threw to him, and the ball of string, and then went to hold the step-ladder steady while Kitty descended.

"Tell me about your house."

"Nothing to tell, really. We're living in a caravan."

"Will you show me the house?"

"Of course I will. You can come and see me tomorrow. I'll probably give you a job of work to do."

"Do you think if we went and made the right sort of noises somebody would give us a cup of tea?"

They turned off the light and made their way back across the landing and through the big door that led to the kitchen. Here a couple of stalwart ladies were engaged in every sort of culinary preparation for the party the following day. A roasted turkey was just coming out of the oven; egg whites were beating in an electric mixer; soup steamed in an enormous pan. In the middle of all this, at the end of the long table, eating pastry scraps, sat Crispin. He looked amazingly like Kitty.

She introduced him.

"This is Tom, and he's a sort of cousin. I don't know whether you call him Tom or Uncle Tom or Cousin Tom or what."

"Just Tom," he said, pulling out a chair and sitting down. Kitty had joined the stalwart ladies at the other end of the kitchen.

"We live in a caravan," Crispin told him.

"I know."

"We're going to live in a house."

"I've been hearing about it. I'm going to come and see it."

"You're not allowed to walk on the floor because it's all sticky. Mummy's been varnishing it . . ."

"It'll be dry by now."

Kitty had wandered back again to inform them that a tray of tea had been taken into the library, so they trooped off and found Aunt Mabel sitting by the fire, sharing ginger-bread with four tail-waving dogs.

Tom slept that night in a brass bedstead, in a bedroom that had only a single dim light hanging from the middle of the ceiling and a howling draught which whistled across the floorboards. Investigation disclosed the fact that this was coming from a hole in the roof of an adjoining tower room, where a row of coat hooks and some wire hangers indicated that this was the closet where he was expected to put his clothes. Tom, unpacking, did this, got into his pyjamas and then made the long journey to the nearest bathroom in order to clean his teeth. Finally he got into bed. The sheets were linen, much darned and icy to touch, the pillowcase so heavily embroidered he knew that he would awake in the morning with the pattern embossed upon his cheek.

It rained in the night. He awoke and lay listening to it; first a patter of drops and then a steady drumming on the roof and then, inevitably, the drip, drip, drip of the leak in the tower room. He lay and thought about his dinner jacket hanging there, and wondered whether he should get up and rescue it, and then decided that he couldn't be bothered to leave his bed. He thought about Mabel, and tried to imagine how much longer she could continue to live in this vast and primitive place. He thought about Kitty and Crispin, cosy and warm in their caravan. He thought about Elaine and was glad, under such circumstances, that she had decided not to accompany him. He thought about Kitty again. That face . . . the mouth with the dimple when she smiled. Still thinking about Kitty, he went to sleep, lulled by the peaceful sound of the rain.

It had stopped raining by the morning. Tom awoke late and came downstairs to find a plate of bacon and eggs kept warm in the oven, and a flurry of domestic activity already in progress. Chairs were being shunted to and fro, crates of glasses manhandled up the stairs, tables set out, draped in immense damask cloths unused for years. Small vans burst into the forecourt through the arch of the gatehouse, to park at the front door and unload pot-plants, piles of plates, crates of wine, trays of freshly baked rolls.

One particularly disreputable van disgorged two long-haired young men and all the trappings of the disco. Tom left them, twined about with electrical wires, to set up their speakers and woofers and tweeters. Then, when he asked for a job to do, he was given the exhausting task of carrying big sackfuls of logs up the back stairs, as fuel for the many open fires.

Aunt Mabel was everywhere, large-footed, wrapped in a hessian garden apron, apparently tireless. On his fourth trip upstairs with a sack of logs on his back, Tom came upon her on the kitchen landing, peacefully mixing up dinners for her vast entourage of dogs as though it were the most important task of the day.

He set down his sack and straightened his aching shoulders.

"This is worse than the salt mines. How many more of these do I have to bring up?"

"Oh, my darling, I'm sure you've brought enough. I didn't realise you were still doing it. I thought you'd stopped."

He laughed. "Nobody told me to stop."

"Well, stop now. Stop doing anything. There's nothing more to do, and if there is, somebody else can do it." She looked at the massive watch on her wrist. "Go and buy yourself a drink in the pub. And have something to eat as well. The caterer doesn't provide luncheon, and I daren't go into the kitchen and cook for you, I'm sure I'd be turned out."

"I thought," said Tom, "I might drive over and see Kitty's new house at Caxford."

"What a good idea! You can take her out for lunch as well. I'm sure she never eats enough. I sometimes wonder if she ever eats anything. That's why she's got so thin. And as for that little Crispin, when he comes here he never has his hand out of the biscuit tin. Starved, most likely," she added tranquilly, and beamed down at her drooling dogs. "Who's ready for din-dins?"

32

Caxford lay on the edge of the moor, with a distant view of the North Sea, and a small and beautiful church surrounded by trees which all leaned inland, away from the prevailing wind. Kitty's house lay at the far end of the main street, set away by itself, a little distant from the last straggling row of cottages. Tom drew up at the side of the road, got out of the car, smelt the peaty tang of the moor and heard the distant baa-ing of sheep. He saw the little house, the old walls and the new roof, the chaos of building that had churned up what had once been a front garden.

Tom carefully opened a sagging wooden gate and went up a stone path that led around the side of the house. At the back of it was a great deal more land. He looked about him with interest and saw the border hedge of hawthorn, a line of derelict outbuildings which had probably once been piggeries; in front of these was parked Kitty's caravan, which was serving as their temporary home while the cottage was being renovated, and a battered old car, along with a cement mixer and a selection of shovels and wheelbarrows.

Picking his way across the churned mud, Tom now had a view of the back of the house, and saw that on this side a whole new extension had been constructed, the new roof tiles blending with the slope of the old. Planks led across pools of mud at the side of the house to the main door at the front, which stood open. It was a very beautiful panelled door of stripped pine and from beyond it came the cheerful sound of pop music.

He made his way across the plank and banged on the door. "Kitty!"

The music stopped. She had switched off her transistor. A moment later she appeared at the door, looking much as she had looked yesterday except for a smear of brown varnish down one cheek.

"Tom! I didn't think you'd really come today."

"I said I was coming."

"I thought you'd be too busy helping Mabel."

"I've been working like a slave, but thank heaven she turned me out. She said I was to come and buy you lunch." He stepped through the door and looked about him with interest. "What are you doing?"

"I've just finished Crispin's bedroom floor."

"Where is Crispin?"

"He's gone to spend the day with the schoolmaster's family. They're terribly kind. My best friends, really. The schoolmaster's wife is keeping him for tonight as well, and she says I can change for Mabel's party in her house, and have a bath. It's not very easy getting dressed for a dance if you're living in a rather cramped caravan."

"No, I can see that. When are you moving in here?"

"I think it ought to be ready in about two weeks."

"Have you got any furniture?"

"Enough. Enough for just the two of us to start with. It's just a cottage. Not very grand."

"It's got a frightfully grand front door, though."

Kitty looked delighted. "Isn't it beautiful? I got it from a scrap merchant. I got all the doors from scrap merchants or junk-yards. You know, people pull down lovely old houses because they're falling to pieces or somebody wants to build a factory in the garden, and sometimes somebody has the wit to save all the doors and the window frames and the shutters. This one was so handsome I immediately decided to make it my front door."

"Who stripped the paint off?"

"I did. I've done a lot of other things as well. I mean, the builders have done all the professional work, but they're terribly nice men and they don't seem to mind having me under their feet all the time. And if you have to pay people to strip paint off doors it costs the earth and, you see, I haven't got very much money. Anyway, come and look round. This is the kitchen, and we're going to have to eat in here as well, so it's got to be a kitchen-dining-room . . ." Kitty explained.

Slowly they inspected the house, going from room to room, and Tom's natural interest grew to a sort of amazed admiration, for Kitty had somehow managed to see in a derelict cottage the possibilities of creating a house that was unique. Every room had its charming, unexpected feature. An odd little window, a recess for books, a soaring tongue-and-grooved ceiling, a skylight.

The kitchen was flagged with red quarry tiles and an open stair rose to Crispin's attic bedroom, which had a long, low window where his bed would be, so that he could watch the sun rising in the mornings.

The sitting-room had not only a small and charming Victorian fireplace but a gallery as well, with access by means of a ladder which Kitty had had riveted to the wall.

"That's where Crispin can go to watch television. He can get away by himself and not have to be quiet when I have friends in."

A fire burned and crackled cheerfully in the grate.

"I lit the fire to see if it would draw properly."

"Was the fireplace here?"

"No. I rescued that from a dump, too, and set the blue and white tiles in around it. I think it looks just right, don't you?"

She showed him a pine dresser that she had bought and was going to fill with coloured china. She showed him a chair that she had made from a barrel, sawn in two. She showed him her own bedroom, which was on the ground floor and had french windows leading out on to what would one day be a terrace.

He stood and looked out at the churned mud and the piles of bricks. "Who's going to put the garden straight for you?"

"I'll do it myself. I'll have to dig it, because there are all sorts of hideous treasures buried there. Like old bedsteads. I thought of putting a cultivator through it, but I think a cultivator would be broken in a matter of minutes."

He said, "Are you going to live here with Crispin?"

"Of course. What else do you think I would do?"

"Sell it. Make an enormous profit. Move on."

"I couldn't sell it. I've put too much of myself into it."

"It's very isolated."

"I like it."

"And Crispin? What will happen to him? Where will he go to school when he's older?"

"Right here, in the village."

He turned from the window and faced her. "Kitty, are you sure you haven't taken on too much?"

For a moment she met his gaze; her eyes were enormous in her thin face, their blueness startling. Then she turned away from him.

"Look, Tom, these are my fitted cupboards. See how huge they are. And I've only got one pair of jeans and a dress to put in them, I'm afraid. But you see, we used old shutters for the doors. They're really lovely, aren't they?"

She laid her hand on the satiny, honey-coloured wood, and it was like watching a person caress some living creature. "There's this pretty plaster moulding. At first I thought it was carved wood and I nearly rubbed it off . . ." He saw her hands, the nails broken, the skin roughened and engrained with dirt.

"Kitty, are you sure this is what you really want?"

She did not at once reply to this. He waited and after a little she said, "In a moment, Tom, you're going to say, 'Kitty, you don't want to live here.' It's what people have been saying to me all my life. 'Kitty, you don't want to ride that horse.' 'Kitty, you don't want to buy that old bicycle.' 'Kitty, you don't want to wear that dreadful dress.' Whatever I really wanted to do, my parents always told me that I didn't. How could they know? It wasn't any good telling them that I didn't want to go to Paris and be an *au pair* girl, but if I hadn't gone, then I'd have been sent to some dismal place to be taught how to cook or type or arrange flowers. I'm not that sort of person, Tom. That's why, when I got chucked out of that job in Paris – and it wasn't my fault, Monsieur didn't seem to be able to keep his hands off me and when Madame caught him at it, I was obviously to blame! – I didn't come home. I knew that if I didn't escape then, I never would. And as for Terence, my ex-husband ... if only everybody had just left me alone, I know I'd never have married him. But it started right away, just as soon as they'd set eyes on him. 'Kitty, you don't want to have anything to do with a man like that.' 'Kitty, you don't want to spend the rest of your life living on a boat.' 'Kitty, you don't want to marry him.' So in the end, I did. It's as simple, and as stupid, as that."

Tom leaned his shoulders against the cold glass of the french windows, and put his hands in his pockets. He said, cautiously, "I wouldn't ever tell you what you want. I wouldn't know what you want. I just don't want to see you make another mistake, get into a situation that's way over your head."

"I've been making mistakes all my life, but still, I must be allowed to go my own way. I've got Crispin and I don't need a lot of money. And I like it here in Caxford. I like being near Mabel. I like being near Kinton and remembering all the fun we had when we were children."

"I'm filled with admiration for you," Tom said. "I'm astonished at what you've achieved, Kitty. I just can't bear to think of you struggling on endlessly on your own . . ."

"You mean the house? But that's been a sort of therapy. It's got me over Terence." She closed the doors of her cupboards and turned the latch, as though she were shutting Terence away. "You know, Tom, when I knew that you were coming north this weekend, I wished that you weren't. I didn't want to be reminded of that terrible evening when you took us out for dinner and Terence got so drunk. I suppose it makes me feel embarrassed and ashamed. Nobody ever likes to feel ashamed. Or guilty."

"You have nothing to feel guilty about. I think you've come through a long dark tunnel, all on your own, and you're still in one piece, and you've got Crispin. As for Terence, well, you can simply write him down to experience."

"Then you don't think this house is another mistake?"

"Someone who never made a mistake never made anything. And even if it is a mistake, it's a magnificent one. As I told you before, I'm filled with admiration."

"You mustn't say that. You mustn't be too kind."

He realised, with some surprise, that she was on the edge of tears. He could not remember ever having seen Kitty cry.

"I'm ... I'm not used to people being so kind ..."

"Oh, Kitty ..."

"It's just talking about it. Even Mabel thinks I'm insane. I haven't been able to talk to anybody. Not like this. Not to someone like you."

"You mustn't cry."

"I know, but I can't help it."

She felt helplessly for a handkerchief which did not materialise, and he gave her his own and she blew her nose and wiped her eyes. "It's just that so many things have gone wrong that sometimes – like this winter – when I'm tired and the car won't start, and the caravan's icy cold, and there's nowhere for Crispin to play ... I lose confidence in myself and begin to wonder if I'm really as irresponsible as everybody keeps telling me I am. 'Kitty, you don't want to bury yourself in Northumberland.' 'Kitty, you must think of Crispin.' 'Kitty, you're so selfish to cut yourself off from your family.' 'Kitty, what are you doing with your l-life?' "

Tom could bear it no longer. He crossed the floor, turned her towards him and pulled her into his arms. He could feel the skinny ribs beneath the wool of her sweater, and her hair was soft beneath his chin.

He said, "Don't cry any more. I don't associate you with tears and having you cry makes me feel that the world is falling to pieces."

"I don't mean to be so stupid."

"You're not stupid. I think you're fantastic. You're beautiful, you've survived and you've got your child. That's what I think. And I need a drink. Let's go down to the pub and sit by the fire and talk about cheerful things, like summer coming and Mabel's party. And after we've had something to eat, I'll take you for a drive, and we'll go and walk on the moor; or we'll go down to the beach and throw pebbles into the sea, or we'll go into town and find an antique shop and I'll buy you something marvellous for your house. Whatever you'd like to do, Kitty. You only have to say the words. You only have to tell me . . ."

❦

Dusk was falling as he drove back to Kinton. The first of the lights came on as he turned the corner of the village street, and the castle loomed ahead of him, silhouetted against a turquoise sky.

It was odd to realise that tonight, perhaps for the last time ever, Kinton would be *en fête*. Lights would shine and music would play. Cars would roll through the arch of the gatehouse, their headlights flashing on the ancient walls. The old and shabby rooms, flower-filled and soft with candle-light, would ring with voices and laughter.

But never again. It was a miracle that the old ways had endured so long. Kinton was a ridiculous, out-dated anachronism, perhaps, but no more of an anachronism than Mabel herself. It was she who had achieved so much by sticking to what she believed in; by knowing what she wanted out of life; by being prepared to pay for it. She had turned the castle into a home, filled it with other people's children, seen only beauty in the cold lofty rooms. She had tended her garden, walked dogs, gathered friends around her fire-side. She had, by some stubborn contrivance, managed to hold together the tattered fabric of threadbare carpets and recalcitrant boilers and crumbling walls. She had been, for so long, indomitable.

Driving slowly down the street, up the ramp and through the arch, Tom thought about that word, indomitable. And it occurred to him, then, that Kitty and Mabel had a lot in common. They were both unconventional to the point of eccentricity, their actions incomprehensible to ordinary beings. But they were survivors, too. In one way or another, whatever happened, instinct told him that they would both survive.

❧

He was in his bedroom, standing at his dressing-table and trying to tie his bow tie in the inadequate light, when there came a tap at his door.

"Tom."

He turned. It was Mabel. She looked magnificent in a long brown dress of old-fashioned cut, with family diamonds in her ears and the pearls Ned had given her on their wedding day around her neck.

Tom stopped struggling with his bow tie. He said, "You look wonderful," and meant it.

She closed the door and came towards him. "You know, Tom, I feel rather wonderful. Quite youthful and festive. Do you want me to help you with your tie? I always used to have to do Ned's for him, poor man. He was incapable of deciding which end was which."

Tom, who had already made his decision, stood obediently while she dealt with it for him. "There," she gave the finished effort a little pat. "That's perfect."

They stood looking at each other, smiling broadly.

He said, "Perhaps this is as good a time as any to give you your present." He went to take it from the top of the dressing-table, a large, flat parcel, painstakingly wrapped in crisp white paper and tied with a flourish of gold ribbon.

"Oh, Tom, you are a dear boy. You shouldn't have brought me anything. Just having you here is quite gift enough."

But she carried it, in obvious pleasure and anticipation, to the bed, where she sat herself down and proceeded to undo the wrappings. He went to sit beside her. The ribbon and the paper fell away; the old print, mounted and framed, was suddenly revealed.

"Tom! Oh, Tom, it's Kinton. Where did you find it?"

"By some extraordinary chance, in an antique shop in Salisbury. There were two or three in a sort of job-lot and this was one of them." He recalled the pleasure he had had in buying them, in finding such a perfect present for Mabel. "I took it back to London and got it mounted and framed there."

She peered at it short-sightedly because, with her evening gown, she was not wearing her glasses. "It must be very old. At least two hundred years, I should think. How very kind of you. I shall be able to take it with me . . ."

"Take it with you?"

"Yes." She laid the picture carefully on the bed and turned to him. "I wasn't going to tell you tonight, but perhaps I will, after all. It's right that you should be the first to know. I'm going to leave Kinton. It's become, all at once, too much for me. It's too big and too old." She laughed. "Rather like me."

"Where will you go?"

"There's a small house in the main street of the village. I've had my eye on it for a little while. I shall do it up and put in some central heating, and the dogs and I will move there just as soon as possible, and live out the rest of our lives with the pork-butcher on one side and the newsagent on the other."

Tom, picturing this, smiled. He said, "I'm not surprised, you know. Sorry, but not surprised. Coming home this evening, driving down the street, I saw the castle and I knew then that there was no way it could carry on for very much longer."

"I'd have liked to die here. But then, I might have to be very ill and old first, and what a tiresome worry I should have been to all my good friends and relations."

"You've got years to go yet."

"I'm not sorry, you know. There comes a time to end everything; like leaving a party when you're really enjoying yourself. And we've had good times here, haven't we? It's so full of happy memories for me, and I would hate to sit around and grow old, and let them all turn stale."

"What will happen to Kinton?"

"I've no idea. Perhaps someone will want to buy it for a school, or a hospital, or a remand home, but I doubt it. Perhaps the National Trust will take it over. Perhaps it will just crumble to bits. It's not far from that already. Dry rot in the basement. Death-watch beetle in the west tower." She laughed and struck him a loving blow on the knee. "Bats in the belfry!"

Tom laughed with her. He said, "If you want to do up the house in the village, why don't you ask Kitty to help you?"

"Oh, yes," said Mabel. "I thought we'd come round to the subject of Kitty sooner or later."

"That little house of hers . . . I was wordless with admiration. The work she's put into it absolutely beggars belief."

"I know. She's a maddening, pig-headed child, but one has to take off one's hat to her."

"She's not as tough as she likes people to think."

"No. She's been through a bad time. After the divorce, I asked her and Crispin to live with me for a little, but she wouldn't. She said she had to sort out her own mess for herself." She fell silent. Tom, looking up, found himself on the receiving end of her thoughtful, calculating gaze.

Before he could speak, Mabel asked him, "What did you do today, you and Kitty?"

"Looked at the house. Had lunch in Caxford, drove into town and did some shopping. I bought her some blue and white Spode plates for her dresser. Then I took her home."

"You were always very close to Kitty. I think perhaps you were always the only person who really understood her."

"You told me once that I should marry her."

"And you said that it would be incestuous because she was like a sister to you."

"And you said that one day she would be beautiful."

"And you told me that you'd be able to wait."

"I've waited," said Tom.

Mabel sat, vastly patient, waiting to see if he was going to enlarge upon this. When he didn't, she simply said, "Don't wait too long."

From far away, in the depths of the castle, came the faint sound of music. They listened. As though in deference to the occasion of the party, the long-haired boys with the disco had chosen to start off this particular evening with a selection of Strauss waltzes.

Mabel was pleased. "How pretty! But I thought," she added, as though the complicated stereo system was an instrument on which the two young men were going to perform, "that they could only play rock and roll music."

He was about to explain when there came yet another knock at the door of his room.

"Mabel!"

"I'm in here, come along."

The door opened slowly, and Kitty's head appeared around the edge of it. Tom got to his feet.

"Mabel, I've been looking for you everywhere. You'll have to hurry. The first cars are beginning to arrive and you've got to be downstairs to greet your guests."

"Heavens!" Mabel heaved herself off the bed, tidied her bun, smoothed down the brown lace front of her skirt. "I had no idea it was so late." She looked keenly at Kitty. "And when did you get here?"

"About five minutes ago. Oh, Mabel, you look marvellous. But do hurry. You've got to be there."

"I'm on my way," said Mabel. She gathered up her picture and the paper and the golden ribbon. She kissed Tom on the cheek and made for the door, kissing Kitty *en passant* in an abstracted sort of way, and then was gone, her back erect, her diamonds flashing, her brown lace trailing on the threadbare carpet.

❦

Across the room, Tom and Kitty smiled at each other. Tom said, "Mabel is not the only one who looks marvellous." Kitty wore a dress so utterly romantic and feminine that she was, all at once, a totally different person. Slipper satin, white and pale blue, with a skirt that rustled when she moved and a neckline cut low to reveal her delicate shoulders, her vulnerable neck. Her pale, thick hair, clean and shining and very fair, hung in a soft curtain to frame her face and there were pearl studs in her ears and a tiny jewelled watch encircling one of her narrow wrists.

"Where on earth did you get that lovely creation? It's sensational."

"It's terribly old. I had it when I was eighteen and my mother was trying to turn me into a deb."

Tom smiled. "Come in and shut the door. I'm not ready yet, but I won't be a moment."

She did as he said, coming to sit on the bed where Mabel had sat. She watched while he put on his shoes, picked up his jacket and put that on too, disposed of money and keys and handkerchief in various pockets. She said, "What did you give Mabel for a birthday present?"

"A print of Kinton. She says she's going to take it with her."

"Where is she going to take it?"

"To a small house in the village. She's leaving the castle."

After a little, "I thought she might be," said Kitty.

"I don't know whether I was meant to tell you or not. You don't need to say anything."

"I'm just full of wonder that she's stuck it out – living here, I mean – so long. I ... I'm glad that she's going, though."

"So am I. Like she said, it's best to leave a party while you're still enjoying yourself. And she doesn't want to become ill or infirm, and so an anxiety to all her friends."

"If she does become old and infirm," said Kitty, "then I shall look after her."

"Yes," said Tom. "Yes, I believe you will."

From below them, the music still played. But now, as well, there was the sound of cars approaching, of voices mingling.

He said, "We should go down. We should be there to give Mabel some moral support."

"All right," said Kitty.

She stood up, smoothing down her skirts as Mabel had done, and Tom took her hand and together they went out of the room and down the long passage to the head of the stairs.

Now the music sounded more clearly. *Tales of the Vienna Woods.* Side by side, they started down the stairs. But as they descended, rounding the curve beneath the beautiful arched window, the hall below them revealed itself. He saw it, candlelit and firelit, the flickering flames reflected in the curved surfaces of dozens of champagne glasses lined up upon a table.

Suddenly it was a moment so important that he wanted to savour it, to spin it out, to remember it for always. He stopped and held Kitty back. "Wait," he told her.

She turned to look at him. "Why, what is it, Tom?"

"There'll never be an instant quite like this again. You know that, don't you? We shouldn't hurry away."

"What should we do?"

"Enjoy it."

He lowered himself down on to the wide lap of the stone stair and drew her down beside him. She sat, sinking down in a whisper of satin skirts, wrapping her arms about her knees. She was smiling at him, but he knew that she understood. A combination, perhaps, of everything that could fill him with pleasure and satisfaction. The time, the place and the girl.

Kitty – whom he had known for the best part of his life and yet had never known at all. She was part of it all; part of this evening, part of Kinton. He looked about him, at the painted ceiling, the soaring splendour of the arched window, the perfectly proportioned curve of the stone staircase upon which they sat together. He looked into her face and all at once was filled with joy.

He said, "When are you going to move out of your caravan and into your house?"

Kitty began to laugh.

"What's so funny?" Tom asked.

"You. I thought you were going to come out with something enormously flattering or romantic."

"I'm keeping the romance and the flattery for later on in the evening. But this is the moment for humdrum affairs."

"All right. I told you, in about two weeks."

"I was thinking ... if you could wait for a month, I'm due for a few days off. I thought I might go to Spain, but I'd much rather come to Northumberland and perhaps give you a hand with your move. That is ... if you'd like me to."

Kitty had stopped laughing. Her eyes were unblinking, enormous, very blue. She said, "Tom, you must never be sorry for me."

"I couldn't be sorry for a person like you. I might admire, or be envious, or even be maddened. But pity would never come into it."

"You don't think we've known each other for too long?"

"I don't think we've known each other nearly long enough."

"I've got Crispin."

"I know you have."

"If you did come and help me – and I can't think of anything I'd like more – and at the end of it, you decided you'd had enough ... I mean I wouldn't want you to feel that I wasn't able to be on my own ... be independent. Couldn't do things for myself ..."

"You know something, Kitty? You're floundering."

"You don't understand."

"I understand perfectly." He took one of her hands and

sat looking at it. He thought of Mabel and Kinton. Kinton a ruin, and Mabel and the dogs living in a small centrally-heated house and probably warm for the first time in their lives. He remembered Kitty as a child sleeping out on the battlements for a dare, stubborn and resolute and brave, and he thought of her son lying in his bed in their new house and watching, through the window, the sun rise.

Kitty's hand was scratched and rough and broken-nailed, but he thought it beautiful. He raised it to his lips, planted a kiss in her palm and folded her fingers over it.

"What's that for?" she asked him.

"Endings," he told her, smiling. "And beginnings."

# ⚜ *Flowers in the Rain* ⚜

Through thick, wetting mist and a cold east wind, the slow, stopping country bus finally ground its way up the last incline towards the village. We had left Relkirk an hour before and, as the winding road climbed up into the hills, the weather had worsened, turning from an overcast but dry afternoon, to this sodden cheerless day.

"Aye, it's driech," the conductor commented, taking the fare from a fat country woman with a pair of carrier bags filled with her morning's shopping. And the very word, 'driech', took me back into the past and made me feel that I was almost coming home.

The window was misty with condensation. I rubbed a patch clear and looked out hopefully; saw stone walls, the vague shapes of silver birch and larch. Small turnings led to invisible farmsteads, lost in the murk, but by now I recognised the road and knew that in a moment we should cross the bridge and draw, at last, into the main street of the village.

I was sitting by the window. "Excuse me," I said to the man next to me. "I have to get out at the next stop."

"Oh, aye." He heaved himself out of his seat and stood in the aisle to let me pass. "It's no' a very good day."

"No. It's horrible."

I made my way to the front of the bus. We crossed the bridge and the next moment were there, halted by the pavement in front of Mrs McLaren's shop.

*Effie McLaren*
*Lachlan General Stores*
*Post Office*

read the sign over her door, as it had read ever since I could remember. The door of the bus opened. I thanked the conductor and stepped down, followed by one or two other passengers who were alighting.

"Aye, aye," we all agreed. "It is a terrible day."

They went their separate ways but I stayed where I was, standing on the pavement by the bus stop. I waited until the bus pulled out; until the sound of its grinding engine had died away, up and around the next bend in the road. The silence filled up with other sounds. The bubbling, watery chuckle of the river. The bleat of unseen sheep. The sough of wind through the pines on the hillside above me. All blessedly familiar. Unchanged.

❧

I and my three brothers had first come to Lachlan one Eastertime, with our parents, when I was about ten. After that the holiday became an annual event. Our home was in Edinburgh, where my father was a schoolmaster, but both my parents loved fishing, and each year rented the same little cottage from Mrs Farquhar who lived in what was always known as the 'Big Hoose'.

They were wonderful times. While my mother and father sat by the river, or for hours in a boat in the middle of the loch, we children were left to our own devices, running wild over the heathery hillsides, swimming in icy pools, guddling for trout, or hiking, professionally haversacked, to some distant beauty spot. As well, we were absorbed into the local village life. My father sometimes played the harmonium in the Presbyterian church on Sunday mornings; my mother

50

was asked to demonstrate Italian quilting to the Women's Rural Institute, and my brothers and I were included in school outings and concerts.

But the best – and this added real glamour to our yearly excursions – was the endless hospitality of Mrs Farquhar herself. A widow, and quite elderly, she genuinely loved people and there was always a selection of friends, their children, nephews and nieces, perhaps a godchild or two, staying in the house.

But only one grandson, the only son of Mrs Farquhar's only son.

We were, from the first, automatically included in any ploy that might have been planned. Perhaps tennis, or a tea-party, or a paper-chase, or a picnic. I remembered how the front door of the Big House stood, always, open; the dining-room table laid for the next generous meal; the fire in her sitting-room always lighted, blazing and welcoming. I think of daffodils and I think of the Big House at Lachlan at Eastertime. Drifts of them in the wild garden, bowlfuls of them indoors, filling the rooms with their heavy scent.

When I told my mother, over the telephone, that I was coming to Relkirk to work for a month, she had said at once, "I wonder if you'll be able to get up to Lachlan."

"I'm sure they'll give me a day off. They'll have to, some time, or I'll collapse. I can catch a bus and make a visit. Go and see Mrs Farquhar."

"Yes . . ." My mother didn't sound too sure about this.

"Why shouldn't I go and see her? Do you think she wouldn't remember us?"

"Darling, of course she would and she'd adore to see you. It's just that I don't think she's been awfully well . . . I heard something about a stroke, or a heart attack. But perhaps she's better now. Anyway, you could always ring up first."

But I hadn't rung up first. Presented with a day to myself, I had simply got myself to the bus stop in Relkirk and boarded the country bus. And now I was here, standing like a lunatic in the driving rain and already drenched. I crossed the pavement and went into the post office; the bell above the door went ting, and I was met by the familiar smell of paraffin mixed with oranges and cloves and the sugary smell of sweets.

❧

The shop was empty. It was always empty. It always had been empty, unless there were actually some customers there, buying stamps or chocolate, or cans of peaches, or button thread. Mrs McLaren preferred to live in her back room, beyond the bead curtain, where she drank cups of tea and talked to her cat. I could hear her now. "Well, now, Tiddles, and who will that be?" A few shuffling steps and she appeared through the beads, with her flowered pinafore and her brown beret, worn well down over her eyebrows. We had never seen her without that beret. My brother Roger insisted that underneath it, she had no hair, was as bald as Kojak.

"Well, and what a terrible day it's turned into. And what can I be doing for you?"

I said, "Hello, Mrs McLaren."

She eyed me across the counter, frowning. I pulled off my woollen hat and shook out my hair and at once recognition dawned in her face. Her mouth opened in delight, her hands went up in the classic gesture of astonishment. "And if it isn't Lavinia Hunter! What a surprise. My, you've grown! However long is it since you were last here?"

"It must be five years."

"We've missed you all."

"We've missed coming, too. But my father died and my mother went to live in Gloucestershire, near her sister. And my brothers seem to be living all over the world."

"I'm sorry to hear about your father. He was a dear man. And how about yourself? What are you doing?"

"I'm a nurse."

"But that's splendid. In a hospital?"

"No. I was in a hospital. But now I do private nursing. I'm with a family in Relkirk, just for a month, helping to look after two older children and a new baby. I'd have been up to see you all before, but it's not very easy to get time off."

"No, no, you'll be busy."

"I thought I might go and see Mrs Farquhar."

"Oh, dear." Mrs McLaren's cheerful expression changed to one of sadness and gloom. "Poor Mrs Farquhar. She had a wee stroke and she's been going downhill, by all accounts, ever since. The house is changed now, not the way it used to be with all of you running around. Just the old lady upstairs in her bed, and two nurses, night and day. Mary and Sandy Reekie are still there, she doing the cooking and he taking care of the garden, but Mary says it's a chilling business cooking for just the nurses, for poor Mrs Farquhar takes no more than a wee cup of baby food."

"Oh, I am sorry. You don't think there's any point my going up to see her, then?"

"And why not? She might just be having a good day, and then, who knows the good it would do her to see a cheerful young face?"

"Doesn't anybody come to stay any more?" It was sad to think of the big house so bleak.

"Well, it wouldn't work, would it? Mary Reekie told me the one person Mrs Farquhar wanted to see was Rory, and she told the minister, too, and he wrote to Rory, but Rory's in America and I don't know if there was ever any reply to the letter."

Rory. Mrs Farquhar's grandson. What had prompted Mrs McLaren to suddenly come out with his name? I looked at her across the counter and tried to detect some glimmer of unexplained Highland intuition. But her faded eyes remained innocent and met my own with an untroubled gaze. I told myself that she could not guess at the pounding that started up in the region of my heart at the very mention of his name. Rory Farquhar. I had always thought of him as Rory, and will write of him that way, but in fact his name was spelt with Gaelic inconsistence, R-u-a-r-a-i-d-h.

I fell in love with Rory, one remembered sunny spring, when I was sixteen and he was twenty-two. I had never been in love before and it had the effect of making me, not dreamy, but intensely perceptive; so that objects, previously unnoticed, became beautiful; leaves and trees, flowers, chairs, dishes, firelight – everything was touched with the magic of a spell-binding novelty, as though I had never known any of these ordinary day-to-day things before.

There were many picnics that spring, and swimming in the loch and tennis parties, but the best was the idleness, the casual getting to know each other. Lying on the lawn in front of the Big House, watching somebody practising his casting, with a scrap of sheep wool instead of a fly to weight the line. Or walking down to the farm in the evenings to fetch the milk, or helping the farmer's wife to bottle-feed the abandoned lamb who lived by her kitchen fireside.

At the end of those holidays Mrs Farquhar arranged a little party. We cleared the old billiard room of furniture and put on the record player, and danced reels. And Rory wore his kilt and an old khaki shirt that had belonged to his father, and showed me the steps and spun me till I was breathless. It was at the end of that evening that he kissed me, but it didn't do much good because he was going back to London the next morning, and I could never be sure if it was a kiss of affection or a kiss of goodbye.

After he went I lived in a fantasy world of getting letters and phone calls from him, and having him realise that he could not live without me. But all that happened was that he started working in London, with his father's firm, and after that he did not come back to Lachlan for Easter. If he did take a few days off in the spring, Mrs Farquhar told me that he was going skiing, and I imagined rich and elegant girls in dashing ski-clothes, and felt sick with jealousy.

Once I stole a photograph of Rory out of an old album I found in a bookcase in Mrs Farquhar's library. It had come loose and fell out of the shabby pages, so it wasn't really stealing. I picked it up and put it in my pocket and later between the pages of my diary. I always kept it, although I never saw Rory again, and since my father died and we stopped coming to Lachlan, I had heard no news of him.

And now, Mrs McLaren said his name, and I remembered that young Rory, with his worn kilt and his brown face and his dark hair.

I said, "What's he doing in America?"

"Oh, some business or other, in New York. His father died too, you know."

"I expect Rory's a married man now, with a string of children."

"No, no. Rory never married."

❧

We talked a little longer, and then I bought some chocolate from her, said goodbye and went out of the shop, and set off in the direction of the Big House. I tore the paper off the chocolate and bit off a chunk. Eaten thus, in the open air, it tasted just the way it used to.

'I'll just go and see,' I told myself. 'I'll just go and ring at the door, and if the nurse sends me packing, it won't matter.'

A woman was coming towards me down the street, carrying a shopping basket and dressed in the country woman's uniform of headscarf, tweed skirt and sleeveless quilted waistcoat in that horrible sludgy green colour.

'I can't come all this way and not just try.'

She stopped. "Lavinia."

I stopped, too. It was certainly a day for being recognised. My heart sank. "Hello, Mrs Felham."

I *would* meet her. Stella Felham, the one woman in the village my mother could never bring herself to like. She and her husband, who had been a lawyer, had built themselves a house in Lachlan after his retirement and had settled permanently. He was a manic fisherman and always said "Tight lines" instead of "Cheers" when he took a drink, and she was enormously efficient and spent most of her time trying to dragoon the village ladies into attending philosophical lectures, or involving them in money-making events for charity. The village ladies were polite and charming but, despite Stella Felham's enthusiasm, the events were never very lucrative. She could never think why, and they were all far too kind to tell her.

"What a surprise! I couldn't believe it was you. What on earth are you doing here?"

I told her, as I had told Mrs McLaren.

"But my dear, you must come and see us. Lionel would love to have a glimpse of you." *Tight lines*. "Anyway, he's bored stiff today. He was meant to be fishing but it was called off."

"It . . . it's very kind of you, but actually I'm on my way to see Mrs Farquhar."

"Mrs Farquhar!" Her voice rose an octave. "But hasn't anybody told you? She's dying."

I could have hit her.

"Had this appalling stroke a couple of months ago. My

56

dear, nurses, day and night. It's no good going to see her, she just lies like a log. We do what we can, of course, but I'm afraid social visiting is just a waste of time. So sad, when you remember how wonderful she was, and how much she's always done for the village. And as for that Rory – there he is, sitting in New York, and he's never been to see her. You'd think, when he'll obviously inherit the place . . ."

I couldn't bear to listen to anyone talking about Rory, and certainly not Stella Felham.

I said, "I am sorry. I really must be on my way. I haven't much time before the last bus back to Relkirk."

"You're going to the Big House, then?" She made it sound as though I were deliberately defying her.

"Yes, I am."

"Oh, all right. But if you have a moment to spare before you do catch the bus, be sure to pop in. Lionel will give you a snifter."

"So kind . . ."

I backed away from her and then turned and left her standing there, gazing after me as though I were mad. Which I probably was.

I wouldn't think about Rory, sitting in New York. If he hadn't come home, if he hadn't answered the minister's letter, there was probably some very good reason. I walked, in long, warming strides, on up the hill, along the narrow lane which led to the gates of the Big House. I came to them and they loomed before me, standing open. I did not walk up the drive, but took the short-cut through the wild garden, through the sodden drifts of daffodils. They were still in bud, closed against the rain, their trumpets unopened. I went beneath the trees and opened the tall gate in the deer fence. Beyond lay the rough grass, the azaleas and the hybrid rhododendrons, and then the lawn, sloping up to the gravel terrace in front of the house.

Through the mist the house took shape. The old, ugly, red stone house with the conservatory tacked on to one side and the pepper-pot turret over the front door. The outer door stood open and I went up the slope of the grass and crossed the gravel and went into the porch and rang the bell. Then, with the jangling of the bell still sounding from the back regions, I opened the inner glass door and let myself in.

It was very quiet. Very tidy. No flowers stood upon the table in the hall; no dogs barked; no children's voices broke the quiet. There was the smell of pine and polish and, as well, a faint aura of disinfectant, nursing, hospitals, so familiar to me that I noticed it at once. I went into the centre of the hall and pulled off my hat. I looked up the empty staircase. I said, not wanting to call too loudly, "Is anyone around?"

Out of the silence came footsteps, along the upper passage. Not the quick, rubber-heeled footsteps of a professional nurse but heavy, masculine footsteps. Sandy Reekie, I decided, upstairs to fill the log baskets for the invalid's fire. I waited.

The footsteps started downstairs. Reached the half-landing and stopped. He was silhouetted against the light of the stair window. Not Sandy Reekie, whom I remembered as wiry and stooped. But a tall man, dressed in a kilt and a thick sweater.

"Who is it?" he asked, and then he saw me, my face tilted up to his. Our eyes met. There was a long silence. Then, for the third time that day, a person said my name. "Lavinia."

And I simply said, "Rory."

He came on down the stairs, his hand trailing on the banister. He crossed the hall and took my hand.

"I don't believe it," he said, and then he kissed my cheek.

"I don't believe it, either. Everybody tells me you're in New York."

"I flew over a couple of nights ago. I've been here a day."

"How is your grandmother?"

"She's dying." But he didn't say it the way Stella Felham had said it. He made it sound rather peaceful and nice, as though he were telling me that Mrs Farquhar was nearly asleep.

I said, "I came to see her."

"Where from? Where have you come from?"

"Relkirk. I'm working there, nursing for a month. I got a day off. I thought I'd come to Lachlan. My mother told me Mrs Farquhar had been ill, but I thought perhaps she would be getting better."

"There are two nurses with her, around the clock. But the day nurse wanted to go and do some shopping in Relkirk, so I lent her the car and said I'd watch out for my grandmother." He paused, hesitating, and then said, "There's a fire in the sitting-room. Let's go there. It'll be more cheerful. Besides, you're wet through."

✵

It was more cheerful. He put logs on the fire and the flames crackled up. I pulled off my wet anorak and warmed my swollen, scarlet hands at the blaze. He said, "Tell me about you all," so I told him, and by the time I had finished with all the family news I was truly warm again, and the clock on the mantelpiece struck four, so he left me by the fire and went off to put the kettle on for a cup of tea. I sat by the fire, very cosy and happy, and waited for him. When he returned, with a tray and cups and a teapot and the heel of a gingerbread he had found in a tin, I said, "And what about you? I've told you all about our family. Now you've got to tell me about you."

"Not much to tell, really. Worked with my father for a bit and then, when he died, I went out and joined the American office. I was in San Francisco when my grandmother became so ill. That was why I've been so long in getting back."

"You had a letter from the minister."

I was pouring tea. He sat in an armchair and watched me, grinning. "Lachlan grapevine never gets anything wrong. Who told you that?"

"Mrs McLaren in the shop. I also met Mrs Felham."

"That woman! She's been more trouble than she's worth. Endlessly telephoning and rubbing the nurses up the wrong way, organising everybody, telling the Reekies what they ought to be doing."

"She told me that Mrs Farquhar was lying like a log and there was no point in coming to see her."

"That's because she hasn't been allowed near the house, and she's furiously jealous if anybody else is."

"I'm sure she means well. At least that's what my mother always used to say about her. Go on about America."

"Well, anyway, I had a letter from the minister, but I didn't get it until I returned to New York. I caught the first possible flight home."

"And if she . . . when she dies . . . what will happen to the house?"

"It'll come to me, and I'm very lucky. But what on earth am I going to do with it?"

"You could stop being a high-powered businessman and retire to the country and take up farming."

"Perhaps I'd end up like Lionel Felham, saying 'Tight lines' every time I took a drink."

I considered this. "No. I don't think you would."

He grinned again. "And farming is just about the most

high-powered business that's going these days. I'd have to go back to college, start at the bottom, learn a whole new trade."

"Lots of people do that. You could go to Cirencester. Take what they call the gin-and-tonic course. That's what people call the course for mature students, retired army officers, those sorts of people."

"How do you know so much about it?"

"My mother lives no more than five miles from Cirencester."

He laughed, and all at once looked just as young as I had remembered him. "And then I should be near you all again. That's just about the biggest carrot you could dangle in front of this old donkey. I shall have to think seriously about it." And then he became grave again. "I would rather hold on to this place than anything else in the world. What good times we used to have. What good times we could have again. Remember walking down for the milk? And how you fed the lamb from a bottle?"

"I was remembering that."

"And the evenings when we danced reels . . ."

We talked on, sharing memories, until the clock struck five. I could not believe the hour had passed so swiftly. I laid down my empty teacup and got to my feet. "Rory, I must go, or I'll miss my bus."

"I'd drive you back, only the nurse has borrowed the car, and anyway, I can't leave my grandmother." He hesitated. "Do you want to come up and see her?"

I looked at him. I said, "I don't want to be like Stella Felham. I just wanted to see her again. I wanted to talk to her. I suppose, now, I just want to say goodbye."

He took my hand. "Then come," he said.

We went out of the room and up the stairs, hand in hand. Along the passage. At the end of the passage a door stood open, and now the hospital smell was stronger. We went through the doorway and into the big, pretty, faded bed-room, where Mrs Farquhar had slept since coming to Lachlan as a bride. Even with the familiar evidences of professional nursing, it was still a warm and welcoming room, essentially feminine with silver brushes on the dressing-table, photographs everywhere, frilled curtains drawn back from the long windows.

We went to the bedside. I saw her face, serene and beauti-ful still, the eyes closed, the wrinkled hand lying peacefully on the fold of the linen sheet. I took her hand in mine and it was warm, and I felt still that strong persistent throb of life. She wore a pale pink Shetland bed-jacket, lined with silk chiffon. A satin ribbon lay across her throat, provocative as if she had set it there herself.

Rory said, "Grandmother." I thought she was sleeping, but she opened her eyes and looked up at him, and then she turned her head and looked at me. For a moment those blue eyes stayed puzzled and empty, and then, slowly, came alive. Recognition sparked. Her fingers closed upon mine, a smile touched her wrinkled mouth, and quietly, but quite dis-tinctly, she said my name.

"Lavinia."

We stayed only for a moment. We spoke, exchanging a word or two, and then her eyes closed once more. I bent quickly and kissed her. Her fingers loosened and I slipped my hand away and straightened up.

I said goodbye, but I didn't say it aloud. Then Rory put his arm around me and turned me, and we went out of the room and left her by herself.

I was in tears. I couldn't find a handkerchief but Rory had one, and he mopped me up, and finally I managed to stop crying. We went downstairs and back into the sitting-room, and I picked up my anorak and put it on. I pulled on my woollen hat. I said, "Thank you for letting me see her."

"You mustn't be sad."

I said, "I have to go. I have to catch that bus. Let me know what you decide to do."

"I will. When I've decided."

We went out of the room and across the hall and out through the open door. It was colder and wetter than ever, but the air smelt of heather and peat and across the sky, somewhere beyond the rain-clouds, an invisible oyster-catcher flew, crying his lonely song.

"You'll be all right?" said Rory.

"Of course."

"You know the way?"

I smiled. "Of course." I put out my hand. "Goodbye, Rory."

He took my hand, and pulled me close, and kissed me. "I'm not going to say goodbye," he told me. "I'm going to say what the Americans always say. Take care. It doesn't sound so final. Just take care."

I nodded. He let go of my hand and I turned and walked away from him, down across the grass and into the misty tunnel beneath the trees, where the azaleas grew and the daffodils tossed their heads in the wind, waiting for the first of the sunshine, the first of the warmth.

# ≷ *Playing a Round with Love* ≷

This, then, was the real beginning of their life together. The honeymoon was over and behind them. This morning Julian had returned to work in his London office, and now he was on his way home to Putney.

Feeling like an old married man, he found his latch-key, but Amanda opened the door before he had time to put it into the lock and one of the best things that had ever happened to Julian was stepping inside his own house, shutting his own door behind him, and taking his own wife into his arms.

When she could speak, she said, "You haven't even taken off your coat yet."

"No time."

He could smell something delicious cooking. Over her shoulder he saw the table laid in the tiny hall that they used as a dining-room. The wedding present glasses and table-mats, the silver that his mother had given them gleaming in the soft lighting.

"But, darling . . ."

He could feel Amanda's ribs, her narrow waist, the round curve of her neat behind. He said, "Be quiet. You have to realise I only have time to deal with essentials . . ."

The next morning in the office, Julian's telephone rang. It was Tommy Benham. "Nice to have you back in London again, Julian. Are you okay for Wentworth on Saturday?

I've fixed Roger and Martin and we've got a starting time at ten."

Julian did not reply at once.

Amanda knew about Tommy and golf. Before they were engaged, and after, she had philosophically accepted the fact that Saturdays and sometimes Sundays, too, belonged to the golf course. But this Saturday was the first of their real life together, and she might want to spend it with him.

"I'm . . . I'm not sure, Tommy."

Tommy was outraged. "What do you mean, you're not sure? You can't change your lifestyle just because you've got a wife! Besides, she's never minded before, why should she mind now?"

That was a good point. "Perhaps I should have a word . . ."

"No discussions, therefore no arguments. Present it as a *fait accompli*. Can you be there by ten o'clock?"

"Yes, of course, but . . ."

"Fine, we'll see you. Till then."

And Tommy rang off.

On his way home that evening, Julian stopped and bought his wife flowers.

'She'll love them,' he told himself smugly.

'She'll smell a rat the moment she sees them,' answered a sneering voice inside his head. 'Probably think you've been flirting with one of the typists.'

'That's ridiculous. She knows I play golf at the weekends. It's just that . . . well, this is the first time since we were married. And Tommy was right. Present it as a *fait accompli*. Getting married doesn't mean changing one's lifestyle. Compromises, okay, but not a total change of habits.'

'Who's going to make the compromises?' sneered the voice. 'Her or you?'

Julian didn't reply to that.

In the end he was completely honest. He found Amanda in the garden, mud-smeared and with her fair hair all over her face.

Julian produced the flowers, which he had been hiding behind his back, with the panache of a successful conjurer.

"I have bought them," he said, "because I feel a louse. Tommy rang up this morning, and I've said I'll play golf with him on Saturday and my conscience has been pricking ever since."

She had buried her face in the flower-heads. Now she looked up, astonished and laughing. "But why should your conscience prick, darling?"

"You don't mind?"

"Well, you can't say it's the first time it's happened!"

He knew a great surge of love for her. He took her into his arms and kissed her passionately.

Saturday was a beautiful day. Wentworth basked in sunshine, the fairways rolled before them, inviting and velvety. Julian, partnering Tommy, could do no wrong all that day.

His mind was filled with pleasant and generous thoughts as he drove home. He decided that he would take Amanda out for dinner, but when he got in he found that she had already made her special moussaka, so he opened a bottle of wine and they had dinner at home.

Amanda wore a canary yellow caftan which he had bought her on their honeymoon in New York and her hair lay over her shoulders like a curtain of pale silk.

She said: "Shall I make some coffee?"

He put out his hand and touched the ends of that fair hair. "Later . . ."

He played golf again the next Saturday, and the next. The following weekend the day was shifted to Sunday, but he accepted this arrangement light-heartedly.

"Not playing this Saturday," he told Amanda when he got home. "Playing on Sunday instead."

"On Sunday?"

"Yes." He poured drinks and flopped into the armchair with the evening paper.

"Why Sunday?"

Engrossed in the share prices, he missed a certain tone in her voice.

"Um? Oh, Tommy's tied up on Saturday."

"I did say we'd go down and see my parents on Sunday."

"What?" She was not angry in any way, just polite. "Oh, sorry. But they'll understand. Ring them and say we'll come down some other weekend." He went back to the share prices and Amanda said no more.

The Sunday was a failure. It rained non-stop, Tommy had a hangover from the previous evening, and Julian played the sort of golf that makes a man swear he will give away his precious golf clubs and take up some other sport. He returned home in a black and dismal mood which was not dispelled by finding his house empty.

He wandered about aimlessly, and eventually went upstairs and had a bath. While he was soaking in the bath, Amanda returned.

"Where have you been?" he demanded angrily.

"I went home. I said I was going to."

"How did you get there? I mean, I had the car."

"I caught a train down and someone very kindly gave me a lift back here."

"I didn't know where you were."

"Well, now you know, don't you?" She kissed him un-enthusiastically. "And don't tell me what sort of a day you've had, because I know. Dreadful."

He was indignant. "How can you tell?"

"Because there is no light in the eye, no frisking of the tail."

"What's for supper?"

"Scrambled eggs."

"Scrambled eggs? I'm starving. I only had a sandwich for lunch."

"I, on the other hand, had a full Sunday lunch, so I am not in the least hungry. Scrambled eggs," she said as she closed the door between them.

Julian supposed this was their first quarrel. Not even a quarrel, really, just a coolness. But it was enough to make him feel miserable and the next day he bought flowers once more on the way home, made love to her as soon as he got home, and then took her out for dinner afterwards.

Everything was all right again. When Tommy rang to fix the next Saturday's game, Julian joyfully agreed to play.

That evening he found Amanda perched on top of a stepladder in the bathroom, painting the ceiling white.

"For heaven's sake, be careful."

"I'm all right." She leaned down for his kiss. "Don't you think it looks better?" Together they stared at the ceiling. "And then I thought we'd have primrose walls to match the bath, and perhaps a new green carpet."

"A carpet?"

"Don't sound so horrified. We can get a cheap one. There's a sale on in the High Street, we can go and look on Saturday."

She went back to her painting. There was a long pause

during which Julian, instantly defensive, took stock of the situation.

He said, evenly, "I can't go on Saturday. I'm playing golf."

"I thought you played golf on Sundays now."

"No. That was last week."

There was another pause. Amanda said, "I see."

She scarcely spoke to him again all that evening. And when she did, it was in the politest possible manner. After dinner they went into the sitting-room and she turned on the television. He turned it off and said, "Amanda."

"I want to watch it."

"Well, you can't watch it because you're going to talk to me."

"No, I'm not."

"Well, I'm going to talk to you. I am not about to become the sort of husband who shops with his wife on Saturday mornings and cuts the grass on Sunday afternoons. Is that quite clear?"

"I suppose I'm meant to do the shopping and cut the grass."

"You can do what you like. We see each other every day . . ."

"What do you suppose I do when you're at the office all day?"

"You don't need to do nothing. You had a marvellous job, but you chucked it up because you said you wanted to be a housewife."

"So what if I did? Does that mean I have to spend the rest of my life on my own, adapting my plans to your beastly golf?"

"Well, what do you want to do?"

"I don't care what I do – but I don't want to do it by myself. Do you understand that? I don't want to do it by myself!"

This time it was a real quarrel, sour and rancorous. By morning the rift was still between them. He kissed her good-bye, but she turned her head away and he went, furious, to work.

The long day droned on, irritating and bugged with frustrations. At the end of it he felt in need of some calm and understanding company. Someone old and wise who would reassure him.

There was one person who fitted this bill and Julian made his way to her. His godmother.

"Julian," she said. "What a wonderful surprise. Come in."

He looked at her with affection. Well into her sixties, she was as pretty and lively as ever. She had been a friend of his mother's and no relation at all, but he had always called her Aunt Nora. Nora Stockforth.

He told her about everything. The honeymoon in New York, the new house.

"And how is Amanda?"

"She's all right."

There was a small silence. Aunt Nora refilled his glass. As she sat down again, he looked up and caught her eye. She said, gently, "You don't make it sound as though she's all right."

"She is all right. It's just that she . . ."

And then it all came out. He told her about Tommy and the weekly golf games. He told her about Amanda always having known about this arrangement, and never minding. "But now . . ."

"Now she minds."

"It's so ridiculous. It's simply one day in the week. It isn't

71

as though she wants to do anything in particular, it's just that she says she doesn't want to do it by herself."

Aunt Nora said, "I hope you're not asking me to make any sort of comment."

Julian frowned. "How do you mean?"

"I would never dream of taking sides. But I think you were right to come over and talk to me. Sometimes just talking about things helps to keep one's sense of proportion."

"You think I've lost mine?"

"No, I don't mean that at all. But I think you must take the long view. I always think a new marriage is a little like a baby. It needs to be cuddled and loved for the first two years, to be wrapped in security.

"Just now you and Amanda only have each other to think about. This is the time that you shape your life together so that when the bad times come – which they will – there'll be something there to remember, to hold you together."

"You think I'm being selfish?"

"I told you I wasn't going to comment."

"You think her complaints are justified?"

Aunt Nora laughed. "I think that if she's complaining, you haven't got too much to worry about. It's when she stops complaining that you have trouble on your hands."

He laid down his glass. "What sort of trouble?"

"I leave you to work that out for yourself. And now I think you should go, or Amanda will think you've had a terrible accident." They stood up. "Julian, do come again. But bring Amanda with you next time."

He was still in a thoughtful mood when he reached home. Amanda opened the door before he had time to find his keys and they stood, eyeing each other, their faces solemn.

Then she smiled. "Hello."

It was all right. "Darling." He stepped indoors and kissed her. "I'm sorry about everything."

"Oh, Julian, I'm sorry, too. Did you have a good day?"

"No – but it's all right now. I'm a bit late because I called in to see Aunt Nora on the way back home. She sent you her love, of course."

Later, Amanda said casually: "Could I have the car tomorrow?"

"Yes, of course. Going somewhere special?"

"No," she said, not looking at him. "It's just that I might need it, that's all."

He waited for her to tell him more, but she didn't. Why did she want the car? Perhaps she was going to have lunch with a girlfriend in town.

The next evening when he got home, Amanda was in the sitting-room watching television, wearing her smartest clothes.

He said: "How did you get along?" and waited to be told all about her day.

But she only said, "All right."

"Would you like a drink?"

"No, thank you."

She seemed intent on the television, so he left her and went out into the kitchen to find himself a beer. As he opened the refrigerator door, he suddenly stopped dead. Aunt Nora's words came clear as a bell: 'It's when she stops complaining that you have trouble on your hands.'

Amanda had, it was obvious, stopped complaining. What was it about her that was different? And why those clothes?

Carefully testing the ground, he said, "Well, how's the bathroom going?"

"I haven't had a chance to get at it today."

"Do you still want to buy the carpet? I could probably call Tommy and he could get hold of someone else to play golf on Saturday."

Amanda laughed. "Oh, it doesn't matter that much. No point in changing your plans."

"But . . ."

"Anyway," she interrupted his self-sacrifice without even bothering to listen, "I shall probably be busy on Saturday myself." She looked at her watch. "When do you want to eat?"

He didn't want to eat. His stomach was a vacuum probed by ghastly suspicions. She didn't mind being left on her own any more. She had occupations of her own . . . appointments. Dates?

But she wouldn't . . . not Amanda.

But why not? She was young and attractive. Before Julian had finally pinned her down, there had been a horde of young men waiting to take her out.

"Julian, I asked you when you wanted to eat?"

He gazed at her as though he had never seen her before. He managed to say, through an unexplained obstruction in his throat: "Any time."

He found himself longing for a cold, for flu – anything would do, provided it gave him a cast-iron excuse not to play golf at Wentworth on Saturday. But his health, perversely, remained unimpaired. When he left, Amanda was still in bed, which was quite out of character.

He played in a stupor. Eventually, Tommy was moved to ask, "Anything wrong?"

"Um? No, nothing."

"Just seem a bit preoccupied. We're seven down, you know."

They were, inevitably, beaten into the ground and Tommy was not pleased. He was even less pleased when Julian excused himself from playing a second round and said that he was going home.

"There *is* something wrong," said Tommy.

"Why should there be anything wrong?"

"Just thought you were beginning to look like a husband. Amanda's not creating, is she? You must assert yourself, you know, Julian."

'Stupid fool,' thought Julian, roaring back towards London. 'What does he know about it? Looking like a husband, indeed. What does he expect me to look like? Miss World?'

But as he turned at last into their own little tree-lined street, all these bolstering blusterings collapsed about his ears. For the house was empty.

He looked at his watch. Four o'clock. What was she doing? Where was she? She might have left him a note, but there was nothing. Only the hum of the refrigerator, the smell of polish.

He thought, 'She's not coming back.' The very prospect left him cold and trembling. No Amanda. No laughter, no digging in the garden, no arguments. No love. The end of love.

He had dropped his bag of clubs at the foot of the stairs. Now, he stepped over them and settled himself on the bottom stair, because there didn't seem to be anywhere better to sit.

He thought back. That Sunday when she had gone to have lunch with her parents and had a lift home ... Who had brought her? Julian had never got around to asking, but now he knew that it had been Guy Hanthorpe.

Guy Hanthorpe had been Amanda's most faithful boyfriend. He had known her all his life, for their parents were neighbours in the country. He was a stockbroker, successful and distinguished. Julian, who was stocky and dark, had disliked and resented the tall, fair Guy on sight.

Perhaps they had been meeting each other, secretly, ever since Julian had brought her back from New York.

He was still there, sitting in the dusk at the foot of the

stairs, smoking himself silly and concocting heart-chilling fantasies, when he heard a car come up the road.

It stopped outside the house, doors opened and shut, he heard voices, footsteps on the path.

He got up and flung the door open.

It was Amanda. And with her was Guy.

"Darling, you're back!" Amanda looked amazed.

Julian said nothing. He simply stood and looked at Guy, aware of rage, like a vice, gripping his ribcage. He thought of hitting Guy; saw himself doing it, like some violent film, slow-motion. He saw his hand come up and smash itself into Guy's amiable face. Saw Guy go down, crumpled, insensible, hitting his head as he fell; lying unconscious on the paving, blood seeping from his mouth, from the ghastly wound in his head . . .

"Hello, Julian," said Guy and Julian blinked, surprised to find that he hadn't hit Guy after all.

"Where have you been?" he asked Amanda.

"Down at my mother's. And Guy was seeing his mother, so he gave me a lift home." Julian said nothing.

Irritated, Amanda continued. "Do you think we could come in? It's rather cool, and it's beginning to drizzle."

"Yes. Yes, of course."

He stood aside, but Guy said, "Actually, I won't, thank you." He glanced at his watch. "I'm going out for dinner tonight, and I must get back and get myself changed. So I'll say goodbye. 'Bye, Amanda." He gave her a peck on the cheek, raised a hand to Julian and was off, plunging down the path on his long legs.

Amanda called: "Goodbye, and thanks for the lift."

She stood in the hall and looked at the bag of golf clubs at the foot of the stairs. At the undrawn curtains. At Julian.

She said: "Is anything wrong?"

"No," he said with fine bitterness. "Nothing. Just that I thought you weren't ever coming home again."

"Never coming . . . ? Have you gone out of your mind?"

"I thought you were with Guy."

"I was."

"I mean, all day."

She laughed, and then stopped laughing. "Julian, I told you. I've been with my mother."

"You didn't tell me that this morning. And where were you the other day, when I came home and found you all dressed up and reeking of perfume?"

"If you're going to be like that, I shan't tell you."

"Oh yes you will!" he yelled.

After the yell, there was a terrible silence. Then Amanda said, very quietly, "I have a feeling we should both take a deep breath and start at the beginning."

Julian took his deep breath. "Right," he said. "You start."

She said: "That day, I went home for the day. I needed the car because I wanted to go and see the doctor. I'm still registered with my parents' doctor and I haven't got a doctor in London.

"And I dressed myself up because I'm sick of wearing paintstained jeans and my mother likes to see me looking smart. And today I had to go back to see the doctor again, because he wanted to give me another check-up and be completely sure."

Was she going to die? "Completely sure of what?"

"And you had the car, so I had to go down by train, and Guy brought me back, very kindly, as he did the time before, and all you did was stand and glower at him. I've never been so ashamed."

"Amanda? What did the doctor say to you?"

"I'm going to have a baby, of course."

"A baby!" He searched for words. "But we've only just got married!"

"We've been married nearly four months. And we had a very long honeymoon . . ."

77

"But we never meant . . ."

"I know we never meant." She sounded near to tears. "But it's happened and if you dare take that horrible tone of voice . . ."

"A baby." He said it again, but this time his voice was filled with wonder. "You're going to have a baby! Oh, my darling, you are the most wonderful girl."

"You don't mind?"

"Mind? I'm thrilled!" He was astonished to find that it was true. "I've never been so thrilled about anything."

"Will the house be big enough for three?"

"Of course it will."

"I don't want to have to move. Our little house . . ."

"We won't move. We'll stay here for ever, and breed an enormous family and have rows of perambulators all the way up the garden path."

She said, "I didn't want to tell you about what I was doing, Julian, because I couldn't be sure myself, so I wanted to wait for a while."

"It doesn't matter. Nothing matters except this . . ."

And it didn't. That evening Julian cooked supper for Amanda, and they ate it off a tray in front of the fire, and she put her feet up on the sofa because he said that that was what all expectant mothers were meant to do.

When at last it was time to go to bed, Julian locked up the house, put his arm around his wife, and then led her gently towards the stairs.

His precious bag of golf clubs still lay where he had dropped it, but he shoved it out of the way with his foot and left it. There would be plenty of time to put it away safely . . .

# ❧ Christabel ❧

Mrs Lowyer awoke, at her usual civilised hour of eight-thirty in the morning, to the hum of the combine harvester in the barley field. It was a good sound to wake up to on a late summer morning. She had always been very fond of this time of the year; loving the precious golden sunshine of Indian summers, the brilliance of laden rowan trees, the first taste of blackberries. She had been married – a long time ago – in September, and her only son Paul had been born a year later in the same month. And now his daughter was going to be married in a week's time. Mrs Lowyer lay in bed and watched the sky through the open window (she had never been able to bear sleeping with drawn curtains) and saw it blue as a robin's egg between soft, slow-moving clouds.

After a little she got up, put on her dressing-gown and slippers and went to the window to inspect the outside world. Her window was at the back of the little house, overlooking the scrap of garden. Beyond the fence was the great, golden field of barley and beyond that again, Shadwell, the old house where her son and his wife now lived, and where Mrs Lowyer had lived and brought up her family for more than thirty years.

The combine was moving across the furthest edge of the field. A huge scarlet monster, eating its way through the waist-high crop. It was too distant to see the driver, but she knew that it was Sam Crichtan. He ran the farm with only sporadic help, and he trusted no one but himself to work that precious, hideously expensive piece of equipment. She wondered how long he had been working. Probably since sun-up, and he would not stop until it was too dark to work any longer. He did this seven days a week.

Mrs Lowyer sighed. For Sam; for changed days; for the fact that at sixty-seven she was too old to go out and give him a hand. And for another, nebulous reason that had been at the back of her mind for some time now, but which she refused to take out and inspect. She shut the window firmly and went downstairs to put out her little dachshund, Lucy, for her morning excursion, and then to light the gas and fill her breakfast kettle.

By ten o'clock, dressed and breakfasted, she was out in her garden snipping a few dead heads off the roses, pulling up a weed or two, staking a straggling clump of Michaelmas daisies. The combine had now cut a deep swathe around the border of the field and, as she fiddled with scissors and string, it came surging up the slope towards the fence at the edge of her garden. She abandoned her flower-bed and went to wave as Sam passed. But he didn't pass. He switched off the engine and stopped the immense machine. All clanking and turning and grinding ceased. The morning was all at once blessedly still. Sam opened the door of the cab and climbed down, and came stiffly and tiredly across the stubble towards her.

She said, "I didn't mean you to stop. I was just waving hello."

"I'm sorry about that. I thought you were going to offer me a cup of tea. I forgot to fill a flask and my throat's as dry as the desert."

"Well, of course I'll give you a cup of tea." 'And something to eat as well,' she decided privately, but she did not say this. "How will you get over the fence?"

"Easy," said Sam. He put a hand on the fence-post and vaulted lightly over. "Amazing what you can do if there's a cup of tea in the offing."

She smiled. She had always liked Sam. For ten years he had been tenant farmer at Shadwell, and she had watched him, by sheer determination and plodding hard work, turn what had been a neglected, run-down property, into a viable proposition. Steadings were repaired, fences mended, profits – and she knew that at first these had been sadly meagre – ploughed back, again and again, into the land. She could not remember him ever taking a holiday, although in the early days he had had two men to help him. Now, with modern streamlined methods and new machinery, he insisted on running the place more or less single-handed, and it was a constant wonder to Mrs Lowyer that he didn't die of exhaustion or become embittered and dour. He had, however, done neither of these things, but he was terribly thin and looked much older than his thirty-two years, and sometimes so tired that she expected him to fall asleep on his feet.

She said, "Come along then, and sit down for a minute."

"I can't stay more than ten. I've the whole field to finish before this evening. The forecast for tomorrow's not too good."

"Well, provided we have a good day next Saturday a little rain won't do any harm."

"That's one of the reasons I'm cutting today. Paul wants to use the field as a car park for the wedding. He's going to build a ramp up over the ha-ha so that the guests can walk from their cars up to the marquee . . ." They had reached the back door, and he paused to toe off his mud-caked wellington boots. There were holes in the toes of his socks, but she did not let on that she had noticed this. She led the way into her miniature kitchen and put on the kettle while Sam shrugged off his oil-stained jacket, pulled out a chair and settled himself with a sigh of relief at the kitchen table.

"What time were you up this morning?" she asked him.

"Six o'clock."

"You must feel as though you've done a day's work already." Without asking him, she took down the frying pan and opened the fridge to get out bacon and eggs and sausages. Behind her, he looked about him with appreciation.

"Best designed little kitchen I've ever seen, this one. Like a ship's galley."

"It does very nicely for one person, but when I have guests to stay it does get a little overcrowded."

He lit himself, luxuriously, a briar pipe, as though it were one of the greatest treats in the world. Mrs Lowyer found an ashtray and laid it on the table. The bacon began to sizzle in the pan.

Sam asked suddenly: "Didn't you mind coming to live here after Paul and Felicity moved into Shadwell?"

"No, I didn't mind. I was fortunate that there was a house available for me, even though it is so tiny. The only thing that made me sad was leaving most of my furniture behind, because there simply wasn't the space for it here. But I've got my favourite bits and pieces. And after all, what is furniture? Nothing worth breaking your heart over. And whenever I go up to the house, I'm able to see it and enjoy it. Felicity loves it too, and probably takes far better care of it than I ever did. She puts me to shame, she's so capable, and of course she's in her element now, planning Christabel's wedding. Lists everywhere, charts pinned up on the kitchen wall, all her girlfriends roped in to do the flowers for her."

Deftly, she broke an egg into the pan, looked at it, and then broke another. She knew, of old, that feeding Sam was like pouring water down a well. His appetite was enormous, but he never seemed to put on an ounce of weight.

He made no comment on this last remark. In order to keep the conversation going, she asked, "When is the marquee going up?"

"Tuesday or Wednesday, depending on the weather."

"Are you going to be roped in to help with that?"

"No. I offered, but the hire firm do the whole thing. However, Felicity said she'd want furniture to be moved in the house, so doubtless I'll be there, heaving sofas as to the manner born."

"And you're going to the party tonight?"

Again, he did not reply. Mrs Lowyer turned to look at him and saw him lean forward to tap out the pipe in the ashtray. He was looking down, his expression shuttered. She said, in sudden concern, "You *have* been asked, haven't you?"

"Yes, and I said I'd go. But I don't know, I'll have to see."

"Sam, you have to go."

"Why?"

"Christabel would be so hurt if you weren't there."

"I don't suppose she'd even notice."

"Don't be so ridiculous, of course she'd notice. And of course she'd be hurt. Besides, you've never met Nigel. This is what the party's all about; so that everybody can meet Nigel before he's suddenly produced at the wedding. He's made a special trip up from London just for this occasion, and it would be very rude if we didn't all turn up."

She put the bacon and eggs and sausages on to a plate and set it, with a steaming mug of tea, on the table before him.

He looked at the spread with satisfaction and some surprise. "What's this? A second breakfast?"

"I'm quite sure you haven't even had a first breakfast." She pulled out a chair and sat down, facing him across the table.

"Well, no, I don't suppose I have." He began to eat.

83

"You're impossible. No man can do everything for himself, certainly not when he's working from dawn to dusk on the farm."

"I'm all right."

"But it must be so cheerless ..."

"Aggie Watson comes in most mornings."

"And what does she do? Scrub a floor and peel a pot of potatoes! That's not what I'm talking about, Sam. You should get a housekeeper. Or a wife. It's time you were married."

He said, "I can't afford a housekeeper."

Mrs Lowyer sighed. "And there's nobody you want to marry."

After a long pause, Sam said, "No."

"Nobody except Christabel," said Mrs Lowyer. She said it very quickly, before she had time to think, before she lost the courage to go treading in where she was obviously not going to be welcome. But she knew that it had to be said. It had to come out into the open if Christabel's wedding day was not to be clouded in any way by any person.

He said, as she knew that he would, "What makes you think that?"

"I suppose I've always known."

"She's just a little girl."

"She was a little girl when you first knew her, but she's twenty now."

Their eyes met across the table. Sam's eyes were a very pale blue, like winter skies. When he was in a cheerful mood they sparkled with good humour, but now they were cold, guarded, giving nothing away.

He said, "She's getting married on Saturday," and went on with his meal.

It was as though he had slammed a door in her face, but Mrs Lowyer knew that this was no time for moral cowardice. She said, "I think you've always loved her. I don't think there was a time when you didn't love her. And she was always so fond of you. I remember you helping her with her first pony, and the way she was always under your feet, trying to do things on the farm, holding the staples when you mended fences . . ."

"Losing the hammer," said Sam.

"She was never remotely interested in any of the young boys who grew up with her. She even took your photograph when she went away to boarding school. Did you know that?"

"Things change," said Sam.

"Do you mean that you've changed, or that Christabel's changed?"

"Both, I suppose. As I said, she was just a little girl. She grew up, and I grew older. Then she went away down to London, got a job, a flat of her own . . ."

"Met Nigel," finished Mrs Lowyer.

"Yes. She met Nigel. And now she's going to marry him."

"Do you blame her?"

"I've never met him."

"He's a very nice, very suitable young man. Any sensible girl would have been a fool to turn him down."

"Christabel never was a fool."

"But I'm beginning to suspect that you are."

"Why?"

"Because it's patently obvious that you're in love with her. You've always loved her, but you've never asked her to marry you."

"I couldn't," said Sam.

"Why not, for heaven's sake?"

"For every reason. That's why not. For every reason. What did I have to offer her? A little farm that doesn't even belong to me. A little house with two bedrooms and no form of central heating. And what about money, material things, all the things that a girl like Christabel deserves? I could never give them to her."

"Did you ever ask her if she even wanted them?"

"No."

"But . . ."

Sam looked despairing. He pushed the empty plate away from him and leaned his arms on the table. He said, "Please. Don't go on about it."

"Oh, Sam." For a moment she wondered if she were going to cry. She hadn't cried for years. She laid her hand over his and felt the horny, calloused skin.

He said, "It's too late, anyway."

She knew that he was right. It was too late. She smiled firmly and gave his hand a little pat. "All right, I won't talk about it any more. But you must come to the party tonight. We're going to be given a buffet dinner, and then there is to be dancing. Disco, I think they call it."

He grinned. "Can you disco dance?"

"I don't know. I've never tried. But if anybody asks me, I shall have a good shot at it."

~ ✦ ~

The day progressed, the morning taken up with small day-to-day chores. After lunch, Mrs Lowyer got her modest car out of the garage and drove to the neighbourhood market town where she had her hair done at the only hairdressers, which was called Huntleys of Mayfair. Miss Pickering, who owned this establishment, had never been near Mayfair in her life, and had chosen the name Huntley because she thought it added a touch of class. Here Mrs Lowyer endured being alternately frozen and scalded by a terrified junior, then had her hair wound around rollers and her scalp speared with plastic pins, and the torture was finally rounded off by being put under a red-hot dryer which she was unable to make cooler, however much she turned the knob on the dial.

At last the ordeal was over. Feeling scarlet in the face and totally exhausted, she drove herself home. She would have a cup of tea and then go to bed for a couple of hours to relax before the evening's festivities. But no sooner had she been greeted by Lucy and put on the kettle than the back door opened, a voice said, "Granny?" and it was Christabel herself.

"Darling," said Mrs Lowyer, and kissed her.

"Are you making tea? Can I have some with you? Gosh, you're looking smashing. Miss Pickering's pulled out all the stops this time. Is there any fruit cake?" She began opening her grandmother's cake tins, found a chocolate biscuit and started to eat it.

She was forever eating. Potato crisps, bars of chocolate, ice-cream in cones, snacking away on all the worst sort of junk food, but not a blemish marred her milky skin and, if anything, she seemed to be more slender than ever. Today she wore her oldest jeans, scuffed cowboy boots, a sagging sweater with darns in the elbows. Her hair, that beautiful hair that was a shade somewhere between chestnut and chocolate, was braided tightly into two pig-tails. Her face was innocent of make-up and she looked like a leggy fifteen-year-old. Impossible, thought Mrs Lowyer, to believe that next Saturday she was going to be married.

She said, "Has Nigel arrived yet?"

"Heavens, yes, he got here for lunch. He left London about four o'clock this morning. That wasn't bad going, was it?"

"Why isn't he with you now?"

"Oh, he and Pa are having a great crack about shooting pigeons and how many of Nigel's relations are coming to the wedding. You haven't seen Sam, have you?"

"I think he's still combining the barley field. Didn't you see him?"

"No. I went along by the river. There wasn't anybody at his house, not even Aggie."

"What did you want to see Sam about?"

"I wanted to thank him for my wedding present." She pulled out a chair and sat at the table, much as Sam had sat this morning. "Do you know what he gave me? It's simply beautiful and he made it all himself."

"No. What did he give you?"

"A walking stick."

Mrs Lowyer said, faintly, "A walking stick," and tried not to sound too astonished.

"Yes, and you know how he used to carve horn handles for walking sticks. He hasn't done it for ages, poor man, because he hasn't had the time, but he's done one for me, and it's all carved with flowers and sheaves of wheat, and it's all polished and gorgeous. And then around the stick there's a little silver band with my name on. Don't you think that was the most lovely thing to give me?"

"Yes, darling, lovely," said Mrs Lowyer, privately deciding that if Sam had considered the problem for a year, he could scarcely have given Christabel anything more unsuitable. A walking stick, for a young girl who was going to get married and go and live in a flat in London.

"I mean, it's so personal. Not just having my name on, but his making it for me with his own two hands."

"I must say, that does make it rather special."

"I hope he'll come tonight. That he won't go on combining after dark, or make some excuse."

"Of course he'll come. He was in this morning having a cup of tea with me, and he said he was coming."

"I can't tell you the spread Mother's laying on. She's put all the leaves in the dining-room table and pushed it against the wall of the dining-room, and there are the best white tablecloths and so much to eat, you just can't imagine."

Mrs Lowyer smiled. "She's in her element," she told Christabel.

She found the cake tin with the fruit cake in it, put the cake on a plate, and set the plate in front of Christabel. She poured tea for Christabel into her own mug, the blue and white striped one that she had used whenever she came to tea, ever since she was a little girl.

"And we're going to have a disco. That was another thing Pa wanted Nigel to do – buff up the old playroom floor."

"I don't quite know what I'm meant to do in a disco."

"Oh, snake around, you know, like they do on the box."

"Couldn't I just sit and watch?"

"Oh, heavens, Granny, don't be so old-fashioned. Just get with it, man." She shrugged her shoulders, tossed her plaits, tilted her chin, looked cool.

"Is that what I'm meant to do?"

"Well, I'll tell you what," said Christabel, cutting a wedge out of the fruit cake and beginning to eat it. "I'll make sure we have at least two Viennese waltzes, and you can whirl away to your heart's content with Colonel Foxton."

"Oh, really, Christabel . . ."

"Now, you know he's madly in love with you. I can't think why you don't marry him."

"What, go and live in that freezing house with all the pitch pine and stained glass?"

"He could come and live here."

"There wouldn't be room."

"You're terribly unkind about Colonel Foxton," Christabel told her. She had been teasing her grandmother about Colonel Foxton ever since the old gentleman had asked her to tea with him, and had spent the time showing her his collection of photographs taken when he was a young subaltern in India. "After all, he's exactly the right age for you."

"No, he's not. If I were to marry someone exactly the right age for me, he'd be over a hundred."

"How do you work that out?"

"Because the perfect age for a marriage is for the girl to be half the man's age, plus seven years. So if the man is twenty, he marries a girl of seventeen. And if the girl is sixty-seven, then she would have to marry a man of . . . um . . ." Mrs Lowyer's arithmetic had never been her strong point. "A hundred and twenty."

Christabel gazed at her. After a little, she said, "But I'm twenty, and Nigel's only twenty-three. That's all wrong. I should be marrying somebody of twenty-six."

"Well, you'd better hurry up, because you've only got a week to find him."

"Do you really think twenty-three is too young for me?"

"No, I don't think it matters at all. It's just a stupid sort of joke people make. It doesn't matter what ages a man and a woman are, provided they are truly fond of each other and want to spend the rest of their lives together."

"You don't say love," said Christabel.

"Darling, I never talk about love at tea-time. And now eat up that cake and drink up that tea, because I'm going upstairs to have a rest before the party. I wonder what time I'm expected?"

"Oh, I should think about eight. Do you want someone to come and fetch you?"

"Of course not. It's going to be a beautiful, fine evening. I shall walk up the lane. And I shall enjoy seeing the house all lit up and festive. There's something very romantic about a house all lit up for a party. Especially a party that's being given for such a happy reason."

"Yes," said Christabel. She did not sound very certain. "Yes, I suppose it is romantic."

At exactly five to eight, wearing her best sapphire blue velvet dinner dress and a cashmere shawl over her shoulders, Mrs Lowyer bid Lucy good night, turned off the lights, and made her way down the garden path, and up the lane which led to her old house. There was a half-moon sailing high in the sky, and overhead the branches of the ancient beeches laced their arms together like the flying buttresses of some great cathedral. Ahead of her, lighted windows shone through the dusk, and the air was filled with the scent of dying leaves, and moss, and the strains of music.

Already cars were arriving, parking on the gravel in front of the house, and as Mrs Lowyer went up the stone steps to the open door she was joined by other guests, the women holding up their long skirts, the men in black ties and dinner jackets.

"Oh, Mrs Lowyer, how lovely to see you! Doesn't the house look pretty, coming along the road, through the trees . . . ? How does Felicity manage even to arrange that the weather is perfect? It never seems to rain when she has a party."

"Let's hope her luck holds for next Saturday."

The hall was filled with people. Mrs Lowyer kissed her son and her pretty daughter-in-law, and then made her way upstairs to leave her shawl. She laid this on Felicity's bed and then went to the dressing-table to check that her coiffure was still a credit to Miss Pickering's hands. Her reflection gazed back at her from the antique triple mirror. It was the mirror that had always stood on that dressing-table – Mrs Lowyer had inherited it from her own mother-in-law. She remembered reflections of herself as she had been, slender and shingle-headed. Now she saw, beneath the careful make-up, the wrinkles of age, the crêpey neck, the silver hair. Her hands, touching that hair, were the hands of an old lady. 'I am a grandmother,' she told herself. 'In a year or so, I may be a great-grandmother.' The prospect she found unalarming. If she had learned nothing else, she had learned that every age brings its own rewards.

"I've caught you preening!"

Mrs Lowyer turned from the looking glass and saw Christabel behind her. She was laughing at her grandmother, her eyes sparkling with amusement.

"I'm not preening. I'm thinking how glad I am that I'm not young any more, that I don't have to worry if some man will dance with me. That I don't have to worry if my husband dances with some other pretty woman."

"I bet you never had any of those worries. And now you look gorgeous."

"Oh, darling, you look lovely too. Is that a new dress?"

"Yes." Christabel straightened up and whirled around to show off her finery. The dress was white, layers of soft, floating lawn. The neck was low, and her hair, released from the plaits of this afternoon, was romantically looped and swathed about her head. Her eyes swam and sparkled.

"Where did you get it?"

"In London. Mother saw it when we were trousseau-shopping and said I had to have it. It's meant to be part of my trousseau, but I thought I'd wear it tonight."

Mrs Lowyer gave her a kiss. "It's perfect. You look lovely."

From outside the open door, from the landing, a voice said, "Christabel!" Christabel went to open the door, and Nigel was revealed, standing outside, looking both embarrassed and faintly put out.

"What are you doing?" Christabel demanded. "Lurking around outside the ladies' room? You'll get a bad name for yourself."

He smiled, but not as though he thought the joke particularly funny. "I've been looking for you all over. Your mother's waiting for you. She sent me to find you."

"Granny and I are having a mutual admiration session."

"Hello, Mrs Lowyer."

"Nigel. How very nice to see you again." She went through the open door, and planted a light kiss on his cheek. With his dark hair and his formal clothes, he looked, not sophisticated as he should have, but like a young boy dressed up for a party. "And I'm sorry Christabel and I have kept you all waiting. Perhaps now we should all go down and join the others."

❧

It was not until halfway through the evening, when most of the guests had had supper and the younger element had already taken themselves off to the disco, that Sam Crichtan appeared. Mrs Lowyer, trapped in a corner by the fireplace with Colonel Foxton, saw him come into the room through the french windows, which had been left open for air, and she knew a rush of relief that he had kept his word to her.

It was a long time since she had seen him dressed for an evening out, and she decided, with private satisfaction, that his dark, formal clothes became him. With his thin, brown face, and his neatly brushed hair, he looked more than presentable – distinguished, even.

". . . it's a funny thing," droned Colonel Foxton. "Damn funny thing, the way some people can get planning permission. Wanted to renovate my gardener's cottage. Wasn't allowed to put a window in the roof. It's a funny . . ."

"I wonder, would you excuse me?" Gracefully, charmingly, Mrs Lowyer got to her feet. "I have an urgent message for Sam, and I must give it to him before he gets swept out of my sight."

"What? Oh, yes. Sorry, my dear. Didn't realise how I'd been going on."

"I loved hearing about your gardener's cottage. You must tell me the rest of the story another time."

She made her way across the room. "Sam."

"Mrs Lowyer."

"I am glad you came. Have you eaten?"

"No. I didn't really have time."

"I thought not. Then come with me right away, and before you do anything else you must have a drink, and some cold salmon and cold roast beef that is out of this world."

She led him through to the dining-room and found him a glass of whisky and a plate which she proceeded to heap with food.

"Have you seen Christabel?"

"I've only just got here."

"But you didn't see her this afternoon?"

"No."

"She was looking for you. To thank you for the walking stick."

"I suppose you thought it was a pretty stupid present?"

"Yes," said Mrs Lowyer, who had never believed in mincing words. "But a very special one. Christabel was not only delighted, she was touched. How about a baked potato with butter? Or even two?"

"You didn't tell her? What we talked about this morning?"

"Of course not. A roll?"

"I wouldn't want her to know."

"No," said Mrs Lowyer. "Of course not." Across the room, through the open door, she could see Christabel and Nigel. He had his arm around her shoulder, her amazing hair glinted in the candlelight. "Nigel is a very nice young man. She is a very lucky girl."

Sam glanced up, saw that she was looking over his shoulder and turned. Nigel bent and kissed the top of Christabel's head. Somebody made a remark and everybody laughed. For a second Sam was still, and then he turned back to the table. He said, "And some of that mayonnaise, too, if I may. I was always very fond of Felicity's mayonnaise."

❦

But, later again, taken to inspect the disco by her son, Mrs Lowyer saw Christabel dancing with Sam. All the others on the floor appeared to be dancing by themselves, gyrating to the thumping music, grotesque in the whirling, flashing lights. Only Christabel and Sam seemed a couple. Moving together, their arms around each other, Christabel's head rested against Sam's shoulder.

Mrs Lowyer hoped that her son had not seen. She put a hand on his arm. She said, "The noise is deafening. I'd rather go back to the drawing-room," and, obediently, he led her away. But, at the door, Mrs Lowyer looked back. It did not take a second or more to realise that in that instant, apparently without trace, Sam and Christabel had disappeared.

After that, she went home. Slipped away unnoticed, said good night to nobody. Wrapped in the familiar warmth of her shawl, she made her way down the lane. The sounds of music, the hum of conversation, died away behind her, swallowed into the quiet of a country night. September. Her favourite month.

'This is all a terrible mistake. She is marrying the wrong man.'

Her house, dark and small and quiet, was a sanctuary. She lifted Lucy from her basket, put her out into the garden, got herself a cup of hot milk, let Lucy in again, carried the milk upstairs, slowly undressed and put herself to bed.

Through the open window she saw the half-moon sink from the sky. The world outside was filled with small night sounds. She longed for sleep.

~⚜~

It was four o'clock before the rattle of pebbles sounded like rain against her window-pane. At first she thought that she had imagined it, but it came again. And then, "Granny!"

She got out of bed, took up her dressing-gown, wrapped herself in it, tied the sash. She went to the open window. Below, in the garden, she saw the blur of white. White as a ghost, a wraith.

"Granny?"

"Christabel, what are you doing?"

"I want to talk to you."

She went downstairs, switching on lights. She opened the front door and Christabel came in, shivering with cold, the white dress muddied at its hem.

"What about the party?"

"The party's nearly over. I wanted to talk to you. Everybody thinks I've gone to bed."

"Where's Nigel?"

"Having a second supper."

"And Sam?"

"He went home."

In silence Mrs Lowyer looked into her granddaughter's eyes. They were bright with unshed tears. "Come upstairs," she said.

They went back to her room, her own pretty, fragrant bedroom. Mrs Lowyer got into bed, and Christabel slid in beside her, beneath the eiderdown. Mrs Lowyer could feel the coldness of Christabel's arms, the bony young ribcage, the beat of Christabel's heart.

Christabel said, "I'm afraid."

"What are you afraid of?"

"Everything. Getting married. Being trapped. Doors closing in on me."

"That's what being married is all about," said Mrs Lowyer. "Being trapped. All that matters is that you're trapped with the right person."

"Oh, Granny, why can't everything be easy?"

"Nothing is ever easy," said Mrs Lowyer. Her hand moved against Christabel's shoulder. "Being born isn't easy. Growing up isn't easy. Getting married isn't easy. Having children can be murder. Growing old is just as bad."

"I think . . . I think I don't want to marry Nigel."

"Why not?"

"I don't know."

"Aren't you in love with him?"

"I was. Terribly. Really terribly in love. But . . . I don't know. I don't want to live in London. I don't like being in a flat. I feel as though I'm going to have to live in a box. And . . . there's another thing. I don't like his friends very much. I don't feel I have anything in common with them. Does that matter? Does it matter terribly?"

"Yes," said Mrs Lowyer. "Yes, I think it probably does."

"It's called wedding nerves, isn't it?"

"It is, sometimes."

"Do you think it is this time?"

Mrs Lowyer answered this with another question. "Where did you go with Sam?"

"Into the garden. We just went and sat on the seat under the beech tree. It was quite harmless."

"And then you said good night and he went home?"

"Yes."

"He loves you. You know that, don't you?"

"I hoped he would say that. But he didn't say anything."

"He thinks he has nothing to offer you. He's very proud."

"Why didn't he tell me?"

"Oh, Christabel. Use your imagination."

"I wouldn't mind being poor. I wouldn't mind helping him on the farm. I wouldn't even mind living in that cold little house; I know I could make it bright and comfortable. Nothing would matter provided I was with Sam."

"You'll have to convince him."

"But Granny, the wedding. The marquee and the arrangements and the presents and the invitations. It's all costing so much, and . . ."

"It can be put off," said Mrs Lowyer. "The last thing that your mother and father would want would be for you to marry a man whom you didn't truly love. If you want Sam, you're going to have to go and tell him. You must tell him what you've told me – that you don't mind about his being poor and hard-working and living in that funny little farmhouse. You must tell him that he is the only man in your life that you have ever truly loved."

"You've always known, haven't you?"

"Yes."

"How?"

"I'm old, I'm experienced. I've seen it all happen before."

"When shall I tell him?"

"Now. Go to his house now. You can borrow my car so that you don't get your feet wet. And I'll lend you a cardigan to keep you warm. And if he's asleep, wake him up, get him out of bed. Just tell him. Be truthful to him, but most important of all, be truthful to yourself."

"But Mother and Pa . . . I'll never have the nerve to tell them. I've been so stupid . . ."

"I shall tell them."

"And Nigel . . . ?"

"I shall tell Nigel as well. He's young. He'll be hurt, but he'll recover. Nothing could be worse for him than a half-hearted marriage." She kissed her granddaughter, her heart filled with sympathy and love. "Now off you go, my darling, and good luck. And Christabel . . ."

"Yes, Granny."

"My dearest love to Sam."

❧

She heard Christabel go. Heard her get the little car out of the garage and drive away down the rutted farm lane that led to Sam Crichtan's house. It was now five o'clock in the morning. 'What am I thinking of?' Mrs Lowyer asked herself. 'What in the name of goodness have I done?'

But she could not make herself feel repentant. It had gone, that anxiety which she had been too afraid to take out and examine. She had always known about Sam and Christabel. She had told herself that their destiny was of no concern to her. But now their destiny had been put into her hands, and she had made her decision. Right or wrong, there could be no going back.

She lay sleepless until full light. At eight-thirty, she awoke from a doze, got out of bed and put on her dressing-gown and went to shut the window. The barley field lay shorn and gold under a watery sky. She knew that Sam and Christabel were right for each other. She thought of Paul and Felicity and Nigel. She dressed and went downstairs; said good morning to Lucy and put her out into the garden, cooked her own breakfast, drank her coffee. Then she put on her coat and, taking Lucy with her, let herself out of the house. It was a sweet, damp morning. Mrs Lowyer went down the path and through the gate, and then, briskly, set off up the lane towards the big house with her little dog at her heels.

# The Blackberry Day

The night train moved out of Euston, heading north. Claudia, already changed into her nightgown and robe, pulled up the blind and sat on the edge of the narrow bunk, watching the city slip away, lights and dim streets and high-rise flats wheeling off into the past. It was a cloudy evening, the clouds stained bronze by a million street lamps but, as she watched, the clouds parted for a moment and a moon sailed into view, a full moon, round and shining as a polished silver plate.

She turned off the lights, got into the bunk, with its cotton sheets all crisp and tight as a hospital bed, and lay and watched the moon and was lulled by the smooth, gathering speed of the train. Inevitably she recalled other, long-ago journeys and, for the first time, thought of tomorrow and felt a mild stirring of excitement. It was as though what she was doing had become a positive action, not simply a compromise. Not simply the next best thing.

This did something to bolster her bruised pride and enabled her to bundle, for the moment, anxious uncertainties out of her mind. They were still there and would remain so, lurking around the edge of her subconscious, but for the time being she allowed herself the luxury of knowing that she had taken the right course.

She was immensely tired. The moon shone into her eyes.

She turned on her side, away from its disturbing brilliance, buried her face in the pillow and, surprisingly, slept.

At Inverness she alighted from the train into a climate so different that the night train could have carried her not only north, but abroad. The day was Saturday, the month September, and she had left London on an evening warm as June, the air muggy and stale, the sky overcast. But now she walked out into a world that glittered in the early light and was arched by a high and cloudless sky of pale and pristine blue. It was much colder. There was the nip of frost in the air and leaves on trees were already turning autumn gold.

Here she had an hour or two to wait for the small stopping train that would carry her, through the morning, even further north. She filled this in by going to the nearest hotel and eating breakfast, and then walked back to the station. The news-stand had opened, so she bought a magazine and made her way to the platform where the smaller train waited, already gradually filling with passengers. She found a seat, stowed her luggage, and was almost at once joined by a pleasant-faced woman who settled herself across the table in the seat opposite. She wore a tweed coat with a Cairngorm brooch in the lapel and a furry green felt hat. As well as her zipped overnight bag, she was burdened by a number of plastic shopping bags, one of which contained what looked like a hefty picnic.

Their eyes met across the table. Claudia smiled politely. The woman said, "Oh, my, what a cold morning. I had to wait for the bus. My feet turned to stone."

"Yes, but it's lovely."

"Oh, aye, good and fine. Anything's better than the rain, I always say." A whistle blew, doors slammed. "There we are, we're off. Sharp on time, too. Are you going far?"

Claudia, who had picked up her magazine, resigned herself to conversation and laid it down again.

"Lossdale."

"That's where I'm bound, too. I've been down for a night or two, staying with my sister. For the shopping, you know. They've a lovely Marks and Spencers. Bought a shirt for my husband. Are you staying in Lossdale?"

She was not curious, simply interested. Claudia told her, "Yes, just for a week." And then, because it was obvious that she would be asked, she volunteered the information. "At Inverloss, with my cousin, Jennifer Drysdale."

"Jennifer! Oh, I know her well, we're on the Rural together. Stitching new kneelers for the Kirk. Funny she never mentioned the fact that you were coming."

"It was very much a last-minute arrangement."

"Is this your first visit?"

"No. I used to come up every summer when I was young. When her parents were alive, and before Jennifer inherited the farm."

"Do you live in the south?"

"Yes, in London."

"I thought so. By your clothes." The train was rattling over the bridge, the firth spread below them, stretching from the far western hills to the sea. She saw small boats going about their business, delectable houses facing out over the water with gardens sloping down to the shore. "I came up last night on the sleeper."

"That's a long journey, but better than driving a car. My man will scarcely go on the main roads these days, the traffic goes so fast. Like taking your life in your hands. But then he was always slow. It's his nature. Goes with his job."

Claudia smiled. "What is his job?"

"He's a shepherd. And his mind on not much else but his sheep. I just hope he remembers to come and pick me up

103

at the station. I left a note over the cooker to remind him, but that's no certainty that he'll remember." She was not complaining. In fact, she looked quite smug about her husband's shortcomings, as though they made him special. "And is Jennifer coming to meet you?"

"She said she would."

"She's a busy girl, with the farm and the animals and the children. They're lovely bairns."

"I've only seen photographs. I haven't been to Inverloss for twenty years. Jennifer wasn't even married then."

"Well, she's got a lovely man in Ronnie. Mind, he comes from south of the border, but for all that he's a good farmer. Just as well, with that great place to run."

The conversation lapsed. Claudia gazed from the window. They were into the hills now, snaking away into a country desolate save for isolated farmsteads and flocks of sheep, and rivers flowing through wide green straths. The sun rose in the sky and long shadows grew shorter. Claudia's companion opened her picnic bag, poured tea into a plastic mug, munched genteelly on a ham sandwich.

The small stations came and went, the train idling for moments while passengers alighted or climbed aboard. They passed the time of day, and dogs barked, and porters trundled trolleys of parcels. Nobody hurried. It was as though there was all the time in the world.

The journey progressed and Claudia began to count the stops, as once she used to. Three more to go. Two more. One more. Nearly there. The train ran alongside the sea. She saw ebb-tide beaches and distant breakers. The shepherd's wife packed up her picnic, dusted shortbread crumbs from her pouter-pigeon bosom, rummaged in her capacious handbag for her ticket.

The train slowed, and the sign *Lossdale* sailed past the window. The two women stood, gathered up their belongings, stepped down on to the platform. The shepherd was there, with his dog. He had not forgotten, but greeted his wife with little fuss. "You're here," he told her unnecessarily, took her bag from her and strode away. She followed him, turning back to wave at Claudia. "See you around, maybe."

No sign of Jennifer. The train drew away and Claudia was left alone on the platform. She stood by her suitcase in her London suit, and decided that there is nothing more letting down than to have no person to meet one at the end of a journey. She determined not to become impatient. There was no hurry, no pressing appointment. Jennifer had just been held up . . .

"Claudia!"

A man's voice. Startled, she turned, full into the sun, needing to shade her eyes. She saw him coming at her out of the dazzle, unrecognised for an instant and then, astonishingly, familiar.

Magnus Ballater. The last person she had ever expected to see. Not forgotten, but out of mind for longer than Claudia cared to think about. Magnus, in dark corduroys and a hugely patterned sweater; taller and more heftily built than she remembered, with a head of unfashionably long, dark, thick hair, and that old irrepressible grin on his suntanned, weather-seamed face.

"Claudia."

She knew that she was gaping, and had to laugh at her own amazement. "Magnus. For heaven's sake. What are you doing here?"

"Come to meet you. Jennifer's been held up at Inverloss. Something about the boiler. She gave me a ring and asked me to come and collect you." He stood there, looking down at her. "Do I get a kiss?"

Claudia reached up and planted a peck on his cold cheek. "I didn't know you'd be around."

"Oh, yes, I'm around. A local inhabitant now. Is this all your luggage?" He swept it up. "Come along now."

She followed him, almost running to keep up with his long legs, through the gate and out into the station yard where a large and battered estate car awaited them. A dog looked out of the back window. Its nose had made smeary marks on the glass. Magnus flung open the boot and tossed Claudia's suitcase in with the dog, and then came around to open the front door for her. She got in. The car smelt of dog and the inside looked as though it hadn't been cleaned out for months, but Magnus made no apologies as he settled himself beside her, slammed the door and started up the engine. Gravel shot from behind the back wheels and they were away. She remembered that he had never been a man to waste time.

She said, "But what do you do here?"

"I run my father's old woollen mill."

"But you always swore you'd never do that. You were going to be independent, go out on your own."

"And so I was for a bit. Worked in the Borders and then Yorkshire. Then I went to Germany for a couple of years and ended up in New York as a wool broker. But then my father died, and the mill started running down and was going to be sold, so I came home."

There was an air of tremendous confidence about him. She said, and it was a statement and not a question, "And pulled it all together."

"Tried to. At least we're out of the red now and we've got some important orders coming in. Doubled the workforce. You must come and see it. See if you approve of our end product."

"And what is that?"

"Tweeds, but much finer than the ones my father used to make. Closer weaves, lighter weights. Hard-wearing, but not hard. Malleable, I think the word is. And some amazing colours."

"Are you designing?"

"Yes."

"And where are the important orders coming from?"

"All over the world."

"That's marvellous. And where do you live?"

"In Pa's old house."

Old Mr Ballater's house. Claudia remembered it, built high on the hill above the town. It had a large garden and a tennis court. Many energetic afternoons had been spent there, for Magnus, a year or so older than Claudia and Jennifer, had been one of a pack of youngsters who had spent all their time together. Leaving school, he had studied textile design and that last summer of all he was already a first-year student.

That had been a special summer for a number of reasons. The weather was one of them, for it had been exceptionally warm and dry and the long, light northern evenings had seen many fishing expeditions, walks up the river bank and quiet hours spent casting for trout. The social life was another. They were all grown up now, and never had there been such an endless round of picnics and golf matches and tennis tournaments and reel parties and midnight barbecues on the beach. But Magnus, perhaps, had been the most important reason of all, for his enormous energy and his appetite for new diversions had swept them all up in his wake. A young man who never tired, was never bored nor out of humour, who owned his own car, and generally gave the impression that never for one moment did he doubt that life was for living and every day to be filled with enjoyment.

"But tell me about yourself." Driving at an alarming rate, they were already through the little town and out into the countryside beyond. "Jennifer says you haven't been north for twenty years. How could you stay out of touch for so long?"

"We weren't out of touch. We've always written to each other and telephoned, and every now and then Jennifer comes to London for a day or two and stays with me and we go shopping and to the theatre . . ."

"But twenty years. So long since we were all together. What times those were." He turned to smile at her, and Claudia prayed that a car was not bombing towards them around the curve of the road. "Why didn't you come? Were you too busy?"

"Like you. Learning a trade. Getting experience. Starting a business."

"Interior designing. Jennifer told me. Where do you operate?"

"London. The King's Road. I've got a shop and my own workrooms. Lots of commissions; too many, sometimes."

"Who runs it while you're away?"

"I have an assistant."

"You sound successful."

Claudia thought about this. "I suppose I am."

His eyes were back on the road. He said, "You never married?"

"I suppose Jennifer told you that, as well."

"Of course. I found it hard to believe."

Claudia knew a stirring of feminine irritation. Her voice was cool. "I suppose you imagined that my only potential was a house, a husband and children?"

"No," Magnus replied calmly, "I didn't imagine anything of the sort. I was just surprised that a girl so beautiful hadn't been snapped up years ago."

He spoke so naturally, so reasonably, that Claudia was ashamed of her own thoughtless words. She said, "I'm doing what I want to do," but thought of Giles, and then did not think of Giles because Giles was in America and this place and this moment and this man beside her had no part of Giles. "I am being independent."

"May I say that it suits you?"

She was touched. "Yes, I should like that very much." She smiled, and smoothly changed the direction of the conversation. "And you, Magnus? A wife?"

"Still unresolved."

"What does that mean?"

"That I never actually gathered up the courage to make the great commitment. A certain amount of dabbling has taken place, of course, but not the dreaded plunge." Once more he turned his head to look into her face, and his blue eyes gleamed with amusement. "It would appear that we are birds of a feather."

Claudia turned away, made no comment. She knew that he was mistaken, and they were not birds of a feather, but she was not going to tell him so. *A certain amount of dabbling has taken place*. It was not difficult to imagine the extent of these dabblings for he was, and always had been, an extremely attractive man. But she had not dabbled. Since meeting Giles eight years ago she had remained constant to him; seen him through an unsatisfactory marriage and an acrimonious divorce and, staunchly, been around ever since. And Magnus's dreaded plunge, the final commitment of marriage, she did not fear, but longed for.

Inverloss lay back from the road, reached by a rutted track and sheltered by a stand of ancient beeches and oaks. Bumping down the lane, Claudia looked for change and was grateful to see little. A new barn had been built, and there was a cattle grid between the road and the garden, but otherwise all was just the same. Beyond the cattle grid, sea pebbles did duty as gravel and approaching the house had always sounded just like driving across a beach. Magnus put the heel of his hand on the horn in a long blast, and before Claudia could open the door of the car Jennifer was there, erupting out of the house with dogs at her heels and a toddler on her hip. She wore jeans and a sweatshirt, her freckled face shone with good health, her hair was a curly mop, and she looked no different from the tomboy teenager she had once been.

"Oh, Jennifer . . ."

Jennifer set the toddler down and they hugged. All the dogs, including Magnus's, began to bark, and the child's face crumpled and he began to howl, so Jennifer picked him up again and he gazed at Claudia with baleful, tear-brimmed eyes.

"I'm sorry I couldn't get to meet you but Ronnie's fishing, and the man came to see about the boiler. We've been waiting for days and he had to come on a Saturday!"

"No problem. I'm here."

"Magnus, you are a saint. Stay and have lunch with us. It's such a gorgeous day, we're going to go blackberrying. We decided this morning that this is going to be our blackberry day. Jane and Rory are riding their ponies but they'll be back soon."

There had always, every year, as far back as Claudia could remember, been a blackberry day. A traditional expedition to pick the dark fruit for a twelve months' supply of jellies and jams.

She said, "Are we going to Creagan Hill?"

"But of course. Where else? Do come, Magnus. We can always do with an extra pair of hands."

"All right. But I have to go back to the mill first – there are a few things I have to sort out. What time's lunch?"

"Around one."

"I'll be there."

The inside of the house was no different. Such comfort. It smelt the same, a bit musky and smoky and peaty, and there were worn bits on the carpets and grubby marks on the wallpaper, just the height of children's hands.

"Isn't it great that Magnus has come back to Lossdale to live? It's like old times. He and Ronnie are tremendous buddies, and he's doing wonders at the mill. Were you surprised to see him?"

Jennifer, hefting her baby, led the way upstairs and Claudia, carrying her suitcase, followed. Across the wide landing, then Jennifer flung open a door and walked into the sunlight beyond.

"I put you in here, it's the room you always had." Claudia went to lay her suitcase on the seat of a chair. "Don't you adore the new bedspreads? I found them in a trunk in the attic. You must be longing to get out of your trainy clothes. I can't wait to introduce you to Ronnie. I can't believe you've never met him! And Jane and Rory. This one's called Geordie." She set him on his feet and sat herself down on the edge of the bed. Geordie, tottering slightly, made his way to the chest of drawers, thumped down on his bottom and began to play with one of the brass handles. "He's such a love."

Claudia was at the window, standing with her back to her cousin, looking down over the fields to the distant sea. She said, "I was so afraid everything would be changed, but it isn't." She turned back to smile at Jennifer. "Nor have you. You never do."

"You've changed," said Jennifer bluntly. "You've lost weight. You're dreadfully thin."

"That's just London. And we're both thirty-seven now. Not girls any longer."

"I didn't say you looked old. Just thin. And sort of polished." Jennifer's gaze was steady and unblinking. "Why did you suddenly decide to come, at a day's notice? Or don't

111

you want to talk about it?" There had never been secrets between them. Claudia lowered her head and began to unbutton the jacket of her suit. "It's Giles, isn't it?"

And it was a relief to have her say his name; to have it said so that it did not have to hang, like a spectre, between them.

Jennifer knew about Giles. Had gleaned what she could from letters, and had met him once in London when Giles had taken the pair of them out for dinner. At that time he had been divorced for nearly a year. "Is he going to marry you?" Jennifer had asked, but Claudia had laughed and told her that it was not like that at all, they were simply good friends.

Giles. Handsome, successful, charming, but paranoiacally elusive. He and Claudia each kept their separate establishments but they were lovers. They were a pair, accepted as a couple and, when asked away for country weekends, went together and stayed together.

But Giles's job as a money-broker was far-reaching. Much of his time he spent in New York where he had an apartment in the city, and often he was away for three or four months at a time. She did not know when he was returning until he called her. "I am back," he would say. "I am here." Whereupon, as if their separation had never taken place, the pattern of a shared life was taken up again: the dinner party in Giles's house which Claudia was glad to organise; the contacting of mutual friends; the intimate evenings in their favourite Italian restaurant; the magic nights, their love shared in Claudia's huge, downy bed.

And life changed colour and became vital, with energies to spare so that the day-to-day demands of home and job and business presented no problems, rather, were a challenge which Claudia gladly met. She felt fulfilled, each tomorrow bright with promise. So much so that it was hard to believe that it was not the same for Giles. One day, she told herself, tomorrow he will discover that he cannot exist without me. But then that tomorrow would bring a telephone call to let her know that Giles was once more on his way, his flight dictated by the vagaries of his job. And he would be gone, across the Atlantic, leaving her alone to get on as best she could with her single, lonely existence.

Jennifer was waiting. Claudia said, at last, "Yes, it's Giles. We were going to Spain with a party of friends. Everything booked. But he's been held up in New York and we had to cancel. I could have gone, but it would have been pointless on my own."

"How long has he been away this time?"

"A few months. He was due back three days ago."

"How mean."

Claudia sprang to Giles's defence. "It's not his fault."

"You make excuses for him. Does he ever write to you? Is he ever in touch?"

"He telephones. Sometimes. He's a busy man."

"More excuses. I suppose you love him. Would you marry him?"

"I . . ." Claudia sought for the right words. "Yes. Yes, I do. I mean, I want to be married. I want to have children. Everybody thinks I'm a dedicated career woman, but I would love to have children. Soon I'll be too old."

"Are you certain," Jennifer asked with disconcerting frankness, "that you are not simply his London lady?"

The feared, unacknowledged suspicion. As she had always done, Claudia shrugged it away. "There's a possibility, I suppose."

"Do you trust him?"

"I don't think about trust."

"But Claudia, trust is the most important thing of all. Don't waste your life."

"How could I walk away from Giles? It's too big a decision. I can't handle it. He's part of me now, I've loved him for too long."

113

"Yes. Too long. Cut loose."

Claudia said, "I can't."

They fell silent. This silence was shattered by doors opening and slamming shut, footsteps, high-pitched voices calling up the stairs. "Mummy! We're back. We're starving!"

Jennifer sighed. She got to her feet and went to gather Geordie up into her arms. She said, "I must go and see to lunch. We'll talk some more."

She went. Claudia, alone, unpacked and changed into old jeans and trainers. She cleaned her face, brushed her hair. As she did this she heard a car drawing up outside the front door and, looking from the window, saw Magnus, returned from his mill.

He got out of the car and started towards the house. Claudia watched him but, as though she had called out his name, he suddenly stopped and looked up and saw her there, framed in the upstairs window.

He said, "Are you not ready, yet, for lunch?"

"Yes, I'm ready. On my way."

Creagan Hill lay three miles from Inverloss on the far side of the little town. From a rounded summit, crowned with scree and rock, it swept down, heather-clad, to the coastal plain, there giving way to a scattering of small drystone-dyked fields where bracken grew and sheep grazed. Narrow lanes wound around the margins of these fields, sheltered from the prevailing wind and in the full face of the sun. Here were the bramble thickets and the fat, dark blackberries clustered, ripening, upon the thorny stems.

The prospect of the expedition filled Jennifer's children with unsophisticated anticipation.

"We go every year," Jane explained through a mouthful of cottage pie. "And we get absolutely filthy, and the person

114

who's picked the most gets a prize. I got it last year . . ."

"You stole some of mine," Rory pointed out. He was a stolid child, with blue eyes and his mother's hair.

"I didn't, you gave them to me."

"I'd filled my bucket. I didn't have any more room."

Magnus tactfully intervened. "Never mind. Perhaps this year everybody will get a prize."

"Even Geordie?"

"Why not?"

"He'll just be a nuisance and get under everybody's feet, and eat berries. He'll probably make himself sick."

Geordie banged a spoon on his highchair and, when they all looked at him, dissolved into delighted laughter.

"In fact," Jennifer said, when they had all stopped laughing at Geordie, "Jane's got a point. Geordie certainly won't last the whole afternoon. So I think we should take two cars and then I can bring him home when he starts to flag."

"I want to go with Magnus," Jane announced. "I'm going in his car."

Rory was not to be outdone. "Me, too."

Their mother sighed. "I don't mind who goes with who, but how about getting the plates into the dishwasher and then we can make a start?"

⌒✦⌒

And so Claudia found herself once more seated beside Magnus in his car, with Rory and Jane on the back seat and Magnus's dog in the boot. The expression on the dog's face was long-suffering and Claudia did not blame him. Jennifer went ahead, the baby strapped into his chair behind her, and Magnus, at a more prudent speed than their drive that morning, brought up the rear of the little procession.

The afternoon fulfilled the promise of the early morning and remained incredibly bright, clear and warm. Once they

115

had left the town behind them Claudia saw the shape of the hills, the brilliance of the sea. Sunlight streamed down over tawny bracken and the plum-bloom of the heather. They turned off the road and plunged into a maze of small lanes heading away from the sea, and Creagan Hill reared up before them so steeply that the summit was lost from view.

Rory and Jane were asking riddles.

"What's green and goes at a hundred miles an hour?"

"A ton-up gooseberry."

"Why did the razorbill raise 'er bill?"

"Because she wanted the sea urchin to see 'er chin. Get it, Rory? See 'er chin."

Screams of laughter.

Claudia opened her window and let the wind blow in on her face. It was cold and smelt of grass and moss and seaweed, and she thought of Spain and was, quite suddenly, glad that she was here and not there.

They reached the chosen spot at last, spilled out of the cars and set to work. Ranged along the roadside, scrambling over dykes into the fields, they picked busily all afternoon. The plastic buckets were slowly filled. Mouths and fingers were stained purple, sweaters snagged, jeans torn, shoes coated with mud. By four o'clock little Geordie had had enough and Jennifer decided that it was time to take him home.

"He's been so good, sitting in that nice bit of bog and looking for ladybirds, haven't you, my poppet?" She kissed his filthy face. "Anyway, I've got to get back and do something about dinner. Come and eat dinner with us, Magnus."

"You've already fed me."

"We'll feed you again. No problem. And Ronnie will want to tell you all about the fish he didn't catch. Who's coming with me?"

Jane and Rory debated and finally decided to go with

their mother. They were sated with blackberries and there was a television programme they wanted to watch.

"How about you two?"

Claudia put her heavy bucket of berries into the boot of Jennifer's car and stretched her aching arms and shoulders. "It's such a beautiful day, I can't bear to waste a moment of it." She looked at Magnus. "Perhaps we could take your dog for a walk? So far, he seems to have had a fairly boring day."

Magnus agreed. "Whatever. We could climb the hill and look at the view. Would you like that?"

It was exactly what she had been wanting to do all afternoon. She said, "Yes, I'd love it."

❧

Jennifer departed, the children waving from the open windows of the car as though they were saying goodbye for ever. When they were gone, Magnus turned to Claudia.

"So. What are we waiting for?"

They set off. Up through the fields, up the gradually steepening slope; through broken gateways and knee-high bracken and on, up again, until they were surrounded by heather. The dog, delighted at last to have some attention paid to it, raced ahead, scenting rabbits, his great tail pluming. A few old sheep, seeing them approach, ceased their grazing and stared. Now Claudia could feel the wind on her cheeks and was grateful for its coolness, and was grateful too for the path which stretched ahead, for the firmness of the close-cropped turf, which made for pleasant walking. She could feel the stretch and pull of the muscles in her legs, and her lungs were filled with air as pure and as cold as fresh spring water.

About halfway up the hill they came upon a grassy corrie cleft by a tiny burn, miniature waterfalls bubbling down over a bed of white pebbles. Claudia was thirsty. She knelt and scooped water up in her palm and drank it. It tasted of peat. She sat then, with her back to the hill and her eyes, for the first time, turned upon the view.

"I had no idea that we had come so far, and climbed so high."

"You've done well." He settled himself beside her, his knees drawn up. He shaded his eyes with his hand. "No need to climb further. We won't get a better sighting than this."

He was right. A spectacular view, remembered from years back, but always breathtaking. It took in the curve of the coastline, the fields and the farms and the inland lochs. All was spread before them like some giant-sized map. So clear was the air that the mountains, some fifty miles to the south, showed themselves, their peaks frosted with the first snows of the winter. And ahead was the sea, on this day blue as the Mediterranean, the wine-dark seas of Homer's Greece.

And the silence. Only the wind, the song of a lark, the long, sad call of a curlew. Sitting still, they were soon chilled by the wind. Claudia, who had taken off her sweater and tied the arms around her waist, now undid the knot and pulled the sweater on again.

He said, "You mustn't get cold."

"I'm all right. And it's good for the soul just to look at a view like that on a day like today. How fortunate we are. You in particular, because now you live here all the time."

"I know what you mean. It gets everything into proportion."

"It makes me feel like an ant."

"An ant?"

"Tiny. Insignificant. Unimportant."

But not just herself. All of life, with its problems: working, making money, loving. Being up here, so high above the world, was like seeing the day-to-day rat-race through the wrong end of a telescope so that all became diminished, weightless and trivial. And if Claudia were an ant, then the Atlantic was no more than a pond, and New York a dot on the globe, yet alive with the millions of teeming insects which peopled that teeming glut of humanity. Giles was one of them.

Magnus spoke. He said, "Would you actually want to live here all the time?"

"I've never thought about it. But there is Jennifer, so happy. With her husband and her farm and her children. Yet I don't suppose it would ever do for me."

"Life is strange. All of us scattered all over the place, and then after all these years ... Why should you and I, of all people, find ourselves here and now, halfway up Creagan Hill and on a God-given day, to boot?"

"I have no idea, Magnus."

He said, "I wonder if you have any idea of how much I was in love with you?"

Claudia, frowning, turned to gaze at him in total puzzlement. His profile was sombre. She could see the lines around his mouth, the crow's feet, the strands of grey in his thick, dark hair. Then he turned and looked into her face, and she saw his eyes, and for once there was no laughter in them.

She said, "You can't be serious."

"You had no idea?"

"I was seventeen."

"You were amazing. So beautiful that I was scared of how I felt because I was so certain that you were unattainable."

"You never said ..."

"Nor let it show."

"But why? Why not?"

"It wasn't the time. We were too young. Scarcely out of school, with all our lives in front of us. Everything to be learned, to be done. The world our oyster, filled with people waiting to love. And all we wanted was to get out and

119

discover it for ourselves. I had a photograph of you. I used to carry it round and show it to my mates. 'This is my first love,' I would say. I didn't say, 'my only love'. That's what I should have said."

"Why do you tell me now?"

"Because I am too old for pride."

Simply spoken. Claudia dropped her eyes, not wishing him to read her thoughts. I am too old for pride as well, but I've hung on to it because, as far as Giles is concerned, it seems to be the only way I can hold on to him. Bleak knowledge. She thought about opening her heart to Magnus and telling him about Giles – explaining, trying to make him understand – but knew that she could never inflict such pain. Not now, not while she was in such a confused and distressed state of mind. Giles was her life and her love but also her problem, and not one to be unloaded on to this man, this old friend, who had just declared his own undying love for her.

No. It must be kept inconsequent, light-hearted. She smiled. She said, "Pride is a nuisance anyway. It just gets between people."

"Yes. And then you say nothing until it is too late. Better perhaps, not to say anything at all."

"Don't feel like that." The afternoon was dying, the sun sinking behind them, the last of its rays casting long shadows. The wind, rising, bent the long grasses which grew on the banks of the little burn. Claudia shivered. She said, "It's getting cold," and then, because he looked so much in need of comfort, she leaned forward and kissed his mouth. "It's time we went home, Magnus."

※

After that it was all right again. He grinned, ruefully, but still it was a smile of sorts, and got to his feet. He held out a hand to help Claudia up, whistled for his dog and they set off. The downward slope was easy going and, by the time they reached the car, he was his old, cheerful self again, and full of plans for the evening ahead.

". . . I must buy some wine for Ronnie. Do you mind if we stop off in the town for a moment while I do a quick bit of shopping? I'm out of bacon, as well, and I need a bag of dog biscuits."

In the last golden light of the afternoon, the main street of Inverloss bustled with the last activities of the day. The shops were still open: the butcher, the greengrocer, the fishing-tackle shop. The Italian café spilled neon light out on to the pavement, and from its interior came the sound of pop music and the evocative smell of frying fish and chips. Girls hung around outside the café, giggling in their Saturday finery, tight jeans and earrings, and the young men sat across the road, outside the pub, and eyed them.

Magnus drew up by the newsagent. "I won't be long."

He disappeared into the shop and emerged almost immediately with a newspaper. Through the open window, he dropped it on to her lap. "This'll keep you amused."

He strode off.

It was this morning's paper he had brought her, a national tabloid printed in London. She cast her eye over the screaming headlines and then slowly scanned the rest of the paper, glancing at items, photographs, advertisements. She turned to the Social Diary and saw the picture of Giles.

It was neither a very large nor a very good photograph, but it leapt at her as a known name will leap from a column of newsprint. He stood with a girl on his arm. A fair-haired girl with a long cascade of hair. She wore a low-necked dress; her arms were bare. She carried a small bunch of flowers. Giles was smiling, showing his teeth. He looked overweight, a bit ponderous. He was sporting a tremendously spotted tie.

The caption: 'Giles Savours with his young bride, Debbie Peyton. See column four.'

Her first instinctive thought was, 'It can't be true. It's a ghastly mistake. They've got it all wrong.' Quite suddenly she felt dreadfully cold, her lips frozen, her mouth dry. 'It can't be true.'

Column four.

The headline in thick black type: 'BUSINESS AS USUAL FOR GILES AND DEBBIE'. And then the story:

There will be no immediate honeymoon for London businessman Giles Savours (44) who was married this week in the Church of St Michael, Brewsville, New York State. Giles, a partner with the City firm Wolfson-Rilke, has work aplenty to keep him at his desk in his New York office, but plans to jet to Barbados for Christmas.

His lovely bride Debbie Peyton (22) is the only daughter of Charlie D. Peyton of Consolidated Aluminium. A petite 5'2", she met Savours for the first time only three months ago, but their whirlwind courtship has not gone unobserved by Giles's New York colleagues. This is his second time around – his previous wife was Lady Priscilla Rolands – and his friends were beginning to doubt if he would ever take the plunge again . . .

She could not read any more. The light was too dim, the newsprint wavered, the words blurred together. Giles, married. She thought of his voice over the transatlantic telephone lines, easy as ever, ripe with reasonable excuses. "Terribly sorry. Something's come up. No possibility of my getting back to London in time for Spain. I know you'll understand. Why don't you go without me? You'll have a great time . . . Yes, of course . . . Just as soon as I can . . ."

And so on. The same voice, the same old let-down. Nothing new. Except this time he hadn't even had the courage to tell her that he was going to be married to another woman. A girl. Young enough to be his daughter. He was married. Gone from Claudia. It was over.

She still felt numb with cold. She thought, 'I am numb with shock.' She sat in Magnus's car and waited for her reactions to make themselves evident. For rage. Perhaps screams of fury. For furious tears of rank humiliation. For a terrible sense of loss. But none of these things happened and, after a bit, she realised that they would not.

Instead, she discovered that she was experiencing the most unexpected emotions of all. Relief, and a sort of gratitude. Relief because all decisions had been taken out of her hands, and gratitude because perhaps this was the last and the best thing that Giles could have done for her.

"Sorry I've been so long." Magnus was back. He hurled a paper sack of dog meal over on to the back seat and then got in behind the wheel, placing a grocer's carrier bag on the floor between them. Claudia heard the clank of bottles. He slammed the door shut.

"I got the wine and some sweets for the children. I remembered, just in time, I'd promised them all prizes for blackberry-picking . . ."

Claudia said nothing. She did not turn to look at him, but felt his eyes on her face.

"Claudia?" And then, "Is something wrong?"

After a bit, she shook her head.

"Something is wrong."

She stared at the newspaper. Gently, he reached over and took it from her. "What is it?"

"Just a man I know."

"What's happened to him?" He obviously feared the worst.

"He's not dead or anything. Just married."

"This guy here? Giles Savours?"

Claudia nodded.

"An old friend?"

"Yes."

"A lover?"

"Yes."

"How long have you known him?"

"Eight years."

A long pause while Magnus read what Claudia had already read. "Why are ages and measurements always so vital on these bloody pages?" He folded the newspaper with some force and dropped it on the floor. Then he did a kindly thing. He reached out and took her hand in his own. He said, "Do you want to tell me about it?"

"Nothing to tell. Nothing and everything. It would take too long. But Giles is the reason that I am here. Because we were going to Spain together and he cried off at the last moment. He didn't tell me why, just said that something had come up."

"Didn't you know about this other girl?"

"No. I didn't know anything about her. I suppose because I didn't want to know. I wouldn't let myself think about anybody but myself. There is nothing more unattractive than a suspicious woman, and I knew that if I said anything to Giles, what existed between us would all be spoiled."

"That's not much of a basis for a relationship. You deserve better than that."

"No. It was my own fault. But it would have been more dignified for both of us had he found the courage to tell me himself. In a way I'm rather sorry for him. It must be dreadful to have so little moral courage."

"I'm not sorry for him. I think he sounds a cruel bastard."

"No. Not cruel, Magnus. One of us had to finish it ... it's limped along for long enough. And you mustn't be sorry for me. You think I've been abandoned, but I think I feel as though I've been set free."

Her hand still lay in his. For the first time, she turned her head and looked full into his face, and this time it was he who kissed her.

He said, "It has been, to put it mildly, a remarkable day. And what is more, it is the first day of the rest of your life. So what do you say? Shall we nail our flags to the mast, and make what remains of it just as memorable? After all, we have wine and we have women, and I can always oblige with a song."

Despite everything, she found herself laughing at him. She said, "I'm glad you were the person who was with me. I'm glad that you were the person I was able to tell."

"I'm glad, too," said Magnus.

And that was all. He started up the engine and the car moved forward, down the street and out into the dusky countryside beyond, and Claudia looked out over the sea and saw the moon rising up over the horizon. She felt comforted, and smiled into its silvery face as though she were greeting an old friend.

# ⚜ The Red Dress ⚜

A month after Dr Haliday's funeral, Mr Jenkins, the gardener, sought out Abigail and, with a long face and much scratching of his head, gave in his notice.

Abigail had been half-expecting this for some time. Mr Jenkins was well over seventy. He had gardened for her father for nearly forty years. But still nothing could assuage her dismay.

She thought of the beautiful garden, now with nobody to tend it. She had frightening visions of herself, single-handed, having to mow lawns, dig potatoes, weed flower-beds. She saw herself being overwhelmed by it all, letting the garden go to seed. She saw nettles, brambles, groundsel slowly encroaching, taking over. She thought in a panic: 'What on earth am I going to do without him?'

She said this. "Mr Jenkins, what am I going to do without you?"

"Perhaps," said Mr Jenkins after a long, ruminative pause, "you could find somebody else?"

"I suppose I'll just have to try." She felt defeated, inadequate. "But you know how difficult it is even to find an odd-job man. Unless . . ." But she was without much hope. "Unless you know somebody?"

Mr Jenkins shook his head slowly from side to side, like an old horse bothered by flies. "It's difficult," he admitted, "and I don't like to leave you. But somehow, without the Doctor, I don't have the heart to go on. We made it together, him and me. Besides, I'm getting a bit beyond it and the wet weather does play up my rheumatics. Mrs Jenkins, now, she's been on at me the past year or two to hand in my notice, but I didn't want to leave the Doctor . . ."

He looked more anguished than ever. Abigail's tender heart went out to him. She put out a hand and laid it on his arm. "Of course you must retire. You've worked all your life. It's time you took things more easily. But . . . I will miss you. It's not just the garden. You've been a friend for so long . . ."

Mr Jenkins mumbled something embarrassed and took himself off. A month later he departed for the last time, weaving down the lane on his ancient bicycle. It was the end of an era. Worse, Abigail had still found no one to take his place.

"I'll put a notice in the post office window," Mrs Midgeley had suggested, and together she and Abigail had drafted the wording of a little card. All that came of this, however, was a shifty-eyed boy on a motor-cycle, who looked so untrustworthy that Abigail did not even let him into the kitchen. Too frightened to say that she didn't like the look of him, she told a lie and said that she had already found somebody else. He had then turned quite unpleasant and given Abigail one or two pieces of his meagre mind before roaring away with an offensive blast of smelly exhaust pipes.

"Why don't you get in touch with a gardening contractor?" Yvonne had asked. Yvonne was Abigail's friend, married to Maurice who commuted daily to the City. Yvonne preferred horses to gardening. She spent her life ferrying her children and their ponies to and from gymkhanas and meets, and when she wasn't doing this she was either mucking out, heaving hay bales, cleaning tack, grooming, plaiting manes, or ringing up the vet. "Maurice got fed up with these casual men who never come, so he made a deal with a contractor, and now a team comes once a week and we never even pull up a weed."

But Yvonne's garden was simply a lawn, some beech hedges and a few daffodils. It never looked anything but starkly neat, and bore no relation at all to the beautiful garden which was one of the nicest things old Dr Haliday had bequeathed to his daughter Abigail. She didn't want it licked over once a week by a team of stout, heartless men. She wanted somebody who would not only work in the garden, but would love it as well.

"It would help," said Mrs Brewer, who came in two mornings a week to do for Abigail, "it would help if you had a cottage to offer. Easy to get help if you can offer a house with the job."

"But I haven't got a cottage. And there's no room to build a cottage. And even if there was, I couldn't afford it."

"Makes a difference having a nice little cottage," Mrs Brewer said again. She went on saying it, at intervals, all through the morning, but did nothing to help the situation.

❧

For six weeks Abigail toiled on her own. The weather was fine and this made things worse, because it meant that she never stopped working out of doors until it was almost too dark to see. But despite this, she saw the slow rot already begin. Things became untidy. Chickweed and couch-grass crept in from the neighbouring wood. Dead leaves revealed themselves, skulking beneath the lavender hedge, blown into dismal heaps behind the sundial. The vegetable garden, dug by Mr Jenkins, lay dark and sullen, waiting for the drills which she had no time to make, for the seeds which she had no time to sow.

"Perhaps," she said to Mrs Brewer, "I should forget about vegetables. Perhaps I should just sow it all out in grass."

"That would be a crying shame," said Mrs Brewer sternly. "Took years to make, that asparagus bed. And think of those parsnips Mr Jenkins used to bring in. Could make a meal of them, I used to say. That's what I used to say. Could make a meal of them."

A wind blew, and one of the gates swung open and broke its hinge. The clematis Montana needed to be pruned, but Abigail was frightened of ladders. She knew that she should order peat for the azaleas. She wondered if the motor mower had been serviced.

She met Yvonne in the village. Yvonne said, "Darling, you're beginning to look exhausted. Don't tell me you're trying to cope with that garden on your own?"

"What else can I do?"

"Life is too short to kill yourself over a garden. You've just got to face facts. Your father and Mr Jenkins were unique. Now, you'll have to simplify things. You've got to have some sort of a life of your own."

"Yes," said Abigail, knowing that this was true. She walked home with her basket of groceries and tried to decide what she should do. She thought, 'I am forty,' and this gave her a shock as it always did. What had happened to the dreams of youth? They were gone, slipped away with the years. Years spent working in London, and then coming back to Brookleigh to take care of her father after her mother died. To keep herself busy she had taken a job in the local library but, six months ago, when the Doctor had had a minor stroke, she had given this up as well, and devoted all her time and energy to keeping an eye on the active and determined old man.

And now he was dead, and Abigail was forty. What did one do at forty? Did one stop wearing jeans, buying pretty clothes, feeling cheerful in the sunshine? Did one become a career woman, or did one simply vegetate, moving, without visible effort, from one day to another, until one was fifty, and then sixty? She thought, 'I don't feel forty.' It was nearly middle-aged, and sometimes Abigail felt as though she were still eighteen.

These baffling reflections lasted her all the way home. She came up the lane, and around the corner of the privet hedge, and saw the bicycle. It was a blue bicycle, very spindly and old, with the most uncomfortable-looking seat. An unfamiliar bicycle. Whose?

There was nobody in sight. But, as Abigail approached her back door, a figure came around the house from the front garden and said, "Good morning," and so amazing was his appearance that for an instant Abigail could only stare. He had a great deal of hair and a large, shaggy brown beard. On top of the hair was a knitted hat with a red tassel. Below the beard came a sagging sweater, which reached almost to the man's knees. Then stained corduroys and old-fashioned, lace-up boots.

He came towards her. "That's my bicycle." She saw that he was quite young; his eyes, in all that mass of hair, a remarkable blue.

"Oh, yes," said Abigail.

"I heard you were wanting a gardener."

Abigail played for time. "Who told you?"

"The wife went to the post office, and the lady there told her." They gazed at each other. He added, simply, "I'm needing a job."

"You're new here, aren't you?"

"Yes. We hail from Yorkshire."

"How long have you been in Brookleigh?"

"About two months now. We're living in the Quarry Cottage."

"The Quarry Cottage . . ." Abigail's voice was dismayed. "I thought that had been condemned."

The man grinned. White teeth, very straight and shining, gleamed through the undergrowth of his beard. "It should have been. But at least it's a roof over our heads."

"What brought you to Brookleigh?"

"I'm an artist." He went to lean, gracefully, against the kitchen window-sill, his hands in his pockets. "I've been teaching in a secondary school in Leeds for the past five years, but I decided that if I didn't chuck it up and try to make something of my painting now, then I never would. I talked it over with Poppy – she's my wife – and we decided to give it a try. And I came here because I wanted to be near London. But I've got a couple of kids and they have to be fed, so I need a part-time job."

There was something very disarming about him, with his bright blue eyes and his extraordinary clothes and his composed manner. After a little, Abigail said, "Do you know anything about gardening?"

"Yes. I'm a good gardener. My father had a little plot when I was a boy. I used to garden with him."

"There's a lot to be done here."

"I know," he answered coolly. "I was having a look around. It's time you got your vegetables in, and that climbing rose on the front of the house needs to be cut back . . ."

"I really meant that it's quite a big garden. A lot of work."

"But it's beautiful. It would be a pity to let it go."

"Yes," said Abigail, and her heart warmed to him.

There was another small pause while they eyed each other. He asked, "Have I got the job?"

"How much time can you give me?"

"I could come three days a week."

"Three days isn't very much in a garden this size."

He smiled again. "I have to keep time for my painting,"

he insisted, politely but firmly. "And in three days I can do a right load of work."

Abigail hesitated only a moment longer. And then, impulsively, she made up her mind. "All right. It's a deal. And you can start on Monday morning."

"Eight o'clock, I'll be here." He picked up his bicycle and swung a leg over that dreadful saddle.

"I don't know your name," said Abigail.

"It's Tammy," he told her. "Tammy Hoadey," and with that he was away, pedalling down the drive, with the tassel on his hat blown backwards in the breeze.

❧

The village, when they heard the news, were much concerned. Tammy Hoadey was not a local man. He came from 'up north', nobody knew anything about him. He had set up house in the derelict cottage by the old quarry. His wife looked like a gypsy. Was Abigail sure of what she was doing?

Abigail assured the village that she was quite sure.

Mrs Brewer was more horrified than most. "Not a bit like old Mr Jenkins. Gives me quite a turn seeing him working away with that beard. And the other day, he ate his lunch by the sundial. Sitting in the sun, he was, cool as a cucumber, just eating his sandwich."

Abigail had already noticed this breach of etiquette but had not remarked upon it. After all, just because old Mr Jenkins had incarcerated himself each day in the dank toolshed to sit on an upturned bucket, eat his lunch and read the racing page of the daily paper, there was no reason why Tammy should be expected to do the same. And if a man worked in a garden, why should he not enjoy it as well? She said as much, in her usual diffident manner, to Mrs Brewer, who sniffed and was silenced, but continued to disapprove of Tammy.

For two months all went well. The gate was mended, the lily-pool cleaned, the vegetable garden planted. The grass began to grow and Tammy rode up and down the sloping lawn on the motor mower. He barrowed manure, tied up the clematis, weeded the borders, shifted a straggling rhododendron. And all the time, as he worked, he whistled. Whole arias and cantatas complete with trills and arpeggios. Strains of Mozart and Vivaldi pierced the air, mingling with birdsong. It was like having one's own private flautist.

And then, in the middle of July, he came to Abigail and told her that he was going to be off for two months. She was both hurt and angry. "But, Tammy, you can't leave me without warning. There's the grass, and the fruit to pick, and everything."

"You'll manage," he told her calmly.

"But why are you going?"

"I'm going to work at the potatoes for a contractor. It's good money. I want to get all my pictures framed and that costs a bomb. If they're framed I can try to get them into some exhibition. Unless I exhibit, I'm never going to sell anything."

"Have you ever exhibited?"

"Yes, once, in Leeds. A couple of pictures." He added, with no false modesty, "They both sold."

"I still think it's very unfair of you to walk out on me."

"I'll be back," he told her. "In September."

❦

There was obviously nothing to be done. Tammy duly went, leaving Abigail with no hope of finding, in midsummer, a replacement. No hope, even, of hiring some odd-job man to see her over the crisis. Besides, after her fury had died down and she was able to view the situation in comparative calm, she realised that she did not want another gardener.

No man worked harder than Tammy Hoadey, but what was most important was that Abigail liked him. It was a bore, but the two months would pass. She would wait for him to return.

Which he did. Unchanged, still wearing the same bizarre clothes, thinner, perhaps, but as cheerful as ever. Whistling, he began to sweep up the first of the leaves. Now, it was the Rodrigo Guitar Concerto. Abigail, in jeans and a scarlet sweater, went out to help him. They built a fire and pale smoke rose, a grey plume, up into the still, early autumn air. Tammy stepped back from the bonfire and leaned on his broom. Across the fire and the smoke their eyes met. He smiled at Abigail. He said, "You look really nice in red. Never seen you wear red before."

She was embarrassed, but gratified as well. It was years since she had been paid such a warm and spontaneous compliment.

"It . . . it's only an old jersey."

"It's a good colour."

The compliment stayed with her, warming her, all through the next day. That morning, she walked to the village to do her shopping. Next door to the chemist was a small boutique, recently opened. In the window was a dress. A silk dress, very simple, neatly belted, the skirt a fan of deep pleats. The dress was red. Without allowing herself a second thought, Abigail walked into the shop, tried on the dress and bought it.

She did not tell Yvonne the reason she had been so impulsive. "Red?" said Yvonne. "But, darling, you never wear red."

Abigail bit her lip. "You don't think it's too bright? Too young?"

"No, of course I don't. I'm just astonished at your doing something so out of character. But I'm pleased, too. You can't go on mouldering around in dun-coloured clothes for

135

ever. Anyway, I had a great-aunt who lived to be eighty-four, and she always went to funerals in a sapphire blue hat with feathers."

"What's that got to do with my red dress?"

"Nothing, I suppose." They began to laugh together, like schoolgirls. "I'm glad you bought it. I'll have to throw a party, so that you can wear it."

＊

But, in October, the cheerful whistling suddenly stopped. Tammy came to work silent and uncommunicative. Abigail, terrified that he was going to hand in his notice, gathered up her courage and asked him if anything was the matter. He said, yes, everything. Poppy had left him. She had taken the children and gone to her mother in Leeds.

Abigail was devastated. She sat on the edge of the cucumber frame and said, "For good?"

"No, not for good. Just for a visit, she says. But we had a row. She's so fed up with Quarry Cottage and I can't really blame her. She's scared the kids'll fall down the quarry bank and the little one's been coughing at nights. She says it's the damp."

"What are you going to do?"

He said, "I can't go back to Leeds. I can't go back to living in a city. Not after all this." A tired gesture somehow involved the garden, the wood, the flaming borders, the golden oak leaves.

"But she's your wife. And your children . . ."

"She'll come back," said Tammy, but he did not sound convinced. Abigail ached with sympathy for him. At lunchtime, when he settled down to his meagre snack, she filled a bowl with soup and carried it out to where he slumped, despondent, by the greenhouse. "If your wife isn't here to take care of you, then I must," she told him, and he smiled gratefully and took the soup.

Unbelievably, Poppy and the children returned, but the tuneful whistling was not resumed. Abigail felt herself caught up in some television soap opera: *The Continuing Saga of Tammy Hoadey*. She told herself the problems were between Tammy and Poppy, husband and wife. It was no concern of Abigail's. She would not interfere.

But remaining a bystander was not to be possible. A week or so later, Tammy sought her out and said that he wanted to ask a favour of her. The favour was that Abigail should buy one of Tammy's pictures.

She said, "But I've never seen any of your pictures."

"I brought one with me. On the back of the bike. It's framed." She stared at him, trapped in embarrassment, and he went off and returned with a large parcel wrapped in crumpled brown paper and tied up with binder twine. He undid the knots, and held the picture out for Abigail to inspect.

She saw the silvered frame, the bright colours, the upside-down procession of odd little people, and felt total incomprehension of this new form of art. It was so out of her league, so foreign to any of Dr Haliday's pictures, that she could think of nothing to say. She started to blush. Tammy stayed silent. At last Abigail blurted out, "How much do you want for it?"

"A hundred and fifty pounds."

"A hundred and fifty? Tammy, I haven't got a hundred and fifty pounds to spend on a picture."

"Have you got fifty?"

"Well ... yes ..." Cornered, she was driven to cruel truth. "But ... well, it's just not my sort of picture. I mean, I would never buy a picture like that."

He was undeflected by this. "Well, would you lend me

fifty pounds? Just for a bit? You can have the picture as surety."

"But I thought you'd earned so much on the potatoes?"

"It all went in framing. And it's my little boy's birthday next week, and we owe the grocer. Poppy's come to the end of her rope. She says if I don't start selling pictures and making money, she's going back to her mother for good." He sounded desperate. "Like I said, I don't blame her. It's a hard deal for her."

Abigail looked again at the picture. The colours, at least, were bright. She took it from Tammy. She said, "I'll keep it for you. I'll keep it safely." And she went indoors and up to her bedroom and found her bag, and took from it five crisp ten-pound notes.

'This,' she told herself, 'is probably the stupidest thing I've ever done in my life.' But she closed her handbag and went downstairs and gave the money to Tammy.

He said, "I can never thank you enough."

"I trust you," Abigail told him. "I know you won't let me down."

~❧~

At lunchtime that day Yvonne called. "Darling, it's dreadfully short notice, but would you come and have dinner with us tonight? Maurice has just phoned from the office, and he's bringing a business friend back for the night, and I thought it would be nice if you'd come and help me entertain him."

Abigail did not really want to go. She felt depressed by Tammy's problems and not in the mood for a party. She began to make unenthusiastic noises, but Yvonne thought she was being stupid and told her so. "You're getting terribly old-maidish. What's happened to all that impulsive spirit? Of course you're coming. It'll do you good and you can wear your new red dress."

But Abigail did not wear the red dress. She was keeping the dress for ... something. Some person. Some special day. She put on, instead, a brown dress that Yvonne had seen a dozen times before. She arranged her hair, made up her face, went downstairs. In the hall, Tammy's picture, still in its untidy wrappings, lay on the chest by the telephone. Its presence was somehow pathetic, like a cry for help. *Unless I exhibit, I'm never going to sell anything.* Unless people saw his extraordinary pictures, he was never going to hope to get started. An idea occurred to Abigail. Perhaps Yvonne and Maurice would be interested. Perhaps they would like it so much that they would buy a picture of Tammy's for themselves. And they would hang it in their sitting-room, and other people would see it and ask about him.

It was a faint hope. Maurice and Yvonne did not go in for patronage of the arts. But still, it was worth a try. Decisively, Abigail pulled on her coat, did up the buttons, gathered up the parcel, and set off.

❧

Maurice's friend was called Martin York. He was a very large man, taller than Maurice, and extremely fat. His head was bald, fringed with greying hair. He had come down from Glasgow for a meeting, he told Abigail over sherry, and had actually booked into a London hotel, but Maurice had persuaded him to cancel the booking and instead to spend the night at his home in Brookleigh.

"A charming little village. You live here?"

"Yes, I've lived here all my life, on and off."

Maurice chipped into the conversation. "She's got the prettiest house in the village. And quite the most enviable garden. How's the new gardener doing, Abigail?"

"Well, he's not so new now. He's been working for me for some months." She explained about Tammy to Martin York. ". . . he's really an artist – a painter." This seemed as good a moment as any to broach the subject of the picture. "As a matter of fact, I brought one of his paintings with me. I . . . I bought it from him. I thought you might be interested."

Yvonne came through from the kitchen and caught the tail end of this remark. "Who, me? Darling, I never bought a picture in my life."

"But we could look at it," said Maurice quickly. He was a kind man, and always ready to make amends for his wife's forthright remarks.

"Oh, I'd like to *look* at it . . ."

So Abigail set down her sherry glass, and went out to the hall where she had left Tammy's picture along with her coat. She brought the parcel into the sitting-room, and untied the binder twine and pulled aside the paper. She handed the picture to Maurice, who set it up on the seat of a chair and then stood back, the better to inspect it.

The other two also arranged themselves, standing around in a half-circle. Nobody said anything. Abigail found that she was as nervous of their reaction as if she had herself been responsible for creating those little figures, that brilliant mosaic of colour. She wanted desperately for them all to admire and covet it. It was as though she were the mother of a cherished child, being examined and found wanting.

Yvonne broke the silence at last. "But it's all upside down!"

"Yes, I know."

"Darling, did you really buy it from Tammy Hoadey?"

"Yes," lied Abigail, not having the nerve to disclose the arrangement she had made with Tammy.

"However much did you give him for it?"

"Yvonne!" her husband remonstrated sharply.

"Abigail doesn't mind, do you, Abigail?"

"Fifty pounds," Abigail told them, trying to sound cool.

"But you could have got something really good for fifty pounds!"

"I think it is really good," said Abigail defiantly.

There was another long pause. Martin York had still said nothing. But he had taken out his spectacles and put them on, the better to inspect the picture. Abigail, unable to bear the silence a moment longer, turned to him.

"Do you like it?"

He took his spectacles off. "It's full of innocence and vitality. And I love the colour. It's like the work of a very sophisticated child. I am sure you will have great enjoyment from it."

Abigail could have wept with gratitude. "I'm sure I will," she told him. She went to rescue Tammy's work from the others' unappreciative gaze, to bundle it back into its crumpled wrapping.

"What did you say his name was?"

"Tammy Hoadey," said Abigail. Maurice passed around the sherry decanter once more and Yvonne started to talk about some new pony. Tammy was not mentioned again, and Abigail knew that her first tentative attempt at patronage had been a dismal failure.

The next Monday Tammy did not turn up for work. At the end of the week, Abigail made a few discreet enquiries. Nobody in the village had seen the Hoadeys. She let another day or two pass before getting out the car and driving down the rutted, rubbish-strewn lane which led to the old quarry. The dismal cottage lay by the lip of the cliff. No smoke rose from the chimney. The windows were shuttered, the door locked. In the trodden garden lay a child's abandoned toy, a plastic tractor missing a wheel. Rooks cawed overhead, a thin wind stirred the black water at the base of the quarry.

*'I know you won't let me down.'*

But he had gone back to Leeds with his wife and children. To start teaching again and to forget his dreams of becoming an artist. He had gone, taking Abigail's fifty pounds with him, and she would never see him again.

She went home and took his picture from its wrapping and carried it into the sitting-room. She laid it on a chair and went, with care, to take down the heavy canvas of some Highland glen that had hung for ever above the mantelpiece. Its departure revealed a plethora of dust and cobwebs. She fetched a duster, cleaned these up, and then hung Tammy's picture. She stood back and surveyed it: the pure, clean colours, the little procession of figures, walking up the walls of the canvas and across the top, like those old Hollywood musicals when people danced on the ceiling. She found herself smiling. The whole room felt different, as though a lively and entertaining person had just walked into it. Enjoyment. That was the word that Maurice's friend had used. Tammy had gone, but he had left part of his engaging self behind.

❧

Now it was nearly a month later. The autumn was truly here, cold winds and showers of rain, the beginning of frosts at night. After lunch Abigail, bundled against the cold, went out to tidy the rose-beds, dead-head the frosted blossoms, cut out the dead wood. She was wheeling a barrow of rubbish towards the compost heap when she heard the sound of an approaching car and saw a long, sleek black saloon come quietly around the curve of the lane, and draw up at the side of the house. The door opened and a man got out. A tall stranger, silvery-haired, bespectacled, wearing a formal, dark overcoat. He looked almost as distinguished as his car. Abigail set down the wheelbarrow and went to meet him.

"Good afternoon," he said. "I'm so sorry to disturb you, but I'm looking for Tammy Hoadey and I was told in the village that you might be able to help me."

"No, he isn't here. He used to work for me, but he's gone. I think he's gone back to Leeds. With his wife and children."

"You haven't any idea how I could get in touch with him?"

"I'm afraid not." She took off a gardening glove and tried to push a stray lock of hair under her headscarf. "He didn't leave any address."

"And he's not coming back?"

"I'm not expecting him."

"Oh, dear." He smiled. It was a rueful smile, but all at once he looked much younger and not nearly so intimidating. "Perhaps I should explain. My name is Geoffrey Arland . . ." He felt inside his coat and produced, from an inner breast pocket, a business card. Abigail took it in her earthy hand. *Geoffrey Arland Galleries*, she read, and beneath this a prestigious Bond Street address. "As you can see, I'm an art dealer . . ."

"Yes," said Abigail. "I know. I came to your gallery about four years ago. With my father. You had an exhibition of Victorian flower paintings."

"You came to that? How very nice. It was a delightful collection."

"Yes, we enjoyed it so much."

"I . . ."

But the wind had blown a dark shower cloud over the sun, and now it started, suddenly, to rain.

"I think," said Abigail, "it would be better if we went indoors." And she led the way into the house, through the

143

garden door, directly into the sitting-room. It looked pretty and fresh, the fire flickering in the grate, an arrangement of dahlias on the piano and, over the mantelpiece, the brilliant mosaic of Tammy's picture.

Coming behind her, he saw this at once. "Now, that's Hoadey's work."

"Yes." Abigail closed the glass door behind them and unknotted her headscarf. "I bought it from him. He needed the money. He and his family lived in a gruesome cottage down by the quarry. It was all he could find. It seemed a dreadfully hand-to-mouth existence."

"Is this the only picture you have?"

"Yes."

"Is this the one you showed to Martin York?"

Abigail frowned. "Do you know Martin York?"

"Yes, he's a good friend of mine." Geoffrey Arland turned to face Abigail. "He told me about Tammy Hoadey because he thought I would be interested. What he didn't know was that I've been interested in Hoadey's work ever since I caught sight of a couple of his pictures in an exhibition in Leeds some time ago. But they were both sold, and for some reason I was never able to make contact with Hoadey. He seems to be an elusive sort of man."

Abigail said, "He gardened for me."

"It's a beautiful garden."

"It was. My father made it. But he died at the beginning of spring and our old gardener didn't have the heart to go on without him."

"I'm sorry."

"Yes," said Abigail inadequately.

"So now you live alone?"

"For the moment I do."

He said, "Decisions are difficult at such a time . . . I mean, when you lose someone close to you. My wife died about two years ago, and I've only just had the courage to up sticks and move. Not very far, admittedly. Just from a house in St John's Wood to a flat in Chelsea. But still, it was something of an upheaval."

"If I can't find another gardener, I suppose I shall have to move. I couldn't bear to stay here and watch it all go to rack and ruin, and it's too big for me to manage on my own."

They smiled at each other, understanding. She said, "I could make you a cup of coffee."

"No, really, I must be on my way. I've got to get back to London, preferably before the rush hour. If he does come back, could you get in touch with me?"

"Of course."

The rain had stopped. Abigail opened the door and they moved back out on to the terrace. The flagstones shone wet, the rain clouds had been blown away and now the garden was suffused in misty golden sunlight.

"Do you ever come up to London?"

"Yes, sometimes. To see the dentist or something boring like that."

"Next time you come to the dentist, I hope you'll visit my gallery again."

"Yes. Perhaps. And I'm sorry about Tammy."

"I'm sorry too," said Geoffrey Arland.

November passed and then it was December. The garden lay grey and bare beneath the dark wintry skies. Abigail abandoned the garden and moved indoors to write the first of the Christmas cards, do her tapestry, watch television. For the first time since her father died, she knew loneliness. Next year, she told herself, I shall be forty-one. Next year I will be decisive and competent. I must find a job, make new friends, have people for dinner. No one could do any of these things except herself, and she knew this, but at the moment she had hardly the heart to walk up to the village. She certainly hadn't the energy to undertake a trip to London. Geoffrey Arland's card remained, just as she had left it, tucked into the frame of Tammy's picture. But it was beginning to grow dusty, to curl at the corners, and soon, she knew, she would throw it into the fire.

Her low spirits turned out, inevitably, to be the onset of a bad cold and she was forced to spend two gloomy days in bed. On the third morning she awoke late. She knew it was late because she could hear sounds of the vacuum cleaner from downstairs, which meant that Mrs Brewer had let herself in with her latch-key and started work. Beyond Abigail's open curtains the sky was filling with light, turning from early grey to a pale, pristine, wintry blue. The hours stretched ahead of her like an empty void. Then Mrs Brewer turned off the vacuum cleaner, and Abigail heard a bird singing.

A bird? She listened more intently. It was not a bird. It was a person whistling Mozart. *Eine Kleine Nachtmusik*. Abigail sprang from her bed and ran to the window, holding back the curtains with both hands. And saw, below her in the garden, the familiar figure: the red-tasselled cap, the long green pullover, the boots. He had his spade over his shoulder; he was heading for the vegetable garden, his feet making tracks on the frosty lawn. She threw up the sash, regardless of the fact that she was wearing only her nightdress.

"Tammy!"

He stopped short, turned, his face tilted up towards her. He grinned. He said, "Hello, there."

She bundled herself into the nearest clothes to hand and ran downstairs and out of doors. He was waiting for her by the back door, grinning sheepishly.

"Tammy, what are you doing here?"

"I've come back."

"All of you? Poppy and the children too?"

"No, they're still in Leeds. I've gone back to teaching again. But it's the school holidays, so I'm here now on my own. I'm back in the Quarry Cottage." Abigail stared in puzzlement. "I've come to work off that fifty pounds I owe you."

"You don't owe me anything. I bought the picture. I'm going to keep it."

"I'm glad of that, but even so I want to work off my debt." He scratched the back of his neck. "You thought I'd forgotten, didn't you? Or scarpered with your money? I'm sorry I went off like that, without letting you know. But the little boy got worse, he got flu and Poppy was frightened of pneumonia. His temperature was up so we took him away from that house; it wasn't healthy. We went back to Poppy's mother. He was very ill for a bit, but he's all right now. Anyway, a teaching job came up. They're hard to get nowadays, so I thought I'd better grab the chance."

"You should have told me."

"I'm not much of a one at writing letters and the local telephone box was always being vandalised. But I told Poppy that these holidays I'd be coming back to Brookleigh."

"But what about your painting?"

"I've put that behind me . . ."

"But . . ."

"The children come first. Poppy and the children. I see that now."

"But, Tammy . . ."

He said: "Your telephone's ringing."

Abigail listened. It was, too. She said, "Mrs Brewer will answer it." But it kept on ringing, so she left Tammy standing there and went back into the house.

"Hello?"

"Miss Haliday?"

147

"Yes."

"This is Geoffrey Arland speaking . . ."

Geoffrey Arland. Abigail felt her mouth drop in astonishment at the extraordinariness of the coincidence. Naturally, unaware of her gaping amazement, he went on, "I'm very sorry to ring you so early in the morning, but I have rather a busy day ahead of me, and I thought I'd have a better chance of getting hold of you now rather than later. I wondered if there was any hope of you getting up to town between now and Christmas. We're mounting an exhibition which I would particularly like to show you. And I thought we could perhaps have lunch together? Almost any day would suit me, but . . ."

Abigail found her voice at last. She said, "Tammy's back!"

Geoffrey Arland, interrupted in mid-flow, was naturally disconcerted. "I beg your pardon?"

"Tammy's back. Tammy Hoadey. The artist you came to look for."

"He's back with you?" Geoffrey Arland's voice was at once quite different, imperative and businesslike.

"Yes. He turned up today, this very morning."

"Did you tell him I'd been to Brookleigh?"

"I haven't had the chance."

"I want to see him."

"I'll bring him up to London," said Abigail. "I'll drive him up in my car."

"When?"

"Tomorrow if you like."

"Has he got any work to show me?"

"I'll ask him."

"Bring anything he's got. And if he hasn't got any work at Brookleigh, then just bring him."

"I'll do that."

"I'll expect you in the morning. Come straight to the

galleries. We'll have a talk with him and I'll take you both out for lunch."

"We should be with you about eleven."

For a moment neither of them said anything. And then, "What a miracle," said Geoffrey Arland and he did not sound businesslike any longer, but pleased and grateful.

"They happen," Abigail was smiling so widely, her face felt quite strange. "I am so glad you called."

"I'm glad too. For all sorts of reasons."

He rang off, and after a while Abigail put down her receiver. She stood by the telephone and hugged herself. Nothing had changed and everything had changed. Upstairs, Mrs Brewer continued to move ponderously about behind her vacuum cleaner, but tomorrow Abigail and Tammy were driving to London to see Geoffrey Arland; to show him all Tammy's pictures; to be taken out for lunch. Abigail would wear her red dress. And Tammy? What would Tammy wear?

He was waiting for her, just as she had left him when the telephone started to ring. He was leaning on his spade, filling his pipe, waiting for her to return. As she appeared, he looked up and said, "I thought I'd start in on the digging . . ."

She very nearly said: 'To hell with the garden.' "Tammy, did you take your pictures with you, when you went back to Leeds?"

"No, I left them behind. They're still at Quarry Cottage."

"How many?"

"A dozen or so."

"And there's something else I must ask you. Have you – have you got a suit?"

He looked as though he thought she had gone mad. But,

"Yes," he said. "It was my father's. I wear it to funerals."

"Perfect," said Abigail. "And now don't talk for at least ten minutes because I've got an awful lot to tell you."

Mrs Brewer hoped that Miss Haliday was giving Tammy Hoadey his notice. She had seen him coming up the lane on his bicycle, cool as a cucumber, without so much as a word of warning or explanation. 'Cheeky devil,' she had thought, 'turning up out of the blue, just as though he had never been away.'

Now at the sink, filling the kettle for her morning cup of tea, she watched them at it: Miss Haliday talking nineteen to the dozen (and that wasn't her usual way) and Tammy just standing there like an idiot. 'She's giving him a piece of her mind, at last,' Mrs Brewer told herself with satisfaction. 'It's what he's been needing, all these months. A piece of her mind.'

But she was wrong. For when Miss Haliday stopped talking, nothing happened at all. She and Tammy just stood, quite still, staring at each other. And then Tammy Hoadey let his spade fall to the ground, tossed his pipe into the air, flung wide his arms and wrapped Miss Haliday in a bear-like embrace. And Miss Haliday, far from resisting such impudent goings-on, put her arms around his neck and hugged Tammy, right there in front of Mrs Brewer's eyes, and took her feet off the ground and was swung into the air, careless and graceless as some flighty teenage girl.

"Well, whatever next?" Mrs Brewer asked herself as the stream of water filled the kettle and overflowed, unheeded, into the sink. "Whatever next?"

# ❧ *A Girl I used to Know* ❧

The cable car, at ten o'clock in the morning, was as crammed with humanity as a London bus at rush hour. Grinding, swaying slightly, it mounted, with hideous steadiness, up into the clear, blindingly bright air, high over the snow-fields and scattered chalets of the valley. Behind them the village sank away – houses, shops, hotels, clustered around the main street. Far below lay great tracts of glittering snow, blue-shadowed beneath random stands of fir. Ahead and above – it gave Jeannie vertigo just to think about it – towered the distant peak, piercing the dark blue sky like a needle of ice.

The peak. The Kreisler. Just below it stood the sturdy wooden buildings of the upper cable station, the restaurant complex. The face of this edifice was one enormous window, flashing signals of reflected sunshine, and overhead fluttered the flags of many nations. Both the cable car station and the restaurant had seemed, from the village, as distant as the moon, but now, with every moment, they drew closer.

Jeannie swallowed. Her mouth felt dry, her stomach tight with apprehension. Pressed into a corner of the cable car, she turned her head to look for Alistair, but he and Anne and Colin had become separated from her in the rush to get on board, and he was away over on the other side. Easy to spot because he was so tall, his profile sharp and handsome. She willed him to turn and catch her eye, to give her a smile of reassurance, but all his concentration was for the mountain, for the morning's run down the Kreisler and back into the village.

Last night, as the four of them sat in the bar of the hotel, she had said, "I won't come."

"But of course you must come. That was the whole point of your coming on holiday, so that we could all ski together. It's no fun if you spend the whole time tottering around on the nursery slopes."

"I'm not good enough."

"It's not difficult. Just long. We'll take it at your speed."

That was even worse. "I'll hold you back."

"Don't be so self-abasing."

"I don't want to come."

"You're not frightened, are you?" Alistair had asked.

She was, but she had said, "Not really. Just frightened of spoiling it for you."

"You won't spoil it." He sounded marvellously certain of this, just as he was marvellously certain of himself. He seemed not to know the meaning of physical fear, and so was unable to recognise it in another person.

"But . . ."

"Don't argue any more. Don't talk about it. Come and dance."

Now, crammed into a corner of the cable car, she decided he had forgotten her existence. She sighed and turned back to the window to view the void, the impossible, dizzying height. Far, far below, the skiers were already moving down the *pistes*; tiny, ant-like creatures drawing trails in the virgin snow. It looked so easy. That was the horrible thing, it looked so easy. But for Jeannie it was almost impossibly difficult.

"Bend the knees," the instructor had told her. "Weight on the outside leg."

They had arrived. One moment swinging in the clear air and the brilliant sunshine, the next clanking into the shadowed gloom of the cable car terminal. They stopped with a jerk. The doors opened, everybody flooded out. Up here it was several degrees colder.

Jeannie was the last to emerge, and by the time she did this, the first ones out were already away, down the mountain, anxious not to waste a moment of the morning, reluctant to spend even five minutes in the warmth of the restaurant, with a mug of hot chocolate or a steaming glass of *Glühwein*.

"Come on, Jeannie."

Alistair, Colin and Anne already had their skis on, their goggles pulled down over their eyes, the three of them itching to be off. Her feet felt like lead in the heavy boots, slipping and stumbling across the snow. The cold stung her cheeks, filled her lungs with painfully icy air.

"Here, come on, I'll help you."

Somehow, she reached Alistair's side, and dropped her skis. He stooped to help her, snapping on the bindings. Lumbered with the weight of the skis, she felt even more incapable, helpless.

"All right?"

She couldn't even speak. Colin and Anne, taking her silence for assent, smiled cheerfully, gave her a wave with their ski poles, and were gone. A smooth push sent them over the brow of the slope, and they disappeared into the glittering infinity of space that lay beyond.

"Just follow me," Alistair told her. "It'll be fine." And then he, too, was gone.

'Just follow me.' It was Alistair, and she would have followed him anywhere, but this was an impossibility. Impossible to do anything but simply stand there, quaking. In her

153

wildest imaginings she had never thought up such horror as this. And then in place of panic came, slowly, a calm resolution.

She was not going to ski down the Kreisler. She was going to take off her skis, go into the restaurant, sit down and get warm and have a hot drink. Then she would clamber into the cable car and go back that way, on her own, to the village. Alistair would be furious, but she was beyond caring. The others would think nothing of her, but that had ceased to matter. She was hopeless. A funk. She couldn't ski and never would. At the first possible opportunity, she would get herself to Zurich, get herself on a plane and go home.

<hr>

Having faced up to this, everything suddenly became quite easy. She took off her skis, carried them back to the restaurant and stuck them in the snow, along with the ski poles. She went up the wooden steps and through the heavy glass doors. Here was warmth, the smell of pine and woodsmoke, cigars and coffee.

She bought herself a cup of coffee, took it to an empty table and sat down. The coffee steamed, fragrant and comforting. She pulled off her woollen hat, shook out her hair and felt as though she were taking off some hideous disguise, and was herself again. Putting her hands around the blissful warmth of the coffee mug, she decided that she would concentrate on this moment of total relief, and not think one moment ahead. Most especially, she would not think about Alistair. She would not think about losing him . . .

"Is anybody joining you?"

The question came out of nowhere. Startled, Jeannie looked up, saw the man standing across the table from her, and realised that he was talking to her.

"Nobody."

"Then would you mind if I did?"

She was astonished, but endeavoured to hide her astonishment. "No ... of course not ..." There was no question of being chatted up, because he was quite an elderly man, obviously British, and perfectly presentable. Which made his unexpected appearance all the more surprising.

He, too, had a cup of coffee in his hand. He set it down on the table, pulled out a chair and made himself comfortable. She saw his very blue eyes, his thinning grey hair. He wore a navy-blue anorak with a scarlet sweater beneath it. His skin was very brown, netted with wrinkles, and he had the weather-beaten appearance of a man who has spent most of his life in the open air.

He said, "It's a beautiful morning."

"Yes."

"There was a fall of snow at two in the morning. Quite a heavy one. Did you know that?"

She shook her head. "No, I didn't know."

He watched her, his bright eyes unblinking. He said, "I've been sitting by the table in the window. I saw what happened."

Jeannie's heart sank. "I – I don't understand." But of course she understood only too well.

"Your friends went off without you." He made it sound like an accusation, and Jeannie instantly sprang to their defence.

"They didn't mean to. They thought I was going to follow."

"Why didn't you?"

A number of likely fibs sprang to mind. 'I like to ski alone.' 'I wanted a cup of coffee.' 'I'm waiting till they come up again on the cable car, and then we'll all go down together in time for lunch.'

But those blue eyes were not to be lied to. She said, "I'm afraid."

"Of what?"

"Of heights. Of skiing. Of making a fool of myself. Of spoiling their fun for them."

"Haven't you skied before?"

"Not before this holiday. We've been here for a week and I've spent all that time on the nursery slopes with an instructor, trying to get the hang of it."

"And have you?"

"Sort of. But I think I'm uncoordinated or something. Or else just plain chicken. I mean, I can get down the slopes and turn corners and stop, and things like that, but I'm never sure when I'm going to fall flat on my back, and then I get nervous and I tense up, and then of course I usually do fall. It's a vicious circle. And I'm frightened of heights as well. Even coming up on the cable car I found terrifying."

He did not comment on this. "Your friends, I take it, are all fairly expert?"

"Yes, they've been skiing together for a long time. Alistair used to come here with his parents when he was a little boy. He loves the village, and he knows all the runs like the back of his hand."

"Is Alistair your friend?"

She felt embarrassed. "Yes."

He smiled, and suddenly it was easy to talk, as it is easy to confide in a stranger met by chance in a train, knowing that you will never see that particular stranger again. "It's funny, we have everything in common, and we get on so well, and laugh at the same things . . . but now there's this. I always knew that if I wanted to be with him, and part of his life, I'd have to ski because it's the only thing he really loves to do. And I've always been apprehensive about it because, like I said, I'm the most uncoordinated person in the world. But I thought perhaps skiing would be different, and that it would be something I'd be able to do. So when Alistair suggested we all came out together, I jumped at the chance to prove that I could. But now I know I can't."

"Does Alistair know how you feel?"

"It's hard to make him understand. And I don't want him to think I'm not enjoying myself."

"But you're not?"

"No. I'm hating it. Even the evenings and the fun we have are spoiled, because all the time I'm thinking about what I've got to make myself do the next day."

"When you've finished that cup of coffee, how are you going to get back to the village?"

"I thought on the cable car."

"I see." He considered this, and then said, "Let's both have another cup of coffee and talk things over."

Jeannie couldn't think what there could possibly be to talk over, but the idea of another cup of coffee was a good one, and so she said, "All right."

He took their cups, went to the bar, and came back with them, steaming and refilled. As he sat down again, he said, "You know, you remind me, quite extraordinarily, of a girl I used to know. She looked rather like you, and she talked with your voice. And she was just as frightened as you are."

"What happened to her?" Stirring her coffee, Jeannie tried to turn the whole thing into a joke. "Did she go down in the cable car and then fly home in disgrace, because I think that's what's going to happen to me?"

"No, she didn't do that. She found someone who understood and was prepared to give her a little help and encouragement."

"I need more than that. I need a miracle."

"Don't underestimate yourself."

"I'm a coward."

"That's nothing to be ashamed of. It isn't brave to do something that you're not afraid of. But it's very brave to face up to something which frightens you paralytic."

As he was saying this, the door of the restaurant opened and a man appeared, looked about him, then came across the room towards them. Reaching their table, he stopped, respectfully removing his woollen hat.

"Herr Commander Manleigh?"

"Hans! What can I do for you?"

The man spoke in German, and Jeannie's companion replied in the same language. They talked for a moment and then the problem, whatever it was, was apparently solved. The man bowed to Jeannie, made his farewells, and took himself off.

"What was all that about?" she asked.

"That's Hans from the cable car. Your young man telephoned up from the village to find out what had happened to you. He thought you might have had a fall. Hans came to find you – he recognised you from your friend's description."

"What did you say?"

"I said to tell him not to worry. We'll be down in our own time."

"We?"

"You and I. But not in the cable car. We're doing the Kreisler run together."

"I can't."

He did not contradict her. Instead, after a thoughtful pause, he asked, "Are you in love with this young man?"

She had never actually considered this before. Not seriously. But all at once, faced with the question, she knew the truth. "Yes," she told him.

"Do you want to lose him?"

"No."

"Then come with me. Now. Right away. Before either of us has time to change our minds."

Outside again it was still just as cold, but the sun was climbing into the sky, and the icicles which festooned the balcony of the restaurant and the doorways of the cable house were beginning to thaw and drip.

Jeannie pulled on her hat and gloves, retrieved her skis, fastened the bindings, took a ski pole in either hand. Her new friend was ready before her, and waiting, and together they moved across the beaten, rutted snow to the verge of the slope where the *piste*, like a silver ribbon, wound away down the snowfields before them. The village, reduced by distance to toy-size, lay deep in the valley, and beyond again, the further mountains, ranges of them, shone and glittered like glass.

She said, for the first time, "It's so beautiful."

"Enjoy the beauty. That is one of the joys of skiing. Having time to stop and stare. And this is a magical day. Now. Are you ready to go?"

"As ready as I'll ever be."

"Then shall we make a start?"

"Before we do, can I ask you one thing?"

"What's that?"

"The girl you told me about – the one who was as scared as I am. What happened to her?"

He smiled. "I married her," he said, and then he was gone, gently, smoothly down the slope, traversing a ridge, turning, sailing away in the other direction.

Jeannie took a deep breath, set her teeth, pushed with her ski poles and followed him.

At first she was as stiff and awkward as she had ever been, but every moment that passed increased her confidence. Three turns and she hadn't fallen. Her blood quickened, her body warmed, she could actually feel her muscles relax. There was sunshine on her face and the cool rush of clean air, sparkling, crisp as chilled wine. There was the sweet hiss of her own skis in the snow, the gathering sense of speed, the rasp of steel edges on ice as she manoeuvred a tricky corner.

He was never far ahead. Every so often, he would stop to wait for her and let her get her breath back. Sometimes the way ahead needed a little explanation. "It's a narrow track through the woods," he would say. "Let your skis run in the tracks that other skiers have made, and then you'll be quite safe." Or, "The *piste* circles the edge of the mountain here, but it's not as dangerous as it looks."

He made her feel that nothing could be too difficult or frightening if he were there, leading the way. As they sank down into the valley, the terrain altered. There were bridges to be crossed, and open farm gateways through which they hurtled.

And then, all at once, long before she had expected it, they were in familiar territory, at the top of the nursery slopes, and so the finish of the run was child's play compared with what had gone before. Jeannie came down these slopes, on which she had unhappily struggled for seven solid days, with a flourish of speed, and a sensation of elation and achievement that she had never known before in her life. She had done it. She had come down the Kreisler.

The slope levelled out by the ski school hut and the little café where she had gone each day for a comforting mug of hot chocolate. Here the stranger waited for her, relaxed and smiling, delighted as she was and yet obviously amused by her delight.

She stopped alongside him, pushed up her goggles and

laughed up into his face. "I thought it was going to be horrible and it was heavenly."

"You did very well."

"I didn't fall once. I don't understand it."

"You only fell because you were nervous. Now you will never fall for that reason again."

"I can't thank you enough."

"You don't have to thank me. I enjoyed it. And if I'm not mistaken, I think that's your young man come to claim you."

Jeannie turned and saw that it was indeed Alistair, emerging from the door of the café, down the wooden steps and across the snow towards them. His face was filled with a marvellous relief, and the smile he had for her was a congratulation in itself.

"You made it, Jeannie. Well done, my darling!" He enfolded her in a huge bear hug. "I watched you coming down the last bit of the nursery slope, and you were really good." And then, across her head, his eyes met those of the man who had come to her rescue. Jeannie looked up and saw another expression cross his handsome features – the same respect and reverence that had shown on the face of the cable car man, when he had come to deliver Alistair's message.

"Commander Manleigh." If he had been wearing a hat, he would surely have removed it. "I didn't realise it was you. I didn't even know you were out here." The two men shook hands. "How are you, sir?"

"All the better for having met your charming young lady. I'm sorry, I don't know your name."

"Alistair Hansen. I used to watch you skiing when I was a boy. I had great photographs of you pinned up all over my bedroom walls."

"Well, it's very nice to meet you."

"It was good of you to come down with Jeannie."

"Hans at the cable car station gave me your message."

"I was halfway down the *piste* before I realised she wasn't behind me, and by then it was too late to make my way back."

"I found her in the restaurant. She was feeling a bit cold, so she went to get herself a hot drink. We got talking."

"I was afraid she'd fallen."

Commander Manleigh stooped, loosened his bindings and stepped out of his skis. Shouldering them, he stood erect. He smiled. "Given a little encouragement, young man, she won't let you down. Now I must be off. Goodbye, Jeannie, and good luck."

"Goodbye, and thank you again for being so kind."

He slapped Alistair across the shoulder. "Take good care of her," he told him, then turned and walked away from them, a tall, grey-haired man on his own.

Jeannie was taking off her own skis. "Who is he?" she wanted to know.

"Bill Manleigh. Come on, let's go and have a drink."

"But who's Bill Manleigh?"

"I can't believe you've never heard of him. He's one of the best skiers we've ever produced. When he grew too old to race, he became a coach for the Olympic team. So you see, my darling, you came down the Kreisler with a champion."

"I didn't know that. I only know that he was terribly kind. And, Alistair, it wasn't because I was cold that I went into the restaurant, it was because I was too frightened to follow you. You might as well know."

"You should have told me."

"I couldn't. I just stood there, being terrified, and then I knew I hadn't the nerve to make the run. And I was drinking coffee and he came and talked to me. And he didn't tell me anything about himself at all. Not at all." She thought about this. "Except that he was married."

Alistair lifted her skis on to his shoulder, and took her hand in his other hand. Together, they made their way towards the little café. "Yes, he was," he told her. "To a lovely girl. I used to watch them ski together, and think that they must be the most glamorous couple in the world. They were always such good friends, always laughing together, as though they didn't need anybody but each other."

"You talk as though it's all in the past."

"It is." They had reached the wooden building and Alistair paused to ram her skis into the snow. "She died last summer. She was drowned. I read about it in the papers. They were sailing with friends in Greece and there was some ghastly misadventure. He was devastated and now he must be so lonely without her."

Jeannie looked down the street, the way that he had gone, but he had been swallowed up in the cheerful crowds of holidaymakers, and there was no sign of him. 'He must be so lonely.' For a terrible moment, she thought she was going to cry. A lump swelled in her throat, and her eyes misted with ridiculous tears.

Such a kind man. She would probably never see him again, and yet she owed him an immeasurable debt. She would never forget him.

"But I don't suppose," Alistair went on, "that he would have said anything to you about that."

*You remind me, quite extraordinarily, of a girl I used to know.*

Going hand-in-hand with Alistair up the wooden steps which led to the café door, she realised that she wasn't going to cry after all.

"No," she said. "No, he didn't say anything."

# ⚜ *Whistle for the Wind* ⚜

It was Saturday morning. Blinks of golden light lit the trees, and cloud shadows raced across the face of the hills, chasing each other out to the distant blue line of the sea.

Jenny Fairburn, heading home for lunch after a walk with the two family dogs, was pleasantly tired because she had been a long way – right around the loch and back by the rutted, winding farm road. Home lay ahead, an old Manse alongside a ruined church. It was sheltered from the north by a stand of pines, and the south-facing windows flashed in the sunlight as though sending out signals of welcome. Jenny thought about lunch, because she was hungry as well as tired. She knew that it was roast lamb, and her mouth watered, like a hungry child's.

She was, in fact, twenty, a tall, thin girl with the reddish blonde hair and pale skin that she had inherited from her father's mother, a true Highlander. Her eyes were dark, her nose narrow and tip-tilted, and her mouth wide and expressive. When she smiled, it lit up her face, but she knew that when she was feeling cross or depressed she could look sulky and plain.

In the back porch, she gave the panting dogs a drink and then toed off her muddy boots. From the kitchen she could hear her mother's voice, presumably chatting on the telephone, because Jenny's father had spent the morning on the golf-course and his car was still not back in the garage.

In stockinged feet, she let herself into the kitchen, and smelt the roasting lamb and the sharpness of mint sauce.

". . . how very kind of you," her mother was saying. She turned, saw Jenny and smiled in an abstracted way. "Yes. Yes. About six-thirty? All of us. Well, we'll look forward to that. 'Bye." She put down the receiver and smiled at her daughter. "Did you have a nice walk?"

She sounded a little too bright. Jenny frowned. "Who was that on the telephone?"

Mrs Fairburn was stooping to open the oven door and inspect the lamb. A fragrant gust of heat escaped into the kitchen.

"Just Daphne Fenton."

"What does she want?"

Mrs Fairburn shut the oven door and straightened up. Her face was pink, but perhaps that was just the heat. "She's asked us all for a drink this evening."

"What's the celebration?"

"No celebration. Fergus is home for the weekend, and Daphne's asked a few people in for a drink. She particularly wants you to come."

Jenny said, "I don't want to go."

"Oh, darling, you must."

"You can say I'm doing something else."

Her mother came over to Jenny's side. "Look, I know you were hurt, and I know how much you loved Fergus, but it's over. He's marrying Rose next month. At some point you've got to let everybody see that you've accepted this."

"I think I will once they're married. But they're not yet, and I don't like Rose."

They gazed hopelessly at each other, then they heard Mr Fairburn's car coming up the road, turning into the gate.

"There's your father. He'll be starving." Mrs Fairburn gave Jenny's hand a loving pat. "I must make the gravy."

After lunch, with the dishes washed and the kitchen tidy,

they dispersed on their various ploys. Mr Fairburn changed into his gardening clothes (in which no self-respecting gardener would be seen dead) and went out to sweep leaves; Mrs Fairburn disappeared to work on the new sitting-room curtains which she had been trying to finish for a month and Jenny decided to go fishing. She collected her rod and her fishing bag, pulled on her father's old shooting jacket and the rubber boots, and firmly told the dogs that this time they couldn't come.

"Is it all right if I borrow your car?" she asked her mother. "I'm going up to the loch to see if I can catch anything."

"Catch at least three trout. Then we can have them for supper."

As Jenny came to the loch, she saw the stillness of the brown water, scarcely touched now by the breeze. 'Too still for fish,' Fergus would have said. 'We'll need to whistle for the wind.'

About a mile down the loch, a grassy track led off the road and down towards the water. Jenny took this, letting the small, battered car bump and bounce its way over tussocks of turf and heather. She parked a few feet from the shore, collected her rod and the bag, and made her way down to where the little rowing-boat was pulled up on a sickle of shingle.

But she didn't get into it at once. Instead, she sat on the bank, and listened to the silence, which was not a silence at all but a stirring and murmuring of tiny sounds. The buzz of a bee, the distant baa-ing of sheep, the sigh of a breeze, the whisper of water against pebbles.

'We'll need to whistle for the wind.'

Fergus . . . What could you do about a man who had been part of your life since you were a little girl? A boy in patched jeans, collecting shells on the beach. A young man in a worn kilt, walking the hill. A grown man, immensely sophisticated and attractive, with a smooth dark head and eyes as blue as the loch on a summer day. What could you do about someone with whom you had quarrelled and laughed, who had always been your friend and your rival and finally turned out to be – she knew – the only man she could ever love?

He was six years older than Jenny, which made him now twenty-six, and the son of her parents' friends, the Fentons, who farmed Inverbruie, two miles down the road.

"He's like a brother," people used to say to Jenny who was an only child. But she knew that it had never been like that. For what brother would spend patient hours teaching a small girl how to fish? What brother would dance with a gangling teenager at parties, when the room was filled with older, more charming and prettier girls?

And when Jenny, sent to boarding school in Kent, hated being away from Scotland so much that every letter home begged to be allowed to return, it was Fergus who eventually persuaded her parents that Jenny would do just as well, and be a thousand times happier, at the local Creagan High School.

'One day,' she had promised herself, 'I shall marry him. He will fall in love with me and I shall marry him, and I'll move down the road to Inverbruie and be the young farmer's wife.'

But this happy prospect was slightly dimmed by Fergus deciding that he did not want to follow his father into farming, but would go to Edinburgh to learn how to be a chartered accountant.

So what. Jenny's private schemes for the two of them did a quick change of direction. 'One day he will fall in love with me and I shall marry him, and go with him to live in Edinburgh and we'll have a little house in Ann Street and go to symphony concerts together.'

The thought of living in Edinburgh was, truth be told, fairly daunting. Jenny hated towns but perhaps Edinburgh wouldn't be too bad. They could come home for weekends.

But Fergus did not stay in Edinburgh. After he qualified, he was offered a transfer to the main office of his firm, and moved to London. London? For the first time Jenny knew a nudge of doubt. London. Could she bear to go so far away from her beloved hills and loch?

"Why don't you go to London?" her mother asked when Jenny finally left school. "You could go to college there. Perhaps share a little flat!"

"I couldn't bear it. It would be worse than Kent."

"Edinburgh, then? You ought to get away from home for a bit."

❧

So Jenny went to Edinburgh and learned shorthand and typing, studied French and went to art galleries, and when she became homesick, climbed Arthur's Seat and pretended she was on the top of Ben Creagan. By Easter, she had finished the course and been duly presented with a Certificate, and it was time to go home. Fergus would probably be home for Easter as well and she wondered if he would notice a change in her.

He would probably look at her, like people did in books, as though seeing her for the first time, and perhaps then he would recognise what Jenny had known for years. That they were made for each other. And at last all those elusive daydreams would come true. It would, of course, mean living in London, but by now Jenny knew that living anywhere without Fergus was no fun at all.

As her train drew into Creagan, she hung out of the window and saw her mother waiting for her, which was odd, because usually it was her father who met her.

"Darling!" They hugged and kissed, and there was the business of getting cases off the train and making their way out into the yard where the car waited. It was now nearly dark, street lights were on, and the air smelt of hills and peat.

They came through the little town and turned on to the side road which led to home. They passed Inverbruie.

"Is Fergus back?"

"Yes. He's home." Jenny hugged herself. "He's – he's brought a friend with him."

Jenny turned her head and looked at her mother's neat profile. "A friend?"

"Yes. A girl called Rose. You may have seen her on television. She's an actress." A friend. A girl. An actress? "He met her a couple of months ago."

"H – have you met her?"

"No, but we've all been invited to a party there tomorrow night."

"But – but –" There didn't seem to be any words for the shock and the desolation which she felt. Mrs Fairburn stopped the car and turned to Jenny. "This is why I came to meet you at the station. I knew you'd be upset. I wanted to talk it over."

"I just – I just don't want him to bring anyone here to Creagan." Even to herself this sounded pathetically juvenile.

"Jenny, you don't own Fergus. He has a perfect right to make new friends. He's a grown man with his own life to live. Just as you have a life to make for yourself. You can't spend it looking over your shoulder and mourning for childhood fancies."

The worst bit was not that she actually said this, but that she had been so perceptive in the first place.

"I – I really do love him."

"I know. It's agony. First love is always agony. But you'll have to grit your teeth and see it through. And don't let

170

anybody see how much you mind." They sat in silence for a bit. Then, "All right?" her mother asked, and Jenny nodded. Mrs Fairburn started the car up again, and they moved on.

"Do you think he'll marry her?"

"I've no idea. But from what Daphne Fenton tells me, it sounds perfectly possible. She says he's bought himself a flat in Wandsworth and Rose is making his loose covers."

"Do you think that's a bad sign?"

"Not bad, exactly. But indicative."

Jenny fell silent. But as they turned into the gates of the Manse, she stirred herself. "Perhaps I shall like her."

"Yes," said Mrs Fairburn. "Perhaps you will."

And she did try to like Rose. But it was difficult, because, without realising it, she had seen Rose on television in a hospital drama, where Rose had played a nurse. Even then Jenny had thought that she was a bore, with her heart-shaped face struggling with a variety of emotions, an unbearable distress being conveyed by a slight tremor in her well-bred voice.

In real life, Rose was pretty enough. Her hair was silky black, loose and curly around her shoulders, and she wore a low-waisted dress with unexpected bits of beading and glitter stitched to its loose folds.

"Fergus has told me so much about you," she said to Jenny when they were introduced at Inverbruie. "He says you were practically brought up together. Is your father a farmer too?"

"No, he's the bank manager in Creagan."

"And you've always lived here?"

"Born and bred. I even went to school here. I was in Edinburgh for the winter, but it's heaven to be back."

"Don't you get – er – rather bored in such a desolate spot?"

"No."

"What are you going to do now?"

"I don't know."

"Come to London. Nowhere else on earth to live, I always say to Fergy. Come to London and we'll keep an eye on you –" She reached out and closed her fingers around Fergus's arm. Fergus was at that moment engaged, happily, in conversation with somebody else, but she drew him physically away from this person and back to herself. "Darling, I was just saying, Jenny must come to London."

Fergus and Jenny looked into each other's eyes; Jenny smiled and found to her surprise that it was remarkably easy.

Fergus said, "Jenny doesn't like city life."

Jenny shrugged. "It's a matter of taste."

"But you can't stay here always." Rose sounded incredulous.

"I will for the summer." She had not, in fact, thought about it, but now discovered, in an instant, that her decision was made. "I'll get a holiday job in Creagan, I expect." She decided to change the subject. "My mother was telling me about the flat in Wandsworth."

"Yes . . ." Fergus began, but that was as far as he got because Rose took over.

"It's heavenly. Not very big, but full of sunshine. Just a few little touches and it will be quite perfect."

"Has it got a garden?" Jenny asked.

"No. But there's a window box or two. I thought we could plant geraniums. Real scarlet ones. Then we can pretend we're in Majorca or Greece. Can't we, darling?"

"Whatever you say," said Fergus.

Scarlet geraniums. 'Dear heaven,' thought Jenny, 'he really is in love with her.' And suddenly she couldn't bear to stand there any longer, watching them. She made her

excuses and turned away. She did not speak to either Rose
or Fergus for the rest of the evening.

But she could not escape Fergus, because he sought her out
the very next day, spring-cleaning the summerhouse.

"Jenny."

She was actually shaking dust out of a rush mat when he
appeared, unexpectedly, around the side of the summerhouse, and for an instant she was startled into immobility.

"What do you want?" she managed at last.

"I've come to see you."

"How nice. Where's Rose?"

"She's at home. She's washing her hair."

"It looked perfectly clean to me."

"Jenny, are you going to listen to me?"

She sighed noisily and looked resigned. "It depends on
what you've got to say."

"I just want you to understand. To understand the way
things are. I want you not to be angry. I want to feel that
we can still at least talk to each other. And be friends."

"Well, we're talking, aren't we?"

"And friends?"

"Oh, friends. Always friends. Friends whatever we do to
each other."

"And what have I done?"

She glared at him accusingly, and then threw down the
rush mat.

"All right, so you don't like Rose. You might as well admit
it," he said.

"I don't feel about Rose one way or the other. I don't
know Rose."

"Then isn't it a little unfair – on both Rose and myself –
to make a snap judgment?"

"I just don't feel I have anything in common with her."

"That's just because she told you that you ought to get away from Creagan."

"And what possible business is it of hers?"

Now his temper was rising to match her own. She saw his jaw muscles tighten, a familiar sign, and she was pleased because she had made him angry. It somehow eased the hurt inside her.

"Jenny, you stay here for the rest of your life, and you'll end up a country bumpkin in a seated tweed skirt with nothing to talk about except dogs and fishing."

She turned on him. "You know something? I'd rather be that than a third-rate actress with a mouth like a button."

He laughed, but he was laughing at Jenny and not with her. He said unforgivably, "I do believe you're jealous. You always could be quite impossible!"

"And you, perhaps, could always be a fool, but I never realised it until now."

Fergus turned on his heel and walked away, across the lawn. Jenny watched his progress, her temper dying as swiftly as it had blown up. Words spoken in heat and haste were all very well, but they could never be taken back. Nothing could ever be the same again.

~❦~

Jenny found a job in Creagan, working in a shop which sold Shetland pullovers and pebble-jewellery to tourists. Around July, she was told by her mother that Fergus and Rose were engaged, and were to be married in September in London where Rose's parents lived. Just a quiet wedding, with a few of their close London friends. But meantime, they had returned to Inverbruie and there was to be another little party and Jenny could not find the courage to go. After they were married, she told herself again, it would be different.

She would become dynamic; go abroad perhaps; get a job in the French Alps as a chalet girl, or be a cook on a yacht. However, she was growing cold and there were trout to be caught for supper. She stood up, clambered down the heathery bank, untied the painter, pushed the boat out into the water and began to row.

Fishing was special, because when you fished you thought about nothing else. She took the boat a long way up the loch and then shipped the oars and let the wind drift her back towards the shore. Now, there was enough breeze to stir the surface of the water, and she began casting.

She heard the car coming up the road, but was too engrossed to pay attention to it. There was another bite or two, and then at last she hooked a fish, and concentrating on nothing else, began gently to reel it in. She netted it out of the water, and dropped it in the bottom of the boat.

As if on cue, she heard a voice say, "Well done."

Startled by this interruption from the business in hand, she looked up and saw, all at once, a number of surprising things. She had, without realising it, drifted to within yards of the shore; the car she had heard on the road had stopped and was now parked a little way off; and Fergus, a solitary figure, stood on the bank and watched her.

He was bare-headed, the wind ruffling his dark hair. He wore a tweed jacket and a pair of corduroys, tucked into green rubber boots. Not dressed for fishing. Jenny sat in the rocking boat and looked at him, and wondered if he had come upon her by chance, or if, in fact, he had come looking, to ask why she had refused to come to the party, to try to persuade her to change her mind. If he did this, then they would have another argument, another row, and she knew that rather than repeat their last painful set-to, she would prefer never to have to speak to him again.

He grinned. He said again, "Well done. You handled that very neatly. I couldn't have done better myself."

Jenny did not reply. Instead, she busied herself in reeling in the loose line, securing the barbed fly. With care, she laid down the rod, and then looked up again at Fergus.

She said, "How long have you been there?"

"Ten minutes or more." He put his hands in his jacket pockets. "I came to find you. Your mother told me you'd come up here. I want to talk to you."

"What about?"

"Jenny, don't get your hackles up. Let's call it pax."

It seemed only fair. "All right."

"Come and get me then."

Jenny made no move to do this, but even as they spoke she was being blown inshore, and as she hesitated, she felt the first bump as the keel touched stone. Before she realised what was happening, Fergus had waded out and grabbed the bow, thrown one long leg over the gunwale and was aboard.

"Now," he said, "give me the oars."

There didn't seem to be very much alternative. With a couple of clean strokes, he had turned the light craft, and then they were headed back out into the middle of the loch. It was ten minutes or so before he looked about him, decided they had come far enough, shipped the oars, and turned up the collar of his jacket against the cold edge of the wind.

"Now," he said, "we're going to talk."

It seemed sensible to take the initiative. "I suppose my mother told you that I didn't want to come tonight. I suppose that's what it's all about."

"Yes, it's about that. And other things, too."

She waited for him to enlarge on this, but he did not continue. Across the thwarts, they looked at each other, and then suddenly smiled. And all at once Jenny was filled with a curious contentment and peace. It was a long time since she'd sat in a boat with Fergus, in the middle of the loch, with the familiar hills folding away on all sides and the sky arched above them, and have him smile at her like that. It made it easier to be honest, not only with him, but with herself.

"It's just that I don't want to come. I don't want to see Rose again. It'll be different when you're married to her. But now . . ." She shrugged. "It's cowardice, I suppose," she finally admitted.

"That doesn't sound like you."

"Perhaps it isn't me. Perhaps I'm all twisted and back to front. You said that day by the summerhouse that I was jealous, and, of course, you were quite right. I suppose I always thought of you as my property, but that's wrong, isn't it? No person can ever belong to another person, even after they're married."

"No man is an island."

"I always thought that bits of a man had to be an island. You can't creep inside somebody else's head."

"No. You can't do that."

"Just like you can't go on being a child. You have to grow up whether you want to or not."

He said, "Did you get that job in Creagan?"

"Yes, but it folds up in October when the shop closes down for the winter. I've decided that then I shall be enormously enterprising and find myself an occupation that's very well paid and miles away. Like America or Switzerland." She smiled, wryly. "Rose would approve of that."

Fergus stayed silent. His eyes, watching her, were unblinking, intensely blue.

"And how," she asked politely, "is Rose?"

"I don't know."

Jenny frowned. "But you have to know. She's at Inverbruie."

"She's not at Inverbruie."

"She's not . . . ?" A curlew flew overhead, its cry mournful, and the water slapped and whispered against the planking of the boat. "But Mother said . . ."

"She got it wrong. My mother didn't say anything about Rose being here; your mother just took it for granted that Rose was with me. We're not going to get married. The engagement's off."

"Off? You mean –? But why didn't Mother tell me?"

"She didn't know. I haven't got around to telling my own parents yet. I wanted to tell you before I told anyone else."

For some reason, this was so touching that Jenny wondered if she were about to burst into tears. "But, why? Why, Fergus?"

"You just said it. No person can belong to another person."

"Didn't – didn't you love her?"

"Yes, I did. I loved her very much." He could say that, and she didn't feel jealous in the least, just sad for him because it hadn't worked out. "But you marry a life as well as a person, and Rose's life and mine seemed to run along parallel lines, like railway tracks, without ever actually touching."

"When did all this happen?"

"A couple of weeks ago. That's why I came north for the weekend; I wanted to explain it to my parents, and let my mother see I wasn't dying of a broken heart."

"And aren't you?"

"Perhaps a little bit, but not enough to show."

"Rose loved you."

"For a bit she did, yes."

Jenny hesitated, and then said it. "*I* love you."

It was Fergus's turn to look as though he were about to burst into tears. "Oh, Jenny."

"You might as well know. You've probably always known. I never thought I could say that to anybody, least of all to you, but for some reason it seems to be quite easy. I mean, you don't have to do anything about it, but you might as well know. It doesn't change anything. I shall still find that marvellous job and winkle myself away from Creagan into the wide, wide world."

She smiled, expecting him to smile back at her, approving of this sensible, mature scheme. But he did not smile. For a long moment he simply looked at her, and she felt her own smile die beneath the sadness in his face. Then he said, "Don't."

Jenny frowned. "But, Fergus, I thought that was what you wanted. For me to get away from Creagan, and stand on my own feet."

"I couldn't bear you to go away and stand on your own feet," he told her bluntly.

"Well, whose feet am I going to stand on?"

The absurdity of her question somehow made everything all right again. He was caught unawares by this absurdity, and despite himself, began to laugh, wryly, as much at himself as at her. "I don't know. I suppose mine. The truth is, that you've been part of my life for so long that I don't think I can bear the thought of your going away and leaving us all. Leaving me. Life would be so dreadfully dull. There'd be nobody to argue with. Nobody to yell at. Nobody to make me laugh."

Jenny thought about this. She said, "You know, if I had an ounce of pride, I would go away. I'd be the sort of girl who didn't want to be loved on the rebound from some other person."

179

"If you had an ounce of pride, you wouldn't have told me that you loved me."

"You must have known."

"I only know that you were there long before Rose."

"So what was Rose?"

Fergus fell silent. Then he said tentatively, "A pause in the conversation?"

"Oh, Fergus."

"I – I think I'm asking you to marry me. We've wasted enough time as it is. Perhaps I should have had the sense to do it a long time ago."

"No." She was suddenly very wise. "A long time ago would have been too soon. I thought you belonged to me then. But now, like I said, I know that nobody can ever belong to anybody else. Not totally. And yet, it's only when you think that you're going to lose something that you realise how precious it is."

"I found that out too," said Fergus. "What a very good thing that we both found it out at the same time."

Out in the middle of the water, it was becoming chilly. Jenny, despite herself, shivered.

"You're cold," said Fergus. "I'll take you back." He reached for the oars, took his bearings with a glance over his shoulder and turned the little boat.

Jenny suddenly remembered. "But I can't go back yet, Fergus. I've only caught one trout and we'll need three for supper."

"To hell with supper. We'll go out. We'll take all the parents and I'll stand the lot of you dinner at the Creagan Arms. We might even rustle up some champagne and it can be an engagement party – if you like!"

Now they were heading home, back towards the mooring, the little craft skimming across the choppy waters of the loch. The wind blew from behind her. She turned up the collar of her jacket and dug her hands deep into its capacious pockets. She smiled at her love. She said, "I like."

# ◈ *The Watershed* ◈

"Can you manage, now, Mrs Harley?"

"Yes, of course." Edwina draped her handbag over one arm, the bulging basket over the other and, with some effort, heaved the box laden with groceries off the counter. The bag of tomatoes at the top teetered dangerously so she steadied it with her chin. "If you could just open the door."

"Your car there, is it?"

"Yes, right outside."

"Cheerio, then, Mrs Harley."

"Goodbye."

She emerged from the doorway of the village shop and stepped out into the chill February sunshine, crossed the cobbled pavement in a couple of steps, dumped the box on to the bonnet of her car, put the basket alongside, slung her handbag through the open window and went around to the back to open the boot.

As this was Friday and therefore shopping morning, the boot was already half-full. A large parcel from the butcher's; Henry's shoes, picked up from the cobbler's; clean sheets collected from the laundry; and the garden shears, newly sharpened and oiled by the local blacksmith. She lifted the grocery box and basket into the boot, then found that it would not close, and so did a bit of rearranging and finally got it shut.

Finished. All done. No reason now not to drive straight home. Yet she hesitated, standing there by her car in the middle of the small Scottish village, to turn her attention to the stone house which stood across the street. A house with a face as symmetrical as a child's drawing, and a roof tiled with grey slates. A narrow strip of garden, a white wooden gate, and a clipped privet hedge separated it from the pavement. Its curtains were drawn.

Old Mrs Titchfield's house. Empty because, two weeks ago, Mrs Titchfield had died in the local hospital.

Edwina knew the house. She had known Mrs Titchfield for years. Had sometimes called to collect jumble for the church sale, or to deliver a Christmas card and a fruit cake, and be asked indoors to sit by the fire with a cup of tea.

She knew the tiny rooms and the narrow stairway, the garden at the back with its Albertine roses and the clothesline strung between two apple trees ...

"Edwina!" She had neither heard nor seen the other car draw up in the space behind her own. But here was Rosemary Turner approaching; Rosemary, with her shopping basket and her neat, grey hair and her fat, white Peke on a scarlet lead. Rosemary was one of Edwina's closest friends. Her husband, James, played golf with Henry, and Rosemary was godmother to Edwina's oldest child. "What are you doing, standing there, gazing into space?" Rosemary asked.

"Just that."

"Poor old Mrs Titchfield. Never mind – she had a good, long life. Seems funny though, doesn't it, not to see her pottering about in that strip of garden? It must have been the best-weeded plot in the county. Have you done your shopping?"

"Yes. Just on my way home."

"I'm going to get some biscuits for Hi-Fi. Are you in a mad hurry?"

"No. Henry's out for lunch today."

"In that case, why don't we live dangerously and go and

have a cup of coffee in Ye Olde Thatched Café? I haven't seen you for ages. Masses of things to talk about."

Edwina smiled. "All right."

"Hold Hi-Fi for me, then. He hates going into the shop because the cat always spits at him."

Edwina took the lead and, waiting, leaned against the car. Her eyes drifted back to Mrs Titchfield's house. She had an idea, but knew that Henry would hate it, and the prospect of heated discussion filled her with dismay. She sighed, feeling tired and old. Probably, at the end of the day, she would take the easy way out and say nothing.

The little café was cramped and dark and old. But the china was pretty, there were fresh flowers on the tables and the coffee, when it arrived, was fragrant and strong.

Edwina took a sustaining mouthful. "I needed that."

"I thought you looked a bit washed out. Are you feeling all right?"

"Yes. Just overwhelmed by the tedium of shopping. Why does it always have to be such a boring routine?"

"I suppose, after years of marriage, we've become programmed. Like computers. Where's Henry having lunch?"

"With Kate and Tony. He and Tony have spent the morning having horrible financial discussions."

Kate was Henry's sister. Her husband, Tony, was Henry's accountant and his office was walking distance from Edwina and Henry's spacious home in Relkirk.

"Does Henry like being retired?"

"I think so. He always seems to be occupied."

"Do you find him getting under your feet? I nearly went crazy when James first retired. He kept coming into the kitchen and switching off my radio and asking me questions."

"What sort of questions?"

"Oh, the usual. 'Have you seen my calculator?' 'What do you want done with the lawn mower?' 'What time is lunch?'

Who was it said that you marry a man for better, for worse, but not for lunch?"

"The Duchess of Windsor."

Rosemary laughed. Across the table, their eyes met. Her laughter died. "So what's the problem? You're not usually so down in the mouth."

Edwina heaved her shoulders and sighed. "I don't know . . . Yes, I do. I looked in my diary this morning and realised that next month Henry and I will have been married for thirty years."

"So you will! A pearl wedding anniversary. Is it really five years since your silver? How splendid! Another excuse for a lovely party."

"There's no point in having a party if the children can't be there."

"Why can't they be there?"

"Because Rodney's with his ship, patrolling the Straits of Hormuz. And Priscilla's in Sussex, totally occupied with Bob and the two babies. And Tessa's finally found herself a job in London, but she scarcely earns enough to keep body and soul together, so even if she could get the time off, she wouldn't be able to afford the train fare home. Besides, thirty years doesn't seem to be anything to celebrate. To me it feels uncomfortably like a watershed . . . you know, from now on it's downhill all the way . . ."

"Don't say such depressing things!"

". . . and at the end of the day, what has one achieved? I don't feel I've got anything to show for it all."

Rosemary, with characteristic good sense, made no comment on this lament. Instead, stirring her coffee, she turned the conversation to another tack.

"Were you gazing at Mrs Titchfield's house for any particular reason?"

"In a way . . . It's suddenly come home to me that I'm fifty-two and Henry's sixty-seven, and that the day will come when, physically, we won't be able to live at Hill House any longer. As it is, we rattle around in it like a couple of dried peas, and every spare moment is spent trying to keep the garden the way it's always looked."

"Beautiful."

"Yes, it's a beautiful garden, and we love it, and we love the house. But it was always too big for us, even with the three children living at home."

"If you're thinking of moving, you're going to have difficulty persuading Henry."

"You don't have to tell me that." Henry had inherited Hill House from his parents. He had lived there all his life, and remembered the days when there were a large indoor staff and two gardeners. Now there was just Bessie Digley, and she could only manage three mornings a week.

"I can't bear the thought of you not living there. Aren't you jumping the gun? After all, you're not *old* – you've years and years ahead of you. And what about having the grandchildren to stay? You'll need space for them."

"I've thought of that. But isn't it better to make a move before you're too old to enjoy it? Think of the poor old Perrys. They clung on to the manor until they were so decrepit, they simply had to sell up. And then they bought that dreadful little house, and Mrs Perry fell down the stairs and broke her hip, and that was the end of both of them. Supposing Mrs Titchfield's house comes up for sale, and Henry and I buy it. Wouldn't it be fun, doing it up together? Redecorating, and replanning the garden? I know it's tiny, but it's in the village. I wouldn't have to drive seven miles every time I want to buy a loaf of bread or a pound of sausages. And we'd be able to keep it really warm, and not get snowed up in the winter. And the children wouldn't worry about us."

"Do they worry now?"

"No, but they will."

Rosemary laughed. "You know what I think is wrong with you? You're missing those children. They've all fled the nest, even little Tessa, and you miss them. But that's no reason to make a momentous decision about moving. You'll just have to find something else to fill your life. Make Henry take you on a cruise."

"I don't want to go on a cruise."

"Then take up yoga. Do something."

When they finally parted Edwina drove the seven winding miles of country road back to Hill House. She came to the white gate, opened it, and drove up the steep driveway between the tall beeches and the thick clumps of rhododendron. Beyond the trees was the lawn, then the rough grass beneath the white cherry trees which, in spring, would be a riot of yellow daffodils. Beyond it was the big, old Georgian house, its windows blinking in the low February sunshine.

Parking the car in the stable yard, Edwina carried her shopping indoors. The kitchen was huge and homely, with an Aga, a dresser stacked with ironstone china, a basket of laundry waiting to be ironed, and the two Labradors waiting to be taken for a walk.

Without Henry, the house always felt strangely empty. She was suddenly aware, with piercing intensity, of the deserted rooms above and about her. The dust-sheeted drawing-room; the large dining-room, scene of countless cheerful family meals, but now scarcely used, for she and Henry always ate in the kitchen. Like a ghost, her imagination wandered up the stairs to the wide landing and the doors leading off it, into the spacious bedrooms where once the children had slept, or where visitors, often entire families, had stayed; down the passage to the white-painted nurseries, the linen room, the cavernous bathrooms; up to the attic, where the household staff had long ago slept, and where she had stored the outgrown bicycles, perambulators, doll's houses, boxes of bricks.

The house was a monument to family life. To a family of children who were children no longer. How had the years swept by so swiftly?

There was no answer to this. The dogs demanded her attention so she left the groceries on the kitchen table, pulled on her green wellingtons and set off, with the dogs at her heels, for a long walk.

That evening, over supper, emboldened by a glass of wine, Edwina broached the subject of Mrs Titchfield's house.

"I expect it will be coming up for sale."

"I expect it will."

"You don't think we should buy it?"

Henry raised his handsome white head to stare at her in disbelief. "*Buy* it? For heaven's sake, why?"

Edwina gathered her courage about her. "To live in."

"But we live here."

"We're getting older. And Hill House seems to be getting bigger."

"We're not that old."

"I just feel we ought to be sensible."

"And what do you intend doing with this house?"

"Well ... if Rodney wants it one day, we could let it. And if he doesn't, we could sell it."

At this he laid down his knife and fork and reached for his Scotch and soda. She watched him. He set down the glass, then asked, "When did you get this brilliant idea?"

"Today. No, not today. It's been in the back of my mind for some time. I love Hill House, Henry, just the way you do. But face it, the children are gone. They have their own lives to live. And we're not going to be able to stay here for ever ..."

"I can't see why not."

"But there's so much to look after. The garden . . ."

"If I didn't have the garden, what would I do with myself? Imagine me in Mrs Titchfield's house, banging my head every time I went through a door. If I didn't die of brain damage, I'd go dotty with claustrophobia. Probably end my days as one of those seedy old men you see ambling down to the pub at midday and not emerging until closing time. Besides, this is our home."

"I just feel . . . perhaps . . . that we should look ahead."

"I look ahead all the time. To the spring, and the bulbs coming up. To the summer, and seeing my new rose-bed bloom. I'm looking ahead to Rodney finding himself a wife, and Tessa getting married from this house. I'm looking forward to having them all back to stay, with their families. We've survived the traumas of bringing them all up; now let's allow ourselves to reap some of the rewards."

After a bit, Edwina said, "Yes."

"You sound unconvinced."

"You're right, of course. But I think I'm right, too." He reached across the table and laid his hand on hers. She said, "I miss the children."

He did not argue with this. "Wherever we lived, we'd miss them."

❧

Two weeks later, Rosemary called. "Edwina, it's about your wedding anniversary. Come and have dinner with James and me, and we'll have a little celebration. That's Saturday in two weeks' time. Shall we say seven-thirty?"

"Oh, Rosemary, you are sweet."

"That's settled, then. If I don't see you before, I'll see you then."

That evening, Edwina's sister-in-law, Kate, telephoned. "Edwina, what are you doing about your thirtieth wedding anniversary?" she asked.

"I didn't think you'd remember."

"Of course I remembered. How could I forget?"

"Well, actually, we're going to have dinner with James and Rosemary. She asked us this morning."

"Splendid. I imagined you and Henry eating a chop in the kitchen and none of us doing anything to mark the occasion. But I'll worry no longer. See you some time. 'Bye."

Thirty years. She awoke to rain pouring down the window-panes and splashing sounds from the bathroom, which meant that Henry was taking his morning shower. She lay and watched the rain, and thought, 'I have been married for thirty years.' She tried to remember that day thirty years ago and scarcely remembered anything, except that her younger sister had tried to iron her wedding-dress petticoat and had scorched the white silk. And everybody had carried on as though it were a total disaster, when, in fact, it hadn't mattered in the very least. She turned her head on the pillow and called "Henry!" and, after a moment, he appeared through the open door with his hair on end and a bath towel tied around his waist.

She said, "Happy day," and he came to kiss her, damply and fragrantly, and produced a small parcel. She unwrapped it, and there was a red-leather jewel box and, inside, a pair of earrings: small gold leaves, each set with a pearl.

191

"Oh, they're so pretty!" She sat up, and he brought her a hand mirror so she could put them on and admire herself. Kissing her again, he went off to get dressed, and she went downstairs to cook breakfast. While they were eating the postman came, and there was a cable from Rodney and cards from Priscilla and Tessa. 'Thinking of you today,' they said. 'Wish we could be with you.' 'Happy anniversary,' they said, 'and lots and lots of love.'

"Well, that's very gratifying," Henry said. "At least they remembered."

Edwina read Rodney's cable for the fourth time. "Yes."

He looked anxious. "Being married to me for thirty years doesn't make you feel old, does it?"

She knew that he was thinking of Mrs Titchfield's house, although they had not spoken of it again. But the idea still hung about at the back of her mind, and she had watched the *For Sale* sign being put up. So far, no one had bought the house.

She said, "No." Just empty and deserted like the rooms upstairs.

"Good. I don't like you feeling old. Because you don't look old. In fact, you look more beautiful than ever."

"That's because of my beautiful earrings."

"I don't think so."

It rained most of the day. Edwina spent it making marmalade and, because they were going out for dinner, did not light the fire in the little sitting-room. By the time the marmalade had set and been stowed away in the storeroom, it was time to go upstairs, and have a bath and change. She made up her face, fixed her hair, and put on her black velvet dress and a great deal of perfume. Then she helped Henry with his cuff links and gave his best grey flannel suit a brush.

"It smells of mothballs," she told him.

"All the best suits smell of mothballs."

Wearing it, he looked handsome and very distinguished. They turned off the lights and went downstairs. They locked the front door, said goodbye to the dogs, locked the back door, and scurried through the rain and into the car. They drove down the hill, leaving the house, dark, cold, and deserted, behind them.

~✱~

The Turners lived in a small and delectable cottage ten miles on the other side of the village. Their front door opened as Henry and Edwina alighted from the car, and light streamed out, turning the rain to a shimmer of silver. Rosemary and James were waiting for them.

"Happy anniversary! Congratulations!" There were kisses and hugs, warmth and brightness. They shed coats and went into Rosemary's sitting-room, where a log fire burned and the white Peke sat on his cushion and yapped. There was a present, too, a new rose for the garden.

"Wonderful," Edwina told them. "That's something we can both enjoy."

Then James opened a bottle of champagne and, after he had raised his glass to them both and made a little speech, they all settled by the fireside in Rosemary's marvellously comfortable chairs, and chatted in the easy manner of four mature people who have been friends for a long time. Their glasses emptied. James refilled them. Henry stole a furtive glance at his watch. It was ten minutes to eight.

He cleared his throat. "James, I'm not complaining, but are we to be the only guests this evening?" he asked.

James looked at his wife. She said, "No, but we're not having dinner here. Just a drink."

"Where are we eating?"

193

"Out."

"I see," said Henry, not sounding as though he saw at all.

"But where are we going?" Edwina asked.

"Wait and see."

Mysterious, but rather exciting. Perhaps they were going to be taken to the new and expensive French restaurant in Relkirk. A pleasing possibility, because Edwina had never been there. Her spirits rose in cautious anticipation.

At a quarter past eight, James set down his glass. "Time to leave." So they all got up, and climbed into their coats, and went out into the rainy darkness. "Edwina, you come with me, and Henry can drive Rosemary. I'll lead the way, Henry."

They set off. James began to tell her about how well old Henry was playing golf these days. She sat beside him, her chin deep in the collar of her coat, watching the headlights probe the winding road ahead. "It's his swing. His swing has really improved since that chat with the pro." In the village she thought he would turn right and head for the road leading to the French restaurant. But he did not do this, and she was mildly disappointed.

"Extraordinary what bad habits one can get into with golf," he was saying. "Sometimes all you need is a little objective advice."

"We seem to be going back to Hill House," she said.

"Edwina, Hill House is not the only establishment in this part of the world."

She fell silent, gazing from the window, trying to get her bearings. Then the car swung around a steep corner, and she saw lights; high above her, shining out over the dark countryside, dazzling as a firework display. But where were they? Listening to James, she had become disorientated. The lights grew larger, brighter. Then they came to a crossroads with two cottages, a familiar landmark, and she realised she had been right all along, the lights were the lights of Hill House, and James was driving her home.

To a house that they had left deserted and dark. A house now with every light on, and every window blazing a welcome.

"James, what's happening?"

But James did not answer. He turned the car in through the gates and roared up the hill. The trees lining the driveway opened out, and the lawn lay illuminated as though floodlit. The front door was open and the dogs came belting out, barking a welcome, and there were two people standing there, a man and a woman. At first she thought it couldn't be true, but it was true. It was Priscilla. Priscilla and Bob.

Almost before the car had stopped she was out of it, for once ignoring her precious dogs, running across the gravel through the rain, heedless of her hair and her high-heeled, satin shoes.

"Hello, Mummy!"

"Oh, Priscilla! Oh, darling!" They hugged enormously. "But what are you doing? What are you doing here?"

"We've come for your anniversary," her son-in-law told her. He was grinning from ear to ear, and she embraced him lovingly and then turned back to Priscilla. "But the children? What have you done with the babies?"

"Left them with my darling neighbour. It's all been the most tremendous conspiracy." The other car had by now arrived, disgorging Henry, who appeared to be pole-axed with astonishment. "Hello, Dad! Surprise, surprise!"

"What the hell is happening?" was all he seemed to be able to say.

Priscilla took his hand. "Come indoors, and we'll show you."

Bemused, they followed her. As they stood in the middle of the hall, a voice floated down from upstairs. "Happy anniversary, you darling old things." They looked up, and there was Tessa, running down the stairs, with her long, silky mane of hair flying behind. She took the last three steps in a single leap, the way she had always done, and Henry scooped her up into his arms and swung her off her feet.

"You monkey! Where did you spring from?"

"From London, where else? Oh, Mum, darling, aren't you looking gorgeous! Isn't this the best surprise ever? No, it isn't the best surprise, there's more . . . come with me!"

"It's worse than *This Is Your Life*," Henry said, but Tessa was not listening. She grasped her mother's wrist, and Edwina found herself being dragged across the hall and through the open door which led into the big drawing-room. The dust-sheets were gone, the fire had been lighted, and there were flowers everywhere. Kate and Tony were there, standing with their backs to the fire, along with a young man with a deeply tanned face and hair bleached blond by the tropic sun. It was Rodney!

"There!" said Tessa and let go of her wrist.

"Happy anniversary, Ma," said Rodney.

"But how did you do it?" Edwina asked, walking into his arms. "How did you arrange everything?"

"It was a conspiracy. Aunt Kate and Uncle Tony were in on it – and Rosemary and James as well, and Bessie Digley. We all met up in London yesterday and flew north together."

"But Rodney, how did you get leave?"

"I was due some anyway. Been saving it up."

"But I got a cable this morning, from your ship."

"I got the First Lieutenant to send it for me."

She turned to her daughters. "And your cards . . ."

"Red herrings," Tessa told her. "To allay any suspicions you might have had. And of course, we're all having dinner here, in the dining-room. Priscilla and I cooked it in Aunt Kate's kitchen, and we brought it all over in the boot of their car. Sort of terribly upmarket Meals on Wheels."

"But ... the fire. This room. The flowers. Everything ..."

"Rodney and Uncle Tony did all that while we flew around laying the table. And Bob went around turning on every single light."

"It was so funny," Priscilla chimed in. "When you left for Rosemary's, we were all waiting in two cars at the bottom of the drive, with everything switched off so you wouldn't see us. Just like playing hide-and-seek. Then, as soon as you were safely on your way, we shot up the drive and set to work."

"How did you get in?" Henry wanted to know.

"Tessa still has her key. And Bessie Digley's here. She's going to make up all our beds. You don't mind if we stay the weekend, do you? Rodney can stay longer, of course, because he's got two weeks' leave, but I can't leave the children too long, and Tessa has to get back to work."

Champagne corks had been popping. Somebody handed Edwina a glass. She hadn't even taken off her coat yet, and she had never felt so happy in her whole life.

A little later, Edwina slipped away from the laughter and talk and champagne. She looked into the dining-room and saw that here, too, the fire had been lighted, and the great mahogany table laid as though for a royal banquet. She moved towards the kitchen and looked in around the door. Bessie Digley turned from the stove. "Now this was a good surprise," she observed, and there was a smile on her face that Edwina had never seen before.

She went upstairs. On the landing every bedroom door was ajar, and every light blazed. She glimpsed open suitcases and clothes lying about in a heartwarming muddle. In her own room, she took off her coat and laid it across the bed.

She thought about drawing the curtains, then decided against it. Let the whole world see and guess what was happening! She stood with her back to the window and surveyed her large, familiar, faintly shabby bedroom. Her dressing-table, the huge double bed, the towering Victorian wardrobe, her desk. She saw the plethora of photographs, which seemed to cover every surface. The children at all stages and ages, and now grandchildren, too, and dogs and picnics and reunions and celebrations.

A thousand memories.

After a little while, she went to the mirror, fixed her hair, and powdered her nose. It was time to join the others. But at the top of the stairs, she paused. From the drawing-room, voices and laughter floated upward, filling the air with happy sounds. Her children were here. They had come to tear the dust-sheets from the empty rooms and fill the vacant bedrooms. Henry had been right. There were still years of life to be lived in this house. It was too soon to be thinking of leaving. Too soon to be thinking of growing old.

Thirty years. She touched her new earrings, found herself smiling, and ran downstairs, excited as a bride.

# ⚜ *Marigold Garden* ⚜

He had not planned to go to Brookclere. It lay deep in the Hampshire countryside, fifteen miles from the motorway between Southampton and London, and he had seen himself simply speeding past the turn-off without a sideways glance.

But somehow – perhaps by memory, perhaps by the familiar countryside drowsing in the afternoon sunshine – he was seduced, beguiled. After all, it was over. Finished. Julia and her new husband would still be away on their honeymoon, basking in the glorious heat of the Mediterranean, or sailing some boat across turquoise blue, glass-clear West Indian waters. She was now out of his reach.

The wide road curved ahead of him, poured behind. On either side villages, orchards, farms, sliced in two by progress, lay untouched, unchanged. Cows stood in the shade beneath clumps of trees, and fields were thick and yellow with ripening corn.

The sign came up at him. *Lamington, Hartston. Brookclere.* Miles eased his foot from the accelerator. The needle on the dashboard dropped from seventy, to sixty, to fifty. *What the hell am I doing?* But the image of the old redbrick house, smothered in wistaria; the lawn, sloping down to the river; the heady scent of roses, pulled him like a magnet. He knew that he had to go back. Now he saw the turn-off, the bridge across the motorway. He glanced into his driving mirror to check the traffic behind him, and then, inexorably, slid across into the slow lane, and so up on to the ramp.

'Perhaps you meant to do this,' he thought wryly. But why not? It was too late for memories. Ten days too late.

Out of sight and sound of the motorway, the surroundings were almost at once familiar. He knew this road, that village; had drunk beer in that pub after a cricket match; had once been to a party in the house that lay behind a pair of impressive gates. It was four years ago that he had first made this journey but, idling along the country lanes, he could remember every moment, every nuance of that drive: he had been excited, and a little anxious, because he was fresh out of agricultural college and going to an interview for his first job as manager of Brookclere Farm, working for Mrs Hawthorne.

When they eventually met, she explained her position. Her husband had recently died. Her son, who would one day take over the farm, had taken a short service commission in the Army, and was at present stationed in Hong Kong.

". . . when he leaves the Army, he plans to go to agricultural college, but meantime I must have somebody to help me . . . just to keep things going until Derek's ready to come home again."

Privately Miles decided that she looked far too young to have a grown-up son, but he said nothing because this was a business matter, and not the time for paying ladies compliments.

"So you can see, I must have a manager. Now, why don't we go and have a look around?"

They had spent the day inspecting the farm. There were good outbuildings and well-kept cattle-courts. Beyond lay arable fields, some stock, sheep and cattle. In a little paddock, horses grazed.

"Do you ride?" he asked Mrs Hawthorne politely.

"No. Julia's the horsey member of our family."

"Is Julia your daughter?"

"Yes. She's got a job in Hartston; she works in an antique shop there. It's nice for me, because she lives at home, but I expect before long she'll get restless and go and find herself a flat in London. That's what all her friends seem to be doing."

"Yes, I suppose they do."

She smiled. "You never wanted to work in London?"

"No. I never wanted to do anything except farm."

She showed him the house where he would live, a brick cottage with a small and totally unkempt garden. "I'm afraid it's rather a mess . . ."

He eyed it. "It wouldn't take long to get straight."

"Are you a keen gardener?"

"Put it this way," he said, "I don't like weeds."

She laughed at that. "I know. I spend most of my time pulling up the beastly things."

"My mother does that, too." They looked at each other, smiling. It was the beginning of friendship.

Finally, they were back in the farm office. She did not sit in the impressive leather chair, but leaned against the desk with her hands deep in the pockets of her cardigan, and turned to face Miles.

"The job is yours if you want it," she told him.

Against all sense, because he wanted to work here more than anything else in the world, he heard himself suggesting that perhaps she would be better with a man older than himself, a man with more experience. But she had thrown back her head and laughed, and said, "Oh, heavens; I'd be terrified of someone like that. It would end up with him telling me what to do."

"Then," said Miles, "it's a deal."

He stayed at Brookclere a year. He would have stayed longer if it had not been for Julia. He was twenty-three. He

201

had never seriously considered meeting a girl, falling in love, and wanting to spend the rest of his life with her. It happened, he knew, to other men. It had already happened to several of his friends. But somehow he had always imagined that, for himself, such an occurrence was a long way off – he would be thirty, or more. The time would be ripe, he would have made his way, built for himself a solid future which he would then offer to some suitable female, as though he were giving her a present which he had made himself.

But Julia was suddenly there, in his life, and all his preconceived ideas, floating like soap bubbles around the back of his mind, instantly burst and disappeared for ever. Why did it have to be Julia? What was it about her that was different? What was it about her that made everything magic? He had heard a word, 'propinquity', and he looked it up in the dictionary, and it said: *Nearness in place. Close kinship.*

They were indeed near. He saw her, if only briefly, every day. Helped her start her little car on frosty mornings; rode with her on April Sundays; swam with her in the river, when the leaves were thick and heavy overhead, and the brown, slow-moving water danced with sun-shafts and midges. They swept leaves together in the autumn, and built bonfires fragrant with woodsmoke. He remembered her at haymaking time, wearing a tattered old straw hat like a hobo, and with her arms sunburnt and her face running with sweat. He remembered her at Christmas, in a red dress, her eyes as excited as a child's.

And as for kinship . . . if that meant laughter and companionship and keeping silence without constraint, then they had been kin. If it meant going to a party with her and glowing with pride because she was more attractive than any other girl in the room, then that was kin. If it meant not minding who she danced with because, inevitably, it was always Miles who drove her home, slowly, dawdling down

the dark lanes, discussing, like an old married couple, everything that had happened – then that was kin.

Propinquity. It was he who had ruined it all.

∗✦∗

It was a Sunday evening, warm and dusky, and they were
sitting down by the river. The sound of church bells reached
them from far across the meadows.

"I love you."

She had said, "I don't want you to love me."

"Why not?"

"Because I don't. Because you're not that sort of a
person."

"What sort of a person am I?"

"You're Miles."

"And is Miles so different from other men?"

"Yes, and a thousand times nicer," Julia had said warmly.

"If you say you think of me as a brother, then I shall
strangle you."

"No, I already have a brother."

"A dog, then. A faithful hound."

"That's a horrible thing to say."

"What do you want me to say? We can't go on like this
for ever."

"I just don't want it to be any other way than this."

"Julia, nothing can stay the same for ever."

"Why me? Why do you have to be in love with me?"

"I didn't actually organise it."

"I'm not ready for falling in love, or for getting married
and setting up house and having babies."

"What are you ready for, then?"

"I don't know. Change, perhaps, but not marriage."

"What sort of change?"

She looked away from him. A lock of dark hair fell

forward and hid her face. "I can't stay at home for ever. I could go to London, perhaps. Sukie Robins . . . you know, you met her at that party. We were at school together. She's getting a flat in Wandsworth – and she's looking for someone to share it with her."

Miles did not say anything to this shattering revelation and Julia suddenly turned and faced him in a sort of rage, but whether it was at him or herself, he could not guess.

"Oh, Miles, it's all right for you. You're doing what you want, you don't want to do anything else. You haven't any doubts. You're on your way, you've made your decisions. But I'm twenty-one and I don't know. I haven't done anything . . ."

He could think of no response to this outburst. At last, "What about your mother?" he asked.

"I adore my mother. You know that. But she would be the last person to be possessive."

"Is that what you think I am?"

"I don't know. I only know that I don't want to get married for years. There are a thousand things I want to do before that happens, and I want to start doing them now."

After a while he said, "I shan't always be a farm manager, you know. One day I'll have a farm of my own. I'll be self-supporting. Things won't always be like this."

"You mean money? You think I don't want you because you haven't got any money? How can you think anything so horrible?"

"Being practical isn't horrible."

"That doesn't come into it."

"We'll see."

"You can't have a very high opinion of me to say a thing like that. I never thought you could be so materialistic."

"Julia – I love you very much."

"Then I'm sorry. I'm sorry!" With that, she burst into tears, springing to her feet. "I'm sorry for you and I'm sorry for me. But I don't want to be trapped ... like a dead butterfly, pinned to a board..." And with this extraordinary statement, she turned from him and fled towards the house.

And Miles sat on, alone, bitten to death by midges, and not caring; he had spoiled everything, and nothing could ever be the same.

He lived with it for a week, and then he went to Mrs Hawthorne and gave in his notice. She was not a stupid woman and he respected her for her outspokenness.

"Oh, Miles. It's Julia, isn't it?"

"Yes."

"You're in love with her?"

"I think I always have been. From the very first moment I set eyes on her."

"I was so afraid that something like this had happened. Julia's going to London. She's got a flat and she's going to get a job there. She told me last night. So there is no reason for you to go, too."

"I must."

"Yes. I can see that. I'm sorry. I've been dreading this, and yet I wanted it too. I've grown so fond of you. I had silly dreams like any sentimental mother. But I wouldn't be any use as a parent if I tried to influence Julia."

"I ... I never meant it to happen," he said.

"You're not to blame. Nobody is to blame for what's happened."

❧

He found another job in Scotland with the Forestry Commission. When he told Mrs Hawthorne, she said with a wry smile, "It could scarcely be further away."

"Perhaps that's what I need."

"Oh, Miles. Dear Miles. How much I shall miss you."

"I'll come back," he promised.

But he did not come back. He went forward to a new life in more senses than one. He went to a solitude he had never known before; to a small granite house in heathery hills that stretched for ever. He went to new attitudes, new problems, new solutions. He made, gradually, new friends. Learned to drive thirty or forty miles for any sort of social contact. Lived with bitter cold and wide skies, endless rain and drifting snow. He planted trees and brushed trees and felled trees; ploughed land which had never known anything but heather and the cries of grouse and curlew. He learned to melt ice when the water from the tap trickled to a standstill, learned to fish for salmon, learned to dance an eightsome reel. He learned to live alone.

He worked, sometimes seven days a week, using self-imposed labour as a sedative, numbing his memories and his heartache. Sometimes there was leisure to read a book or a paper. One morning, more than two years after he had said goodbye to Brookclere, he went the twenty miles to Relkirk for market day and, along with a few crates of necessary groceries, he bought *The Times*. In it he read the announcement of Julia's engagement to a man called Henry Fleet. He had meant to drive straight home, but instead he took himself into the nearest pub with the intention – for the first time in his life – of getting slowly, systematically drunk.

But he did not do this. Because in the pub he met an old friend from agricultural college and, with this extraordinary coincidence, the whole course of his life took a new turning.

Now the road ran downhill and Brookclere lay below him in the valley, a cluster of cottages around a crossroads, surrounded by farmland and shallow hills. He came to the vicarage and the church, passed the Flower In Hand and the grocer's shop that sold everything. He came to the oak copse, the white gates standing open, the cattle grid. Brookclere Farm. He went through the gates, up between the white-painted fences, over the little bridge, and the house revealed itself, rose-red brick, smothered in wistaria, the garden concealed by banks of rhododendrons.

He drew up at the back of the house, stopped the car and turned off the engine. He could smell the rich, sweet fragrance of the farmyard, hear the soft contented squawks of Mrs Hawthorne's free-range hens. He got out of the car, opened the back gate and made his way down to the house and through the open kitchen door. The Aga hummed companionably. There were roses in a lustre jug in the middle of the scrubbed pine table, and all the old lustre plates still ranged upon the dresser.

"Mrs Hawthorne?"

No sound. No reply. He went through the kitchen into the hall; the door to the garden was open to the warm afternoon, and beyond it lay the terrace and the long lawn, sloping down to the river. A wheelbarrow stood in the middle of the grass and, as he stepped out into the sunshine, there was Mrs Hawthorne, on her hands and knees, peacefully weeding her border.

He walked across the grass towards her. She did not hear him, but suddenly became aware that she was not alone. She turned her head, putting up a muddy, gloved hand to push back her hair with her wrist.

He said, "Hello."

"Miles!" Astonishment, delight filled her face. She dropped her weeding fork and got to her feet. "Oh, Miles!"

They had never been on kissing terms, but he kissed her now, and she put her arms around him to give him a hug, then held him off in order to gaze into his face.

"What a wonderful surprise! Where have you sprung from?"

"I was on my way to London from Southampton. I thought I had to call in and see you."

"I thought you were in Scotland."

"Yes, I am. I'm still working there, but I've been on holiday with some friends – they've got a cottage in the Dordogne. Now I'm on my way back. I'm putting the car on the Motorail to Inverness this evening. It saves a long drive."

"But how wonderful that you came. I am touched." She pulled off her gloves and dropped them on to the grass. "Let's go and sit in the shade. Would you like a drink? How about some lemonade?"

"That would be delicious."

<hr />

She led the way back to the house and he watched her go and thought that the years had still not touched her. She remained as slim as a girl, her fair, greying hair cut casually short, her step long-legged and supple. She disappeared indoors, then returned with a tray, a jug of lemonade clinking with ice, and two tumblers.

"Don't look too closely at the garden, Miles. I've been so busy. There's been no time to tie things up or get rid of the weeds."

He turned from his contemplation of the familiar view and sat beside her. "How's the farm going?"

"Splendidly." She poured him a glass of lemonade. "Derek's out of the Army, finished with college, and now he's in charge. So far everything seems to be going according to plan, but I'm afraid you won't meet him because he's gone over to Salisbury today to see about a tractor."

"And the farm manager who took over when I left?"

"He was a great success. He's moved on to work for some friends of ours who farm near Newbury. The only thing was that he wasn't as keen a gardener as you were, and your garden at the cottage has gone back to rack and ruin again."

"There's nobody living in that house, then?"

"No, Derek thought we'd maybe let it. We haven't decided yet. Now, tell me about you. Are you still with the Forestry Commission?"

"No. No, I'm not. I've gone into partnership with a chap called Charlie Westwell. We were at agricultural college together, and met up quite by chance. He'd come north to look at a farm that was for sale, but he couldn't raise sufficient capital to buy it on his own. So, right then and there, we went off together to look at the place. It's a good farm, in the Vale of Strathmore. Sort of place I've always dreamed about. I rang my father that evening, and put the scheme to him, and he came up trumps with just enough cash for the half-share, and a long-suffering bank manager lent me the balance. We've been working together now for four months, and I think it's going to work out." He grinned. "The best thing about having a partner is you can sometimes take a holiday."

"And I'm sure you needed it! He sounds a good friend to have met again. Do you share a house?"

"No. Charlie's married, you see. He and Jenny live in the farmhouse and I've got the farm manager's cottage. It's actually quite a big house, with a new kitchen and central heating and all sorts of luxuries."

"And you . . ." She smiled at him. "You never married?"

"No."

"You should be married, Miles."

He took a long drink of lemonade. It was sour and refreshing and the ice clinked against the glass. When he had drained it, he set down the tumbler and said, as casually as he could, "How did the wedding go?"

She said, "It didn't." Miles looked up quickly, and her blue gaze met his own.

"You mean, it didn't go well?"

"No, I don't mean that. I mean it didn't happen. Five

days before the wedding was due to take place, Henry and Julia came to me and said that they had decided they didn't want to get married, after all. We put an announcement in the paper, but of course, if you were in the Dordogne, you wouldn't have seen it."

"Dear heaven," said Miles.

His voice sounded quite ordinary and calm, but inside he felt as though he had been kicked in the stomach, pushed to the ground, bruised and incapable. A sort of panic knocked in his chest, and it was a second or two before he realised that it was simply the beating of his own heart.

He said, "But why?"

She shrugged and sighed deeply. "I don't know. I simply don't know. They neither of them were able to find any particular reason."

"Did you like him?"

"Yes. Yes, I did. Very much. He was a very nice young man. Everything any mother could wish for. Pleasant-looking, plenty of money, a good job. I always thought, perhaps, that Julia was more in love with him than he was with her, but you know what sort of a person she is. Demonstrative and out-going. She was never any good at hiding her true feelings."

"Is Julia back in London?"

"No. She'd given up her flat, given up her job. She's still here. She won't see anybody. She's very unhappy." Once more their eyes met and held. "I don't suppose," said Mrs Hawthorne, "that you would want to see her."

"What you mean is, that Julia wouldn't want to see me."

"Oh, dear Miles. I don't know what I mean."

❧

All at once she looked exhausted and distraught. As though, suddenly, she felt that she could let down her defences, and stop pretending to be practical and strong.

"Where is she now?"

"Do you remember the raspberry canes you planted at the back of the cottage when you were living here? I don't think you stayed long enough to harvest the fruit, but they produce the most beautiful berries. Julia went down there to see if she could find a bowlful for our supper. Perhaps . . . perhaps if you're not in too much of a hurry, you could go and help her . . . ?"

It was a plea from the heart, and Miles recognised it as such.

He said, "You know, if I'd known what had happened – I mean, about the wedding being called off – I don't think I'd have turned off the motorway today. I'd just have gone on to London."

"Then I'm very glad you didn't know, Miles."

"I don't want to start anything up . . . the same way. I wouldn't want it to end all over again."

"If I didn't know you better I'd say that was a selfish thing to say. Julia doesn't need a love affair. But she certainly needs every friend she's got. You were good friends . . ."

"Until I spoilt it all by saying something stupid like 'I love you'."

"It wasn't stupid. I never thought it was stupid. It was just ill-timed."

A bumpy lane led from the back of the house, down between stone walls smothered in convolvulus. The cottage, where he had lived for those twelve, never-to-be-forgotten months, nestled in the lee of its own garden wall. The little gate had come off its hinges and now hung lopsidedly, and beyond it the weeds had taken over. Where once had grown cabbages, potatoes, carrots, was a riot of groundsel and waist-high grass. Only the raspberry canes bravely raised their heads above the jungle. And there was no sign at all of Julia.

The back door of the cottage was closed and locked. He went around the flagged path, ducking long, thorny branches of bramble, and pushing aside the tall spires of purple willowherb. In the front of the house he had once grown flowers and had a little lawn, but the lawn had disappeared, and the flowers were buried in weed. Only the orange marigolds had somehow survived, seeding themselves to spread all over, a carpet of bitter-smelling sun daisies.

She was there; not picking raspberries, not doing anything. Just sitting waist-deep in fiery flower-heads. Her dark hair was bundled carelessly up at the back of her head; one or two fronds had escaped and fell across her face. She looked very thin. He did not remember her as being so thin. She did not hear his footsteps, and when he said her name, she looked up vaguely, like a person awakened from a dream.

"Julia," he said again.

She pushed a lock of hair away from her eyes and stared fixedly at him. "Miles!"

"Surprise," he said, smiling and squatting beside her. "I thought you were meant to be picking raspberries for supper."

"What are you doing here?"

He explained, simply and briefly.

"Have you seen my mother?"

"Yes, I found her gardening." He settled himself beside her, crushing the flowers beneath his weight. "But she stopped and gave me a glass of lemonade, and we caught up on all the news."

"She told you."

"Yes."

Julia's gaze dropped. She picked a marigold head and began to tear it apart, petal by petal. She said, "You must think I'm mad." She sounded on the verge of tears. He was not surprised. He imagined that she had spent most of the last couple of weeks in floods of weeping. She had always cried easily. For ridiculous reasons like seeing beautiful sunsets, or hearing choirboys raising their sweet, soaring voices in song. It was always one of the things about her that he had most loved.

He said, "Not at all. I think you were very brave. It takes a lot of courage to call off a wedding at the last moment. But it was the only thing to do, if you didn't believe yourself that it was right."

She said, "It was all too awful even to think about. Mother was marvellous, but Derek was furious with me. He kept saying I was selfish, that I wasn't considering anybody but myself."

"Perhaps you were considering Henry, though?"

"I tried to tell Derek that."

"If you truly love a person, sometimes the best thing you can do for them is gently to let them go."

"I did love him, Miles. I wouldn't have said I'd marry him if I hadn't truly wanted to. He was everything I'd ever imagined and never thought would happen to me. When I met him in London, I couldn't believe he'd even noticed me. There seemed to be so many other girls. But then he asked me out one evening, and after that it all just got better and better. It was like living in a whole new world. As though everything was brighter, and had sharper edges. And then when he asked me to marry him I said 'yes' very quickly in case he should change his mind. That was how it was. The sort of relationship that doesn't often happen to people. At least, I'm sure it doesn't often happen. It couldn't."

"But at the end of the day, you decided not to go through with it."

She looked away from him, out over the little garden, the crumbling wall, to the pastoral scene that lay beyond.

213

Shallow hills and stands of trees, with peaceful cattle gathered in the cooling shade around the edge of the river.

He said, "Things pass, you know. You have to remember
that."

"It was the most dreadful thing I've ever had to do. I
felt so conscience-stricken about my mother. She'd been
working so terribly hard for months, and all for me. It was
a nightmare."

"Your mother understood."

"I almost wanted her to be angry, too. I was so ashamed."

"Moral courage is nothing to be ashamed about."

She said nothing to this. He went on, finding it hard to
find the right words but knowing that, somehow, he really
had to.

"Things pass, like I said. Time heals. All the old clichés,
but they're true, or they wouldn't be clichés in the first
place. The most important thing is that you're still yourself.
Julia. A person. An identity. That's what you have to hang
on to."

She stayed silent, motionless, and he ploughed on, talking
to the back of her head, wondering if she even heard what
he said.

"The worst of it's over now. I'm sure things can only get
better."

"I can't believe they'll ever get better . . ." Suddenly she
turned to him and for an instant he saw her face, streaming
with tears, before she flung herself into his arms. "He . . .
he wanted people to think that it was a decision we made
together . . ." It was hard to hear what she was trying to
tell him, so closely was her face pressed to his shoulder.
"But really it was Henry who all at once didn't want any of
it to happen. He said he didn't love me enough to give up
his freedom. He didn't want me any more . . ."

A lump filled his throat. He held her very close, his chin
against the top of her head, his arms tight around her sob-

racked body. He could feel her ribs through the thin stuff of her dress, and her tears were soaking the front of his shirt.

"It's all right." He couldn't think of anything else to say.

"I don't know what I'm going to do now . . ."

"Do you want me to tell you?"

There were a few more sniffs and sobs and then Julia drew away from him, turning up her face to look into his own. Her eyes were swollen with weeping. He thought that he had never seen her look so beautiful.

She tried to brush away her tears with her hands, and he took out his handkerchief and gave it to her.

"What am I going to do?" she asked him.

"If I told you I had a good idea, would you listen?"

She appeared to consider this. She blew her nose. She said, "Yes."

"Well, I think you should get right away, have a holiday, meet new people, see new places, get everything into perspective."

"But where would I go?"

He told her about Scotland. About his farm. About Charlie and Jenny and his own little house. "It's got a honeysuckle growing over the gate, and a marvellous view, and there is everything in the world to be done to it."

"What sort of everything?"

"Making curtains, mowing the grass, building fences, feeding my hens. Having fun."

She blew her nose again, and pushed her hair back from her face.

"Oh, Miles, you were always good for me. I always used to feel that nothing too ghastly could happen if you were around. And I know I made you unhappy. But then I didn't know how unhappy one person could make another."

"I'm sorry you had to find out the hard way."

"I can't think why you came back to Brookclere."

"I think it was like swimming, and being caught in a strong current. Perhaps I couldn't have stopped myself. Perhaps love is more of a constant emotion than I'd ever realised. It becomes a part of you. A heartbeat; a nerve-end."

"When are you going back?"

"Tonight, on the Motorail."

"Could I come with you?"

"If you want to. If you don't take too long to pack."

"I have to pick the raspberries."

"I'll help you."

"It's . . . it's just a holiday, isn't it? Nothing more?"

"You can come home to Hampshire whenever you want."

She suddenly leaned forward and kissed him, briefly, softly, on his cheek. She said, "I think I'd forgotten how nice you are. And comfortable. It's like being with the other half of myself."

He said, "For a start, that's quite a good way to feel."

For a start. He knew events had gone full circle, and now they were back at the beginning again. Except now they had both grown up and were ready to cope with all the problems of the old – and yet new – relationship. He thought of the farm, of his future, of all the work that waited to be accomplished. He thought of Charlie and Jenny and was filled with impatience, as though he could not wait to get home again, to start work, to start building that future which some day he would offer to Julia, like some marvellous present that he had made for her himself.

# ≫ *Weekend* ≪

It was to be a truce weekend. Not a truce from quarrelling, because in the two years they had known each other, they had never quarrelled. So maybe not so much a truce as a gentleman's agreement: that during the weekend Tony should not, once again, ask Eleanor to marry him, thus avoiding the necessity for Eleanor, once again, to turn him down.

He had telephoned her three or four days previously. "I've just been told I've got a few days' leave due. Would you be able to come to the country with me?"

Eleanor, snowed under with printer's proofs, a crammed engagement diary, and a potential author playing hard to get, was taken unawares. "Oh, Tony, I don't know. I don't think I can. I mean . . ."

"Try," he interrupted her. "Just try. Speak to that editor of yours and tell him you've got a sick aunt who has to have her pillow smoothed."

"It's not as easy as that . . ." She gazed at her work-piled desk.

"Then let's just make it a weekend. We'll go on Friday after you've finished work, and get back to London some time on Sunday evening."

"Where did you think of going?"

"To Brandon Manor."

"You mean where you used to work? I thought only millionaires could afford to go there."

217

"Millionaires and employees of my hotel group, who own it. I can get a cut-rate deal. Say yes, and I'll telephone and see if they have a couple of empty rooms."

Eleanor thought about it. A weekend in the country, in comfort and quiet, seemed very attractive. The trees would be bursting into leaf, the grass turning green, the birds beginning to sing.

"You won't . . ." she started to say, and then stopped. "I mean, we aren't going to . . ." She stopped again.

"No," said Tony, "we aren't going to argue. The subject of wedding rings shall be strictly taboo. Let's just get away from everybody and enjoy ourselves."

Eleanor began to smile. "It sounds," she told him, "irresistible."

He said, "I love you."

"Tony, you promised."

"No, I didn't. I only said I wouldn't ask you to marry me. The two things, as we already know, seem to have nothing to do with each other." But he was smiling. She knew from his voice that he was smiling. "See you on Friday."

And so now they were nearly there. It had been a fine day, warm and dry, with the first scent of summer in the air. In London, awnings had started to appear, and there were the first roses on the flower stalls. But in the country the signs of the approaching season were less sophisticated. Orchards of fruit trees were awash with tender pink blossom and cottage gardens were bright with forsythia and neat borders of velvety polyanthus. The road wound ahead of them to the edge of the hills, and then there came a break in the trees, and the view was spread before their eyes, the great flat Vale of Evesham, the distant Malvern hills grey with haze.

"We could go on for ever," said Eleanor. "On and on, till we came to Wales and then to the sea."

"But we're not. We're going to Brandon, and we're very nearly there." The car nosed its way down the steep and winding hill, and at the bottom was the scattering of picture-book houses that made up the village. They came around a corner and the old manor house lay ahead of them, low and rambling, with mullioned windows and steeply sloping roofs of dark slate.

"It's beautiful," she said. "How long did you work here?"

"About four years. I was assistant under-manager, which means general dogsbody, but I learnt everything I know about the hotel business behind those ancient walls."

"How long has it been an hotel?"

"The family who owned it sold up before the war. It's been an hotel ever since. It's even got a honeymoon suite." Gravel crunched as they drew up on the sweep outside the enormous stone porch of the front door. Tony turned off the engine, loosened his seat-belt and turned to smile at Eleanor. "But don't worry. We're not going to be sleeping in it. Not that I don't think that would have been a splendid idea!"

"Tony." Her voice was full of stern warning. "You promised you wouldn't mention anything even remotely connected with honeymoons."

"It's such a romantic spot. I'm going to find it very difficult."

"In that case, you'll have to spend the whole two days playing golf."

"Will you come and caddy for me?"

"No, I shall find some nice, unattached woman guest and sit and talk about the latest fashions with her."

Tony began to laugh. "What an unusual weekend we're going to have." Unexpectedly, he leant forward and kissed her mouth. "I love you even more when you try to look cross. Now come along, don't let's waste a moment."

Inside the stone-flagged, panelled hall the only sounds were the crackle of the fire in the cavernous fireplace and the ticking of a grandfather clock.

Beneath the turn of the Elizabethan staircase a reception desk had been discreetly placed. Behind it a man stood with his back to them, sorting some mail. He had not heard them come in and did not turn until Tony said his name. "Alistair."

Surprised, the man swung round. There was a moment's astonished silence, then his face broke into an incredulous but delighted smile. "Tony! What in heaven's name are you doing here?"

"Come to stay. Didn't you see my name in the book?"

"Yes, of course I did. Talbot. But I had no idea it was you. The receptionist took the booking . . ." He gave Tony a friendly thump on the shoulder. "What a marvellous surprise!"

Eleanor was standing a little behind Tony. Now he moved aside and put out a hand to draw her forward. "This is Eleanor Dean."

"Hello, Eleanor."

"Hello." They shook hands across the polished counter.

"Alistair and I did our training together when we were mere lads. In Switzerland," Tony said.

"You're in London, aren't you?" Alistair asked.

"That's right. But I've been given a few days off, so I thought I'd come back, and see what sort of a job you're making of this place." He looked about him. "Doesn't look too bad. Doing well, are you?"

"Booked to the hilt for most of the year."

"Brisk trade in the honeymoon suite?"

"Well, it's certainly been taken this weekend." A grin crept over Alistair's face. "Why? Did you have designs on it?"

"Heavens, no. None of that sort of rubbish for us."

Alistair laughed and rang the bell. "I'll get the porter to bring your cases in."

※

It was, Eleanor decided, exactly like staying in the very nicest sort of private house, except that one knew one was not going to have to help with the washing-up. All those years ago, when the family who had lived in and loved this house had finally had to leave, they had left behind not only their beautiful furniture, but also a sort of ambience which was hard to define. It was as though they had all gone away for a little while but would soon be back. So cleverly had the house been altered, adapted and redecorated that the modern improvements did nothing to detract from this atmosphere, but rather added to it.

Crisp cotton curtains framed the deep-silled, leaded windows of each bedroom, and although each room now had its own modern bathroom, there were still the original bathrooms to be found down the crooked passages, with marvellous mahogany-encased tubs and brass taps.

Downstairs, the same inspired touch was evident. The lounge had once been the drawing-room of the old house, with french windows which led down a flight of steps to a terrace and then on to the lawns of the garden. The dining-room had been the great hall, with an oriel window that reached to the ceiling, and the bar had been tucked away in some smaller downstairs apartment, perhaps originally a sewing-room.

That evening, Tony was bathed and changed for dinner before Eleanor had even made up her face. Waiting, he came in to sit on the edge of her bed, looking tall and suave in a dark blazer and a fresh shirt and tie.

She said, "You smell delicious. All clean and spicy."

"I may smell delicious, but I'm in need of a drink."

"Go down and get yourself one, and I'll join you later. In the bar. I shan't be more than ten minutes."

He left her, and she began to brush her long pale hair, and then met her own eyes in the mirror, and slowly the strokes ceased. She gazed at herself – almost despising the girl who stared back at her.

'What do you want?' she asked that girl. 'What do you really want?'

'To know that I can give myself to this relationship and yet not be submerged by it.'

'You want everything. You can't have your cake and eat it. You have to make up your mind. You're not being fair on Tony.'

Slowly, she began to brush her hair again. Behind her, the little bedroom, flower-dappled and fresh with white paint, appeared secure as a Victorian nursery. It would be nice, perhaps, to be a child again. With everything arranged for one and no decisions to make.

But she was not a child. She was Eleanor Dean, editor of children's books with a busy publishing house; twenty-eight years old, successful and efficient. She was Eleanor Dean – and far beyond the age of being sentimentally nostalgic for long-gone days. Briskly, she finished her face, sprayed on some scent, picked up her handbag and went from the room, without so much as a backward glance towards the girl reflected in the mirror.

When they had finished their drinks in the bar, Tony and Eleanor walked down the thickly carpeted passage to the dining-room where three-quarters of the tables were already occupied and dinner was in full swing.

When they had ordered from the menu and the waiter had gone, Tony smiled.

"I'll play a guessing game with you. Who, of all the people in this room, are staying in the honeymoon suite?"

His eyes were dancing with amusement. What was so funny? Eleanor, puzzled, looked casually around the room. The young couple, perhaps, in the corner? No, they didn't look nearly opulent enough. The tall, bored-looking pair over by the window? The woman was gazing into space like a highly bred horse, and the man wore an expression of agonised boredom. One somehow couldn't imagine them getting as far as marriage, let alone going on a honeymoon. Or was it the young golfing Americans, she with her tan, and he, immaculate in his maroon blazer and tartan trousers . . . ?

Her gaze came back to Tony's face. "I haven't the faintest idea."

He gave a tiny inclination of his head. "The couple by the fireplace."

Eleanor looked over his shoulder and saw them, old enough to be her parents, or even her grandparents. The woman was silvery headed, her shining white hair swept up into a casual knot at the back of her head; the man quite portly, moustached and balding. Just an ordinary, elderly couple. And yet they weren't ordinary because they were chatting and laughing away together, with eyes for no one but each other.

Amazed, Eleanor looked back at Tony. "Are you *sure*?"

"Yes. Sure. Mr and Mrs Renwick. Honeymoon suite."

"You mean they've just got married?"

"They must have. That's what honeymoons are all about."

"Perhaps," said Eleanor, "they've been friends for years, and then her husband died, and his wife died, and they decided to marry each other."

223

"Perhaps."

"Or perhaps she never married, and when his wife died he was able to confess to her that he'd secretly loved her all his life."

"Perhaps."

"Can't you find out? I long to know."

"I thought they would intrigue you."

The honeymoon suite. She looked at them again, charmed by their obvious delight in each other.

"Do you think," asked Tony, "that seeing them will help you change your mind, or make up your mind, or whatever it is you're trying to do? About us, I mean?"

Eleanor looked down at the tablecloth. Carefully, as though it mattered, she altered the position of her knife. She said, "You promised. You mustn't break your promise."

Their wine arrived.

"Who shall we drink to?" Tony asked.

"Not you and me."

"The newly-weds, perhaps? And a long and happy life to them?"

"Why not?" They drank. Over the rim of her glass their eyes met. 'I love him,' Eleanor told herself. 'I have faith in him. Why can't I have faith in myself?'

❧

In the morning, after a late breakfast, they went out for a walk. The weather, obligingly, was perfect. Eleanor wore white jeans and a pullover over her shirt, and when they had explored the gardens and looked at the massive tithe barn which stood a little way from the house, they wandered down to the lake and found a sheltered hollow by the reedy bank where the wind could not reach them.

The grass was thick and green, starred with the first daisies, and they lay and watched random clouds sail across the pristine blueness of the sky, and were so still and quiet that a couple of inquisitive swans slid across the lake to inspect these strangers in their remote and watery world.

"How wonderful it must have been," said Eleanor, "to own all this. To be a child here, and take it all for granted. To be a man, and know that it was part of you. Part of your life and the person you were."

"But there were responsibilities, too," Tony pointed out. "People to work for you, yes, but people to take care of, too. The land was their responsibility as well and there were buildings to keep up."

"Did you like working here?"

"Yes," said Tony, "but after a bit I felt I was becoming drowned in some gorgeous backwater. Not enough stimulation."

"Aren't people enough stimulation?"

"For me, not entirely."

She said, "If we got married, do you think we should begin to feel we were becoming drowned in some gorgeous backwater?"

Tony opened his eyes, raised his head and looked at her in some surprise. "We weren't going to talk about getting married."

"We seem to be talking about it all the time, without actually saying anything. Perhaps it would be better if we forgot about promises and brought it all out into the open."

He raised himself up on an elbow. "Look, my darling Eleanor, we've known each other for two years. We've proved, to ourselves and the rest of the world, that this is a good thing we're on to. It isn't just some wild infatuation, a fly-by-night affair that's going to turn sour the moment we commit ourselves. Besides" – he grinned – "I don't want to be like Mr and Mrs Renwick and miss all the fun of growing old together."

"I don't either, Tony. But I don't want it to go wrong."

"You mean, like my parents?"

His mother and father had gone through a rancorous divorce when Tony was fifteen, and then had gone their separate ways. He never spoke about this traumatic experience, and Eleanor had not met his parents. He went on, "No marriage can be perfect. And mistakes don't have to be inherited. Besides, your parents were happy."

"Yes, they were happy." She turned away from him, pulling absently at a tuft of grass. "But Mother was only fifty when my father died."

Tony put a hand on her shoulder and turned her to face him. He said, "I can't promise to live for ever, but I'll do my best."

Despite herself, Eleanor smiled. "I believe you would."

On the Sunday morning, like any husband, Tony decided to take himself off and see if he could find some man prepared to play a round of golf with him. Eleanor was invited to accompany him, but she declined and had her breakfast in bed, with all the Sunday papers. About eleven o'clock she got up, had a bath, got dressed and went downstairs and out of doors. It was still sunny, though not as warm as the previous day, and she set off briskly in the direction of the little golf pavilion, with the intention of walking out over the course and meeting Tony on his way in.

When she reached the pavilion she stopped, not sure in which direction she should head, when a voice behind her said, "Good morning," and she turned and saw, sitting in the sheltered veranda which fronted the pavilion, none other than the honeymooner, Mrs Renwick. She wore a tweed skirt and a thick, knitted jacket, and looked content and comfortable in a basket-chair.

Eleanor smiled. "Good morning." Slowly, she went to

join the older woman. "I thought I might walk out, but I don't know which way to go."

"My husband's playing golf, too. I think they come from that direction, but I decided it was more pleasant to sit than to walk. Why don't you join me?"

Eleanor hesitated, and then succumbed. She pulled up another of the basket-chairs and settled herself beside Mrs Renwick, stretching out her legs and turning up her face to the sun.

"This is nice."

"Much nicer than walking in that chilly wind. What time did your husband go out?"

"A couple of hours ago. And he's not my husband."

"Oh, dear, I am sorry. How mistaken can one be? We'd made up our minds that you were married and on your honeymoon."

It was amusing to realise that the Renwicks had discussed herself and Tony, just as they had speculated about them.

"No, I'm afraid not." She glanced at Mrs Renwick's left hand, expecting to see a shining new wedding band, but Mrs Renwick's ring was as thin and worn as the hand which wore it. Puzzled, Eleanor frowned, and Mrs Renwick saw this.

"What's wrong?"

"Nothing. It's just that . . . well, we thought you and your husband were on *your* honeymoon."

Mrs Renwick threw back her head and gave a peal of laughter. "What a compliment. I suppose you found out we were in the honeymoon suite!"

"Well . . ." Eleanor felt embarrassed, as though they had been prying. "It's just that Tony and the manager are old friends."

"I see. Well, I'll put your mind at rest. We've been married for forty years. This is our ruby wedding, and a weekend at Brandon is my husband's little treat instead of throwing a party. You see, we came to Brandon for our honeymoon

227

. . . it was wartime, of course, and my husband only had two days' leave. But we always promised ourselves that one day we'd come back. And it's just as lovely as ever!" She laughed again. "Fancy you thinking we were newly-weds. You must have wondered what on earth a couple of old fogeys like us were up to."

"No," said Eleanor, "we didn't. You looked perfectly believable. Laughing and talking and looking as though you'd just met each other and fallen madly in love."

"An even nicer compliment. And we've been watching you. Last night, when you were dancing together, my husband said he'd never seen a better-looking couple." She hesitated for a moment, then went on, her manner now very down-to-earth. "Have you known each other long?"

"Yes," said Eleanor. "Quite long. Two years."

Mrs Renwick considered this. "Yes," she said thoughtfully. "That is quite a long time. I'm afraid that nowadays men are very spoiled. They seem to get all the advantages of married life handed to them on a plate, without having to bother about any of the responsibilities."

Eleanor said, "It's my fault. Tony isn't like that. He wants to get married."

❧

Mrs Renwick smiled, tranquilly. "He obviously loves you," she said.

"Yes," said Eleanor faintly. She looked at the older woman, sitting there in the pale sunshine, her expression kindly and her eyes wise. A stranger, but all at once Eleanor knew that she could confide in her. She said, "I don't know what to do."

"Is there any reason why you shouldn't marry him?"

"No concrete reason. I mean, we're both free; we neither of us have other commitments. Except our jobs."

"And what are those?"

"Tony's manager of an hotel in London. And I work for a publishing company."

"Perhaps your career is important to you?"

"Yes, it is. But not that important. I mean, I could go on working after I was married. At least, until I started to have children."

"Perhaps . . . you don't feel prepared to spend the rest of your life with him?"

"But I want to. That's what's so frightening. But this thing of becoming part of another person . . . losing one's own identity. Tony's parents divorced when he was a boy. But my parents did everything together, they lived for each other. When they were away from each other, they used to telephone every day. And then my father had a heart attack and died, and my mother was alone. She was only fifty. She'd always been a tower of strength to her family and her friends, and she simply . . . went to pieces. We thought when she'd stopped grieving, she'd pick up and start again, but she never did. Her life simply stopped when my father died. I love her very much, but I simply can't go on being unhappy with her."

"I am sorry," said Mrs Renwick. "But I'm afraid the final parting comes to all of us. I'm sixty now, and my husband is seventy-five. It would be foolish to pretend we have many years left to us, and by the law of averages I shall be left on my own. But I shall have marvellous memories, and being on my own has never frightened me. I am, after all, myself. I always have been. I adore Arnold, but I never wanted to be with him all the time. That's why I'm sitting here now, and not trudging down the fairway, feeling martyred, and watching him miss all his putts."

"You never played golf?"

"Heavens, no. I was never any good at games. But I'm lucky, because when I was a child I was taught to play the piano. I was never very good. Not good enough to become a professional. Mostly I played for myself. It was my private thing. My time on my own. It has sustained me all my life, and will continue to do so, whatever happens. I was lucky. But there are other things. I have a friend who has no particular talents, but she goes out every afternoon for a walk with her dog. She walks by herself, rain or shine, for an hour. Nobody is ever allowed to accompany her. She assures me that more than once it has saved her reason."

Eleanor said, "If I knew I could be like that and not like my mother . . ."

Mrs Renwick sent her a long, measuring look. "You want to marry this young man?" After a little, Eleanor nodded. "Then marry him! You're far too intelligent to let yourself be overwhelmed by any man, let alone that good-looking creature who obviously adores you." She leant forward and laid her hand over Eleanor's. "Just remember. A private world of your own. An independence of spirit. He will respect you for it, and thank you for it, and it will make your life together infinitely more interesting and worthwhile."

"Like your life," said Eleanor.

"You know nothing about my life."

"You've been married for forty years, and you still laugh with your husband."

"Is that what you want?" asked Mrs Renwick.

After a little, "Yes," said Eleanor.

"Then why don't you go and get it? Grasp life with both your hands. I think I can see your Tony now, at the very end of the fairway. Why don't you walk out and meet him?"

Eleanor looked. Saw the two distant figures walking in – one of them, unmistakably, Tony. A ridiculous excitement filled her heart. "Perhaps I will," she said.

She stood up, then hesitated, turned back to Mrs Renwick, stooped and kissed her cheek. "Thank you," she said.

She went down the steps of the pavilion and across the

gravel and on to the springy turf of the fairway. In the far distance Tony, seeing her, waved. She waved back and then began to run, as though, even if they were going to spend the rest of their lifetimes together, there was no longer a single second to be wasted.

# ᐊ A Walk in the Snow ᐅ

Waking to darkness, Antonia, drowsy with half-sleep, at first thought herself back in the flat in London. But then consciousness stirred. No sound of traffic, no pale light seeping through curtains which had never properly fitted, no bundling of a duvet up to her ears. Instead the darkness; silence; extreme cold. Linen sheets, tightly tucked. The smell of lavender. And she knew that it was a Saturday morning at the end of January and she was not in London but home, in the country, for the weekend.

Her mother had sounded a little surprised when she had telephoned to say that she was coming.

"Darling, heaven to see you." Mrs Ramsay adored it when Antonia came home. "But won't it be dreadfully dull? Not a thing going on and the weather's appalling. Terrible gales and bitterly cold. I'm sure we're in for snow."

"It doesn't matter." Without David nothing mattered. She only knew that the prospect of a weekend alone in London was unbearable. "I'll take the train if Pa could meet me at the station."

"Of course he will . . . usual time. I'll race upstairs now and make your bed."

Mrs Ramsay was right about the weather. The snow had begun to fall as the train made its way from Paddington Station and out into the country. By the time they reached Cheltenham the railway platform was two inches deep in snow and Antonia's father, come to meet her, wore rubber boots and the very old tweed coat, rabbit lined, which had once belonged to his grandfather and only came into its own in the most bitter of weather.

The drive home had been dicey, with frozen ruts in the road and the occasional skid, but they made it safely and duly arrived only to be plunged in darkness just as they sat down to supper. Antonia's father, lighting candles, had telephoned the authorities and been told that a main cable was down but repair men were, at this moment, setting out to find the fault. And so they had spent the evening by firelight and candlelight, struggling with the crossword, and grateful for the Aga which simmered comfortingly on, allowing them to boil kettles for hot-water bottles and make warm bedtime drinks.

And now, the next morning ... still darkness, silence, and cold. Antonia reached out a chilly hand and tried to switch on the bedside lamp, but nothing happened. There was no alternative but to sit up, grope for matches and light the stub of the candle which had seen her to bed. It was astonishing to see, by its pale flamelight, that it was past nine o'clock. With a sort of puny courage, she threw back the covers and stepped out into the icy cold. Drawing back the curtains, she saw the whiteness of snow, black trees etched against the half-light, no glimmer of sunlight. A rabbit had made its way across the lawn, leaving a trail of footmarks like sewing-machine stitches. Shivering, Antonia pulled on the warmest garments she could lay hands on, brushed her hair by candlelight, cleaned her teeth and went downstairs.

The house felt deserted. No sound disturbed the quiet. No washing machine, no dishwasher, no vacuum cleaner, no floor polisher. But someone had lighted a coal fire in the hall fireplace, and it flickered in a welcome fashion and smelt comforting.

Looking for company, Antonia made her way to the

kitchen where she found comparative warmth and her mother, sitting at the kitchen table which she had spread with newspapers and where she was about to embark on the tedious task of plucking a pair of pheasants. As Antonia appeared through the door, she looked up, a small and slender woman with a mop of curly grey hair.

"Darling! Isn't this terrible? We still haven't got any power. Did you have a good sleep?"

"I've only just woken up. It's so dark and so quiet. Like the North Pole. Do you suppose I'll ever get back to London?"

"Oh, yes, you'll be all right. We listened to the weather forecast and the worst seems to be over. Make yourself some breakfast."

"I'll just have some coffee . . ." She poured herself a mugful from the jug which stood at the back of the stove.

"You should have a proper breakfast in weather like this. Are you sure you eat enough? You're dreadfully thin."

"That's just London life. You mustn't start making noises like a mother." She opened the fridge for milk and it was strange having no light go on. "Where is everybody?"

"Mrs Hawkins is snowed up. She rang me up about an hour ago. She can't even get her bike out of the shed. I told her not to bother to come because, without any power, there's not a lot she can do."

"And Pa?"

"He walked over to the farm to get some milk and eggs. He had to walk because the gale we had yesterday blew down one of the Dixons' beech trees, and the lane's blocked. Was it windy in London?"

"Yes, but somehow in London it's different. Just piercingly cold, and rubbish and stuff flying around. You don't think about trees blowing down." She sat at the table and watched her mother, busy at work with deft fingers. Soft grey and brown feathers drifted into the air. "Why are you plucking pheasants? I thought Pa always did that for you."

"Yes, he does, and we're having them for dinner tonight, but after he'd gone and I'd washed up the breakfast dishes I simply couldn't think what to do next. Without electricity, I mean. In the end I decided it was either plucking pheasants or cleaning silver, and I hate cleaning silver so much, I plumped for the pheasants."

Antonia set down her mug, and reached for the cock pheasant. "I'll help you." Its body was cold and solid, the feathers on its well-fed breast thick and downy, but those at its neck blue as peacock eyes, bright as jewels.

She held the bird, spreading its wing like a fan. "I always feel guilty, pulling such a beautiful creature to pieces."

"I know. I do, too. That's why your father always does them for me. And yet there's something comfortingly timeless about plucking birds. You think of generations of country women, doing just this thing, sitting in their kitchens and talking to their daughters. Probably saving all the down feathers for stuffing pillows and quilts. Anyway, we mustn't be sentimental. The poor birds are already dead, and just think of delicious roast pheasant for dinner. I've asked the Dixons and Tom to come and eat them with us." She reached down for a large plastic dustbin bag and bundled the first of the feathers into it. "I thought," she went on, with elaborate casualness, "that David might have been here, too."

David. Mrs Ramsay was a perceptive woman and Antonia knew that this gentle probing was a tentative invitation for confidences. But, somehow, Antonia could not talk about David. She had come home this weekend because she was lonely and desperately unhappy, but she could not bring herself to talk about it.

236

The reason that his name had come so easily into the conversation was because David and Tom Dixon were brothers, and the family were friends and neighbours of a lifetime to the Ramsays. Mr Dixon ran his farm, and Mr Ramsay ran the local bank, but when they could they played golf together, and sometimes escaped for a week's fishing. Mrs Ramsay and Mrs Dixon were equally close, stalwart supporters of the local Women's Rural Institute and members of the same little bridge club. Tom, the older brother, worked now with his father. He had always seemed to Antonia very adult and remote, a responsible sort of person, useful at mending bikes and building rafts, but never a close friend. Not like David. David and Antonia, only a couple of years apart in age, were inseparable.

Like brother and sister, everybody said, but it had been more than that. There had never been anybody but David for Antonia. Going away to school, to college, their ways separating and their lives widening, it was natural to expect that their fondness for each other would mature into simple friendship, but somehow the very opposite happened. Being apart only served to fan the flame of their affection, so that each reunion, each coming together, was more satisfying and exciting than the time before. For Antonia, other boys, and then other men, never stood a chance because, in comparison with David, they seemed dull, or plain, or so demanding that she was sickened by them.

David was her yardstick. He made her laugh. With David, she could talk about anything, because everything important in her life she had shared with him, and if she hadn't, then he knew all about it anyway.

As well, he was the best-looking man she knew; he had grown from a handsome boy to an attractive adult without any of the usual uncomfortable stages in between.

Everything was easy for David. Making friends, playing games, passing exams, getting to university, finding a job.

"I'm coming to London," he told her.

Antonia had already been there for a year, working for the owner of a bookshop in Walton Street and sharing a flat with an old school-friend.

"David, that's marvellous!"

"Got a job with Sandberg Harpers."

She had been terrified that he would go abroad, or to the north of Scotland, or somewhere remote where she would never see him. Now they could do things together. She imagined little dinners in Italian restaurants, trips down the river, the Tate Gallery on bright, cold winter afternoons. "Have you got somewhere to live?"

"I'm going to move in with Nigel Crawston; he's living in his mother's house in Pelham Crescent. He says I can have the attics."

Antonia had never met Nigel Crawston, but when she went first to the house she knew the first stirrings of unease – because Nigel was a young man of much sophistication and the house was beautiful, quite beyond the style of Antonia's little flat. It was a proper, grown-up house, filled with beautiful things, and David's attic proved to be a self-contained flat with a bathroom that looked like an advertisement for high-quality plumbing.

As if all this were not enough, Nigel had a sister. She was called Samantha and she used the house as a sort of pied-à-terre in between sorties to ski in Switzerland, or to join friends on some yacht in the Mediterranean. The Crawstons were that sort of people. Sometimes, when Samantha was in London, she would take some undemanding job just to fill in time, but there seemed no question of her having to earn a living. As well, she was almost unbearably glamorous, thin as a rail and with long, straight fair hair that never looked anything but immaculate.

Antonia did her best, but she found the Crawstons heavy going. Once, they all went out to dinner together, to a restaurant so expensive that she could scarcely bear to watch David forking out his half of the bill.

Afterwards she said, "You can't take me to places like that. You must have spent at least a week's salary on just one meal."

He was annoyed. "What's it got to do with you?"

He had never spoken that way to her before, and Antonia felt as if she had been slapped in the face. "It's just . . . well, it's just a waste."

"A waste of what?"

"Well . . . money."

"How I spend my money is my own concern. Your opinion doesn't interest me."

"But . . ."

"Don't ever interfere again."

It was their first-ever real quarrel. That night she cried herself to sleep, hating herself for having been so stupid. The next morning she rang his office to apologise, but the girl on the switchboard said that he wasn't available, and after that Antonia lost her nerve and it was nearly five days before David called her.

❧

They made it up, and Antonia told herself that everything was the way it had always been but, in her heart of hearts, she knew that it wasn't. At Christmas they drove back to Gloucestershire together in David's car, with the back seat piled with presents for their assorted families. But even Christmas provided its own problems. The holiday, traditionally, is a time for engagement, and, for the first time,

Antonia felt that friends and family expected some sort of an announcement. One or two coy ladies, the Vicar's wife and Mrs Trumper from the Hall, even went so far as to make an arch reference or two, heavily veiled but unmistakable. Ultra-sensitive, Antonia was certain that their beady eyes wandered to her left hand, as though expecting to spy some enormous diamond ring.

It was horrible. In the old days she would have confided in David and they could have laughed about it together but somehow, now, that was impossible.

From this situation she was rescued, oddly enough, by none other than Tom. Tom, uncharacteristically, all at once elected to throw a party in his barn. It was on Boxing Night, and he hired a disco and asked all the young people in the neighbourhood. The dancing and merriment went on until five in the morning, and caused such a stir that people stopped speculating about Antonia and David and discussed the party instead. With the pressure off, things were easier and, at the end of the holiday, she and David returned to London together.

Nothing had changed; nothing was settled; nothing had even been discussed, but she wanted it no other way. She simply wanted not to lose him. He had been part of her life for so long that losing him would be like losing part of herself, and the prospect filled her with such desolation that it didn't bear imagining. Shamingly, she pretended to herself that it would never happen.

But David was stronger than she. One evening, soon after Christmas, he called and suggested coming round to her flat for a meal. Antonia's flatmate tactfully took herself off, and Antonia made a spaghetti bolognaise and went around the corner to the off-licence for an affordable bottle of wine. When the doorbell sounded she ran down the stairs to let him in but, as soon as she saw the expression on his handsome face, all self-deception and reasonless hope seeped away and she knew that he was going to tell her something terrible.

David.

*I thought that David might have been here too.*

Antonia began to tear at the breast feathers of the cock pheasant.

"No . . . he's staying in London this weekend."

"Oh, well," said her mother calmly. "There probably wouldn't have been enough for us all, anyway." She smiled. "You know," she went on, "being like this, without electricity and forced on to our own resources, reminds me so much of when I was little. I've been sitting here wallowing in memories, and all of them so vivid and clear."

Mrs Ramsay had been brought up, one of five children, in a remote area of Wales. Her mother, Antonia's grandmother, lived there yet, independent and wiry, keeping hens, preserving fruit, digging in her vegetable garden and, when forced by darkness or inclement weather to retreat indoors, knitting large, knobbly sweaters for all her grandchildren. Going to stay with her had always been a treat and something of an adventure. You never knew what was going to happen next, and the old lady had passed on much of her enthusiasm and energy for life to her daughter.

"Tell me," said Antonia, partly because she wanted to hear, but mostly because she hoped to get off the subject of David.

Mrs Ramsay shook her head. "Oh, I don't know. Just being without any appliances or labour-saving devices. The smell of a coal fire, and the coldness of bedrooms. We had a range in the kitchen and that heated the bathwater, but all the washing had to be done, once a week, in a huge boiler in the scullery. We all used to help, pegging out lines of sheets, and then, when they were dry, taking turns to iron them. And in winter it was so cold that we all used to dress ourselves in the airing cupboard because that was the only spot that was remotely warm."

"But Granny has electricity now."

"Yes, but it was a long time coming to the village. The main street was lit by lamps but, once you'd passed the last house, that was it. I had a great friend, the Vicar's daughter, and if I had tea with her, I always had to walk home by myself. Most times I didn't mind, but sometimes it was dark and windy and wet, and then I used to imagine every sort of spook, and by the time I reached home I'd be running as though there were monsters at my heels. Mother knew that I was frightened but she said I must learn to be self-reliant. And when I complained about the spooks and monsters she said the thing to do was to walk slowly, looking up at the trees and the infinity of the sky. Then, she said, I would realise how infinitesimal I was, how pointless and puny my tiny fears. And the funny thing was, it really worked."

As she spoke, she had concentrated on the task in hand, but now she looked up and across the littered, feathery table and her eyes met Antonia's. She said, "I still do it. If I'm miserable or worried. I take myself out and go somewhere peaceful and quiet, and look up at the trees and the sky. And after a bit, things do get better. I suppose it's a question of getting your values straight. Keeping a sense of proportion."

A sense of proportion. Antonia realised then that her mother knew that there was something horribly wrong between herself and David. She knew and was offering no form of comfort. Simply advice. Face up to the spooks of loneliness, the monsters of jealousy and hurt. Be self-reliant. And don't run away.

By afternoon, the electricity still had not come on. When the lunch dishes were tidied away, Antonia pulled on boots and a sheepskin coat and persuaded her father's old spaniel to come out for a walk. The dog, having already been exercised, was reluctant to leave the fire but, once out of doors, forgot his misgivings and behaved like a puppy, bounding through the snow and chasing interesting rabbit smells.

The snow was deep, the sky low and grey as ever; the air still, the countryside blanketed and soundless. Antonia followed the track which climbed the hill behind the house. Every now and then there came the clatter of wings in the still air as a pheasant, disturbed, shouted warning, got up and sailed away through the trees. As she climbed she stopped feeling cold and, by the time she reached the top of the hill, was warm enough to clear the snow from a tree-stump and sit there, looking at the great spread of the familiar view.

The valley wound away into the hills. She saw the white fields, the stark trees, the silver river. Far below, the village, darkened by the power cut, lay clustered around the single street; smoke from chimneys rose straight into the motionless air. The silence was immense, broken only now and then by the whine of the chain saw, slicing the crystal quiet, and she guessed that Tom Dixon and one of the farmworkers were still dealing with the fallen beech.

The hill sloped gently down towards the wood. On this hill she and David had sledged as children; in the wood they had, one summer, built a camp and baked potatoes in the ashes of their fire. Where the river curved into the Dixons' land they had fished for trout and, on hot days, bathed in the clear shallows. It seemed that the whole of this small world was littered with memories of David.

David. That last evening: "You're saying that you don't

want to see me any more." Angry, and hurt, she had finally blurted it out.

"Oh, Antonia, I'm being honest. Without meaning to hurt you. I can't go on pretending. I can't lie to you. We can't go on like this. It's not fair for either of us, and it's not fair for our families."

"I suppose you're in love with Samantha."

"I'm not in love with anybody. I don't want to be. I don't want to settle down. I don't want to commit myself. I'm twenty-two and you're twenty. Let's learn to live without each other, and be ourselves."

"I am myself."

"No, you're not. You're part of me. Somehow, you're all entangled with me. It's a good thing, but it's a bad thing, too, because we've neither of us ever been free."

Free. He called it being free, but for Antonia, it meant being alone. On the other hand, as her mother had said, you couldn't be self-reliant until you'd learned to live with yourself. She tipped back her head and looked up through the black winter branches of the overhead trees, to grey and comfortless sky beyond.

*You hold most fast to the people you love by gently letting them go.* Long ago, some person had said this to her – or she had read it. The source of wisdom was forgotten but the words, suddenly, out of nowhere, resurfaced. If she loved David enough to let him go, then, that way, he would never be wholly lost to her. And she had already had so much of him . . . it was greedy to yearn for more.

Besides – and this was a surprising, cool-headed revelation, and something of a shock – she didn't want to get married any more than he did. She didn't want to get engaged, have a wedding, settle down for ever. The world spread far beyond this valley, beyond London, beyond the bounds of her own imagination. Out there, it waited for her, filled with people she had yet to meet and things that she had yet to do. David had known this. This was what he had been trying to tell her.

A sense of proportion. Relative values. Once you had got these worked out, things didn't look so bleak after all. In fact, a number of interesting possibilities began to present themselves. Perhaps she had worked for too long in the bookshop. Perhaps it was time to move on – go abroad, even. She could be a cook on a Mediterranean yacht, or look after some Parisian child and learn to speak really good French, or . . .

A cold nose nuzzled her hand. She looked down and the old dog stared plaintively up at her, telling her, with large brown eyes, that he was sick of sitting there in the snow and wanted to get on with his walk, chase some rabbits. Antonia realised that she too had grown chilly. She got up off the stump and they started for home, not retracing their steps, but setting off down the snow-deep fields towards the wood. After a little, she began to run, not simply because she was cold, but with something of the high spirits of childhood.

She came to the wood, and then to the track which led through the trees to the Dixons' farm. She reached the clearing where the beech had fallen. Already its immense trunk had been sliced into lengths by the chain saw, and a way cleared, but devastation lay all about, along with the smell of newly sawn timber and the fragrance of woodsmoke from a smouldering fire. There was nobody about but, as she stood there, mourning the demise of the noble tree, she heard a tractor coming down the road from the farm, and the next moment it appeared around the bend of the lane, with Tom at the wheel. Reaching the clearing, he killed the engine and climbed down out of the cab. He wore dungarees, an old sweater and a donkey jacket, but, despite the cold, was bare-headed.

"Antonia!"

"Hello, Tom."

"What are you doing here?"

"Just out for a walk. I heard the saw going."

"We've been at it most of the afternoon."

He was older than David and neither so tall nor so handsome. His weather-beaten face did not often smile, but this seriousness was belied by his amused, pale eyes, which always seemed to brim with incipient laughter. "Got rid of the worst of it now." He went to the smouldering bonfire and kicked the grey ashes into life. "At least we won't need to worry about firewood for a month or two. And how are things with you?"

"All right."

He looked up and, across the little flames and the sweet plume of smoke, their eyes met. "How's David?"

"He's all right, too."

"Didn't he come with you?"

"No, he stayed in London." She buried her hands deep into the pockets of the sheepskin coat and said, as she had not been able to say to her mother, "He's going skiing next week with the Crawstons. Didn't you know that?"

"I think my mother said something about it."

"They've taken a villa in Val d'Isère. They asked him to go with them."

"Didn't they ask you?"

"No. Nigel Crawston's got a girl of his own."

"Is Samantha Crawston David's girl now?"

Antonia met his steady gaze. She said, "Yes. For the moment."

Tom stooped, gathered up another branch and threw it on to the fire. "Does that worry you?" he asked her.

"It did, but not any more."

"When did all this happen?"

"It's been happening for some time, only I didn't want to admit it."

246

"Are you unhappy?"

"I was. But not any longer. David says we each have to live our own lives. And he's right. We've been too close for too long."

"Were you hurt?"

"A bit," she admitted. "But I don't own David. I don't possess him."

Tom was silent for a moment. Then, "That's a pretty grown-up thing to say," he observed.

"But it's true, isn't it, Tom? And at least now we know where we stand. Not just David and me, but all of us."

"I know what you mean. It certainly makes things easier." He tossed another armful of branches on to the flames and there was the sizzling sound of melting snow. "There was, without any doubt, a certain amount of covert expectation at Christmas about what the pair of you were up to."

Antonia was surprised. "You felt that, too? I thought I was the only one. I kept telling myself I was over-reacting."

"Even my mother, who's the most sensible of women, caught the bug and started hinting at Christmas engagements and June weddings."

"It was awful."

"I guessed it was awful." He grinned. "I was very sorry for you."

Watching him, a thought occurred to Antonia. "Was it because of that . . . that you threw your party?"

"Well, anything was better than having everybody sitting around, speculating. Waiting for you and David to come prancing in, all bright-eyed and bushy-tailed, saying, 'Listen, listen to our news – we have an announcement to make.'" He said this in a ridiculous voice and Antonia began to laugh, filled with grateful affection.

"Oh, Tom, you are marvellous. You really took the pressure off. You saved my life."

"Well, I don't know. I've been mending your bicycles and

building you tree-houses for long enough. I thought it was time I did something a bit more constructive."

"You've never been anything else. Always. I can't thank you enough."

"You don't have to thank me." He went on working. "I've got to get the worst of this cleared before dark."

She remembered something. "You're coming to dinner tonight. Did you know that?"

"Am I?"

"Well, you've been invited. You must come. I've been plucking pheasants all morning and if you aren't there to eat them, I'll feel the entire effort's been wasted."

"In that case," said Tom, "I'll be there."

She stayed with him for a little, helping with his task and then, as the midwinter afternoon slipped into dusk, she left him, still at it, and set off for home. Walking, she realised that the air had gentled and a soft westerly wind was stirring the trees. Branches which had been frozen in snow were starting to drip. Overhead the clouds were parting, revealing glimpses of a pale evening sky the colour of aquamarines. As she came through the gate which stood at the end of the Dixons' lane, she looked up the hill towards home and saw the lights shining out from the uncurtained windows.

So things were looking up. The power failure was over. And living without David was not going to be impossible, after all. She decided that when she got home she would ring him up and tell him this, putting his mind at rest and leaving him free to make his plans for Val d'Isère without any guilty backward glances over his shoulder.

And it had started to thaw. Tomorrow it might even be a beautiful day.

And Tom was coming for dinner.

## ❧ *Cousin Dorothy* ❧

Mary Burn awoke early in her pretty, flower-sprigged room. Though the sun was shining and the birds were singing, the worry that she had taken to bed with her had not retreated.

She turned over and shut her eyes and longed for Harry to be there; to say, "It's all right. I'll see to it." But he had died five years ago, and now their daughter Vicky was getting married in a week's time and the wedding dress still hadn't materialised.

Harry would have known what to do. With his going, Mary had lost not only a lover and dearest friend, but also a competent and kindly husband who dealt with every problem.

Mary, happily content with the day-to-day demands of house, garden and a small child, had been delighted to let him. Organisation, she was the first to admit, was not her strong point. She was useless on committees, and frequently forgot when it was her Sunday for doing the flowers in church. It was Harry who arranged holidays, ordered coal, interviewed headmistresses, filled the cars with petrol and, when door handles fell off, screwed them on again.

As well, he tackled the problem of Vicky. As a small girl, she had been loving and warm-hearted, a delightful companion, content to make dolls' clothes and bake gingerbread men and dig her own patch of garden. But at around twelve years old, she had changed. Overnight, it seemed, she was no longer the biddable and responsive little girl, but a prickly adolescent, stubborn and contrary. And everything, from the wrong sort of shoes to bad marks for her home-work, was her mother's fault.

Mary was baffled by this metamorphosis. "What on earth is wrong with her?" she whispered furiously to Harry, after a particularly heated exchange with Vicky, concluding with a slammed door. "I don't think she even *likes* me any more."

"She's just growing up, asserting herself. It'll pass, don't worry about it."

"How do you know? You never had a sister. You've only got Cousin Dorothy."

"Now don't start on her."

As far as there could be a bone of contention between them, Harry's cousin Dorothy was it. She was a good ten years older than Mary and, in every way, immensely superior. Unmarried, she had made her career in the Civil Service, attached for some years to the Foreign Office. She spoke three languages and worked for some Under-Secretary of State, with whom she was constantly being sent abroad on important missions. When she wasn't either in Geneva or Brussels, or stalking the corridors of power at Whitehall, she lived in a service flat in Knightsbridge. Mary had never seen her looking anything other than immaculate. She always wore very expensive shoes and carried a briefcase-sized leather handbag bulging, one was certain, with immensely important State secrets.

"I'm not starting on her. It's just that I can't imagine Dorothy being a tedious teenager, or falling in love, or suffering from any sort of emotion. Admit it, Harry, she is fairly awe-inspiring."

"Yes, perhaps, but your paths don't often cross."

"No. But she is your cousin. It would be nice to be friends."

Vicky was seventeen when Harry died. By then, one would have thought the teenage antagonism between mother and daughter would have burnt itself out, but it had simply faded to embers. Where they should have been able to comfort each other, they seemed to do nothing but quarrel.

It was a terrible time. Coping with grief, loss and all the painful formalities of death had been bad enough, but learning to live without Harry was worse. Over the months, through sheer necessity, Mary taught herself to be practical.

Vicky, however, was another matter entirely. She was lost and hurt and angry because her father was gone, and Mary understood this and was deeply sympathetic. The problem was that, though Mary understood exactly what her poor daughter was going through, she couldn't reach Vicky to comfort her.

The worst was having no person to confide in. There were many friends, of course, in the little Wiltshire village where she had lived all her married life, but you couldn't confide in friends about your daughter's shortcomings. It would be too disloyal.

And as for family, there was only Cousin Dorothy. Retired now from the Foreign Office, she had moved to the country to live not ten miles away, run the local Red Cross and play a great deal of golf. Sometimes she and Mary met for a formal lunch, but it was still difficult to think of things to talk about. And Vicky was a touchy subject, for Dorothy had never shown much fondness for her.

"She's a spoiled brat," she had told Harry more than once. "Only child, of course. You've never learned to say no to her. You'll regret it."

The last thing Mary wanted was to give Dorothy the slightest opportunity to say, "I told you so."

Altogether, life went through a phase of being almost impossibly difficult but, just when Mary was deciding she couldn't carry on for another moment, Vicky herself, cool as ever, came up with the solution. At breakfast one morning, she announced she wanted to go to London and learn to cook.

Mary carefully set down her coffee-cup. "Where did you think you might do this training?"

Vicky told her. "Sarah Abbey went there. You remember, she was at school with me. She's living in her own flat now and earning a bomb doing directors' lunches. She says I could stay with her."

Mary, presented with this *fait accompli*, said that she would look into it. But Vicky, it appeared, had already put her name down for the next term.

'She'll be better on her own,' Mary told herself after she'd seen Vicky off on the London train and returned to the empty, but strangely peaceful, house.

But Vicky, true to form, proceeded to do everything possible that would fill her mother's heart with alarm. She moved in with Sarah Abbey, stayed a month and then moved out. To give her her due, she phoned Mary and told her what was happening.

"But, Vicky, I thought you liked her?"

"Mummy, she's turned into the most frightful bore. I'm going to live with another girl who's on the course with me. And two chaps. They all share this house in Fulham. It's going to be much more fun. Look, here's my address . . ." Mary grabbed a pad and pencil and wrote it down. "Got it? Look, I must fly."

"Vicky, how's everything going?" She amended this hastily. "The course, I mean?"

"Oh, like a breeze. Dead easy. I'll do you a crown of lamb next time I come down."

When Vicky eventually came for a weekend visit, she arrived wearing really bizarre clothes which looked as though they had been bought at a jumble sale. Which they had. She came again with a young man whom she had met, she explained, at a disco. He wore a crumpled mauve linen suit and spent the entire weekend plugged into his personal stereo.

The cooking course lasted a year. At the end of it, Vicky passed all her examinations with flying colours and instantly set about finding work. She bought herself a second-hand Mini, and in no time at all was driving herself around London with pots and pans, cooking knives and liquidisers all piled up on the back seat. She cooked for dinner parties, filled deep-freezers, catered for large wedding receptions and concocted enormous luncheons for prestigious board meetings.

With evidence of such industry and success, it was pointless to go on worrying about her, and so Mary stopped, but still could find no good excuse to explain away Vicky's quite eccentric friends. They were brought to Wiltshire at regular intervals, and each was odder than the last, but quite the strangest was a girl called Regina French, who looked like a very thin, young witch, and would eat nothing but raw oatmeal and nuts.

There must be, Mary told herself, some perfectly pleasant, normal young people living in London. Why didn't Vicky ever meet them? And if she did, why didn't she like them? Was she reacting against her own conventional upbringing?

There didn't seem to be any answers.

❧

Dorothy rang. "Mary?"

"Yes. How are you?"

"My dear, I just had to ask. I was in London yesterday in

Harrods and I saw Vicky. At least, I think I did. But she's dyed her hair. It's bright yellow."

"Well, at least it isn't pink!"

"What's she doing with herself? Has she got a job?"

"She's started her own catering business. She's working very hard." Mary was defensive.

"Well, she looks extraordinary. I'm amazed any person employs her to boil so much as an egg."

"How she looks is her affair."

"Oh, well, she's your daughter."

"Yes," said Mary firmly. "She is my daughter."

It was the first time she had ever stood up to Dorothy. It made her feel quite good.

And then, out of the blue, the unimaginable happened. Vicky went to Scotland for a fortnight, to cook for some fishing party in a remote Highland village. There she met a man called Hector Harding. Before long, his name was being mentioned with monotonous frequency and slipped into the conversation on the slenderest of excuses.

Mary's attention was caught. "Who is Hector, Vicky?"

"Oh, just a chap I met in Scotland. I – I've been seeing quite a lot of him."

"What does he do?"

"He's an architect."

An architect. This was breaking new ground. There had never been an architect before. Hope stirred. Hector Harding was invited to Wiltshire for the weekend.

Just another friend, Mary told herself firmly, and made no special preparations, but yet, when the car came trundling up to the front door on Friday evening, she could not suppress a flutter of curiosity as she went out to meet them. They had come, not in Vicky's Mini, but in Hector's car.

He climbed out from behind the wheel, unfolding very long, blue-jeaned legs, and came at once to shake his hostess by the hand. He was tall and thin, and had a lot of thick brown hair. He wasn't particularly good-looking; not particularly anything, really, but he was terribly nice.

On the Saturday morning, he cut the grass and mended the electric toaster, which had been behaving oddly for weeks. That afternoon, he and Vicky took themselves off for a long walk. They returned at five, looking faintly bemused. Later, over drinks before dinner, they told Mary that they wanted to get married.

A few days later Dorothy rang. "Mary, I've just opened the *Daily Telegraph* and read the announcement of Vicky's engagement. When did this happen?"

Mary told her.

"Who is he?"

"He's an architect."

"Do you like him?"

"Very much. And Harry would have liked him, too."

"When's the wedding?"

"In August in the village church with a party here afterwards. Not a big elaborate affair. Just their friends will be there. It's all going to be very simple."

But she was wrong, because it wasn't. Vicky, as always, had a mind of her own.

"We'll have to get invitations printed and make out a guest list."

"Hector and I don't want more than fifty people. Just our close friends. No old relations we don't know."

"Some relatives will have to be asked. Cousin Dorothy, for instance," Mary said.

"Why do I have to have Cousin Dorothy at my wedding?" Vicky protested. "She's never been able to stand the sight of me. I saw her in Harrods one day, and I shot off through the soft furnishings before she could buttonhole me. I knew she'd fix me with that beady stare of hers and ask a lot of probing questions."

Mary was sympathetic. "I know. She puts my back up too, sometimes. But I still think she must be asked."

"Oh, all right," Vicky conceded ungraciously. "She can always sit in a corner and chat to Hector's granny."

Which dealt with Dorothy.

Finally, the most important question of all had to be discussed: the wedding dress.

"Actually, I've seen a picture in a magazine," Vicky told her mother. "It would be perfect."

Mary tentatively imagined white lace and a veil. She might have saved herself the bother. Presented with the magazine, she gazed, wordlessly, at the picture. The model in the photograph was not unlike Vicky, with bright hair and long skinny legs. The dress resembled a tee-shirt with a cotton skirt attached. The skirt fell in points, like handkerchiefs hung out to dry. The model wore ankle socks and tennis shoes.

Vicky broke the silence. "Don't you think it's smashing?"

"It costs three hundred and twenty pounds," was all her mother could think of to say.

"Oh, I wouldn't buy it. I'd get it copied. You remember Regina? I brought her down to stay once, ages ago. Well, she dressmakes."

"Professionally?"

"No, just as a hobby. I'll ask her to do it for me."

"Would she get it done in time?"

"Why shouldn't she?"

"Yes. Well." It was, after all, Vicky's wedding. "Perhaps you'd better get in touch with her right away."

Vicky went off to telephone. But she couldn't get through to Regina, so she rang Hector instead and talked for an hour. Mary, washing up the breakfast dishes, was filled with foreboding.

Her foreboding had been well founded. Each time Vicky went up to London to see how Regina was getting on, or telephoned, there was always some excuse. The material had not come. Her sewing machine was on the blink. She had to go to Devon to look after somebody's baby. But not to worry, it would be all right on the night!

Not to worry ... The thought jerked Mary back to the present. The wedding was a week away and still the problem hadn't been resolved. She got out of bed, dressed and went downstairs, only to discover Vicky down before her, sitting at the kitchen table drinking coffee. The post had arrived.

"Anything from Regina?"

Vicky said, "Yes." She would not look at her mother. Mary glanced around in the hopes of seeing a large parcel which might contain a wedding dress. There was none. "A letter," Vicky enlarged, and held it out. With a sinking heart, Mary took it from her and read it.

*Dear Vicky,*

*Terribly sorry, have been stricken with an awful bout of the flu. Can't even reach a telephone. Sorry about the dress, can't possibly cope with it now. Hope you have a lovely wedding.*

*Love, Regina*

Mary reached for a chair and sat down.

Vicky spoke first. "If you say I told you so, I shall scream."

"I wasn't going to say anything of the sort. At least, now we know how we stand."

"Yes. Stark naked!"

Mary told herself that she must keep calm.

"Shall we go to London, and see if we can buy something?"

"I'll never find anything I like. I know I won't." Vicky's voice rose. She was beginning to sound hysterical. "If I don't get the sort of dress I want, then I'll get married in a boiler suit."

"Oh, darling, don't get worked up."

Vicky sprang to her feet. "What else is there to do? I wish Hector and I could just run away. And not get married at all."

The kitchen door slammed shut between them.

For a moment Mary sat where she was, then before she could break anything, or dash upstairs after Vicky and say something unforgivable that could never be unsaid, she picked up her bag, walked out of the house, got into her car and drove the ten miles to Dorothy's house.

She found Dorothy gardening. Even when she gardened, Dorothy looked neat, in well-cut slacks, and with a net over her white hair. She was forking over her rose border, but when she saw Mary approach across the grass, she instantly laid down the fork and came to meet her.

"My dear." Her face was all concern. 'I must look truly frightful,' Mary thought. She tried to speak but, before she could say a word, she burst into tears.

Dorothy was very kind. She led her gently indoors, settled her in a chair in the sitting-room and tactfully disappeared. The room was cool and orderly, and smelt of polish and freshly-laundered linen loose covers. Gradually soothed by this calm ambience, Mary controlled her weeping. She found a handkerchief and blew her nose. Dorothy returned bearing, not coffee, but a small glass of brandy.

"Drink this."

"But, Dorothy, it's not ten yet."

"Medicinal." Dorothy sat down in the other armchair. "You look totally shattered. Drink it up."

Mary did so. She at once felt stronger and managed a faint smile.

"I'm sorry. It's just that everything's so awful and I knew I had to get out of the house and talk to someone. And you were the only person I could think of."

"Is it Vicky?"

"Well ... yes, in a way. It's not her fault. She's really helped me get this wedding together, and I began to think we were going to be able to do it without a single row." She put down the empty glass. "I know you always thought Harry and I spoiled her, and perhaps we did, but the truth is that Vicky and I are very different people. I don't seem to have anything in common with her. It's all right when things are going smoothly, but this morning ..."

She related the disastrous saga of the wedding dress.

"But it's not your fault," Dorothy pointed out when she'd finished.

"I know. But now, of course, we've only got a week to find another. And Vicky's got such violent ideas about what she's going to wear. She says she's going to wear a boiler suit, or run away with Hector, or even not get married at all."

Dorothy listened to all this, and then shook her head. "It sounds to me like a clear case of wedding nerves. For both of you. A wedding is twice as much work when you haven't got your husband to help you. In fact, I've been on the point of ringing you up, more than once, to suggest I lend a hand with the organisation, but I was frightened you'd think I was interfering. And as for Vicky, you've been splendid with her. It can't have been easy without Harry. I really admired you for letting her go off and make her own way."

To be admired by Dorothy was an entirely new sensation.

259

A silence fell between them. It wasn't a difficult one nor strained in any way. Mary had never felt so at ease with Dorothy before. She glanced at the clock. She said, "I feel better now. I just needed to talk."

"What are you going to do about the dress?"

"I have no idea."

Dorothy said, "I have a wedding dress."

Mary drove home at a tremendous speed, feeling ridiculously light-hearted. She got out of the car, took the huge, old-fashioned box off the back seat, carried it indoors and upstairs to her bedroom. She laid the box on her bed and sat at her dressing-table to do something about her tear-blotched face.

"Mummy?" The door opened and Vicky appeared. "Are you all right?"

Mary did not turn. "Yes, of course I am." She smoothed moisturiser on to her cheeks.

"I couldn't think where you'd gone." Vicky put her arms around Mary's neck and bent to kiss her. "I'm sorry," she said to Mary's reflection. "For flying off the handle like that. It's entirely my own fault that I haven't got a stitch to wear, and I shouldn't have taken it out on you."

"Oh, darling."

"Where did you go? I thought I'd been so beastly I'd made you run away from home."

"Just to see Dorothy."

Vicky went and sat on the bed. "Dorothy? Why did you go and see her?"

"I had a sudden irresistible urge to talk to somebody sane. And she is the sanest woman I know. It worked. She gave me brandy and she gave me a wedding dress."

"You have to be joking?"

"I'm not. It's in the box."

"But whose wedding dress is it?"

"Dorothy's own." She turned to her daughter. "We all think we know so much about other people, and we don't know anything at all. When Dorothy was nineteen she was engaged to a young naval officer. The wedding was to be in September 1939 but then war broke out and it was postponed. He went to sea and was killed almost at once. So that's why Dorothy never married."

"But why didn't we know about this before? Why didn't Daddy know?"

"Harry was only nine. I don't suppose he ever realised it happened."

"And we all thought she was so tough." Vicky sighed.

"I know. But that's not the point. The point is that she says that if you like it, you can have her dress. Circa 1939. A real museum piece and it's never even been worn."

"Have you seen it?"

"No. She just gave me the box."

They sat together on the bed and untied the knot of the string, took off the lid of the box and folded aside the sheets of tissue paper. Standing, Vicky carefully lifted the dress out to hold up in front of her. Folds of pure silk satin whispered to the floor: a flowing skirt cut on the bias, puff sleeves, the shoulders padded, the neckline low and square and embroidered in pearls. There was a faint smell, sweet and musty, like pot-pourri.

"Oh, Mummy, it's blissful!"

"It is rather lovely. But the shoulder pads . . . ?"

"They're high fashion. I think it's perfect."

"It'll be too long."

"You and I can alter it. Dorothy wouldn't mind, would she?"

"She doesn't want it back. She says you can keep it. Try it on."

Vicky did so, tearing off shirt and jeans and slipping the soft silk over her head. It fell into place, and Mary did up the dozens of tiny buttons which ran down the back.

Vicky moved to the long mirror. Aside from the fact that it was far too long, the dress might have been made for her. She turned to see her own back view, to admire the cunningly cut skirt which fanned out into a fish-tail of silk to form a little train.

"It's beautiful," she breathed. "I'm going to wear it. I couldn't have found anything so beautiful if I'd looked for a hundred years. How kind of Dorothy. For the life of me, I can't think why she should be so kind . . ."

They undid all the buttons again and Vicky took the dress off. Mary put it on a padded hanger and hung it on the door of her wardrobe, where it looked impressively rich and significant.

"Goodness, Mum, what a stroke of luck! I'll ring Dorothy right away. How could I have been so horrible about asking her to the wedding?" Vicky hauled on her jeans. "You were right." She zipped them up. "We think we know so much about people and we don't know anything at all." She buttoned up her shirt and hugged her mother. "And as for you, you've been a perfect saint."

She took herself off. Moments later, she could be heard speaking to Dorothy, her voice loud with delight and gratitude. Mary shut the bedroom door and sat down once more at her dressing-table. She looked at the dress, and knew that, for once in her life, Vicky would allow herself to look truly beautiful. She thought about the wedding, in just a week's time, and for the first time found herself looking forward to it. She thought about Hector who was going to become her son-in-law and she thought about Dorothy, and it was like having just met and made a new friend. After the wedding, they would have lunch together. There was much that they had to talk about.

She thought about Harry. Among the bottles and jars on her dressing-table stood a photograph of him. She smiled at it. "You don't have to worry about a thing, Harry," she whispered, feeling full of confidence. "It's all going to be all right."

She looked at her own reflection, powdered her face and then, feeling as light-hearted as the girl she had once been, reached for her lipstick.

# ⚜ *Last Morning* ⚜

Laura Prentiss woke to the unfamiliar hotel bedroom and the sounds of her husband making shaving noises from beyond the open bathroom door. Perhaps out of deference to his sleeping wife, Roger had left the bedroom curtains closed, and when Laura groped first for her spectacles and then for her watch, she saw, with some surprise, that it was already half past eight.

"Roger?"

He appeared, in his pyjama trousers and a face half-covered in lather.

"Good morning."

"I'm afraid to look. What sort of a day is it?"

"Fine."

"Thank heavens for that."

"Cold, with a bit of a wind. But fine."

"Draw the curtains and let me look at it."

He did this with difficulty, first trying to pull the curtains manually, as he did at home, and then realising there was a gadget involved, a string with a handle that was meant to be employed. Roger was not good with gadgets. He tugged at it and was finally successful.

The sky beyond the glass was a pale, clear blue, swept with long, thin, fine-weather clouds, and when Laura sat up she could see the sea – dark blue and flecked with white horses.

She said, "I hope Virginia's veil doesn't blow off."

"Even if it does, she's not your daughter, so you don't need to feel any responsibility."

Laura leaned back on her pillow, took off her spectacles and smiled at him gratefully. He had always been a comfortingly practical man, and this morning was obviously treating the day as though it were a perfectly ordinary one, getting up, shaving, going down to eat his breakfast.

He disappeared back into the bathroom and, through the open door, they continued their conversation.

"What are you going to do this morning?" she asked.

"Play golf," said Roger.

She should have known. The hotel had a fine links on its doorstep.

"You won't be late?"

"Am I likely to be?"

"And leave plenty of time to change. It will take such ages to get you into your morning suit." She might have added: 'Specially since you've put on weight,' but she didn't, because Roger was sensitive about his mildly expanding waistline and had decided to ignore the small insert which the tailor had been forced to let into the back of his trousers.

"Stop worrying about details," said Roger. He appeared once more in the doorway, smelling of after-shave. "Stop worrying about anything. You're a guest at this wedding. You've got nothing to plan, nothing to agonise over, nothing to do. Enjoy it."

"Yes. You're quite right. I will."

She got up and pulled on her dressing-gown and went to the window. She opened it and leaned out and the air was icy and smelt of salt and seaweed. Already there was a single golfer, in a red sweater, out on the fairway. Below her, in the hotel grounds, lay the little pitch-and-putt course, and she remembered, long ago, bringing the children to this very hotel for a summer holiday. Tom had been six, Rose three and Becky a fat baby in a pram, and the weather had been terrible, nothing but rain and wind. They had passed the time playing card games in the leaden sun porch, and every time the rain stopped had dashed across the links to the beach, where the children had crouched, sweatered and chapped of cheek, and built sand-castles of dark, sodden sand.

But some time during that holiday Tom had been introduced to the pitch-and-putt course and the fascinating frustrations of golf, and after that he was out by himself in all weathers, his small form bent against the wind, and golf-balls and divots of turf flying in all directions.

Remembering the small boy he had been, she felt sad, thinking, 'Where have all the years gone?' and immediately was annoyed with herself for being a typical, doting, cliché-ridden mother.

She shut the window when Roger came back into the room. She said, "I thought Tom would have liked a game this morning. Keep his mind off this afternoon."

"I thought of that, too, and I asked him, but he said he had other things to do."

"You mean like recovering from last night's party?"

Roger grinned. "Maybe."

Tom had gone out on a traditional bachelor's spree with one or two of his friends who'd come up for the wedding. Laura hoped, for Virginia's sake, that the party had not been too rowdy. Nothing in this world could be more unattractive than a sheepish and hung-over bridegroom.

"I wonder what he's planning to do?"

"No idea," said Roger. He came over to kiss her. "What about breakfast?" he asked.

"What about it?"

"Do you want it up here? You only have to call Room Service."

She must have looked agonised because he grinned, recognising her horror of asking anybody to do anything for her, and went over to the telephone and ordered her breakfast for her, without asking her what she wanted because, after twenty-seven years of married life, he knew. Orange juice, a boiled egg, coffee. When he put the receiver down she smiled at him gratefully across the room, and he sat on the edge of the bed and smiled back at her, and she had the good feeling that the momentous day had started well.

While she was eating breakfast, propped up with Roger's pillows as well as her own, her two daughters burst in upon her, talking nineteen to the dozen as usual, and come to find out how she was going to spend the morning.

They both had long mouse-coloured hair and clean, shining faces naked of make-up except smudges of eye shadow and mascara. They wore their usual uniform of jeans and sneakers, long shirts and loose sweaters, and sack-like bags. Laura thought they were both beautiful.

They sat on the foot of her bed and ate the bits of toast which had been sent up on the breakfast tray, loading them with butter and marmalade and munching as though they had not seen food for a week.

"It was a super party last night . . ."

"I thought it was meant to be a bachelor party?"

". . . well, of course it started out as one, but this is such a tiny place that in the end we all met up and joined forces. He's terrific, that friend of Tom's . . . what's his name? Mike, or something . . ."

"Yes, he plays the guitar like a dream. Super songs, the

kind we all knew. Everybody joined in, even quite prim-looking people."

"Did Tom come home with you?"

"No, but he wasn't far behind. We heard him come in. Have no fears, Ma. Did you think he was going to die of drink in some Scottish ditch? I say, is there any coffee left in that pot?"

Laura pushed the tray towards them, leaning back, watching them chattering. Why did they have to grow up and get jobs in London and leave home for ever?

In the middle of a sentence Rose suddenly caught sight of her watch. "Gosh, look at the time! We must go."

"Where are you going?"

"There's a beauty salon in the village, believe it or not. We found out last night. We're going to go so that we'll stun all Virginia's smart friends this afternoon, and not be a cause of shame to our brother. Why don't you come, too? We can ring up and fix a time for you."

Laura's hair was short and inclined to curl. She had it cut once a month then dealt with it herself. The thought of spending a morning being rolled and bouffed and sprayed with lacquer, today of all days, was almost more than she could bear. She said, "I don't think I will."

"Your hair looks super, anyway. I'm glad we haven't got curly hair, but I must say when one gets a bit long in the tooth, there's nothing more charming."

Laura laughed. "Thank you very much."

"That was meant as a terrific compliment. Come on, we must go."

They collected their handbags and themselves and climbed off the bed, slim and long-legged and graceful. As they made for the door, their mother said, "You'll get back in plenty of time to get changed, won't you? We really mustn't be late today."

They smiled. "We will," they promised. Rose was going

users, and Becky a long granny-type dress in prune-coloured cotton, with hand-crocheted lace at the wrists and throat. To complement this outfit she had chosen an enormous natural straw hat, which looked to Laura as though the brim had started to unravel. But on making a few tactful enquiries, she had been assured that this was half its charm.

When the girls had gone, Laura stayed where she was for a little, trying to decide what to do next. She thought of Virginia, waking up in her parents' house only two miles away. She wondered if Virginia had had breakfast in bed, too; whether she was feeling nervous. But no, one could not imagine Virginia nervous about anything. She was probably calming down the rest of her family, coping serenely with all the last-minute details.

And Laura tried to conjure up her own wedding morning, but it was all too long ago and she discovered that she could remember very little about it, except that the wedding dress had been very slightly too large, and Laura's Aunt Mary, ever-present in times of crisis, had got on her knees with needle and thread, making the waistline fit.

_____ ❧ _____

Getting up and bathed and dressed took, for some reason, much longer than it took at home. Analysing this, Laura discovered that she was putting off time. Was, in fact, fearful of going downstairs and getting involved with Aunt Lucy and Uncle George, and Tom's godmother and her husband, and the Richard cousins who had come, unexpectedly, all the way north from darkest Somerset to be present at Tom's wedding. It was not that she did not dearly love all these people, but this morning she wanted to be alone. She wanted to go out into that miraculous, fresh morning and walk, and sort herself out and not talk to anybody.

She put on a tweed coat, tied a scarf over her head, cautiously let herself out of her room and went down the wide staircase to the lobby. Thankfully, she realised there did not seem to be anybody about and she made for the main door, but as she passed the glass doors of the dining-room she stopped, for there, in solitary state, sat her son, eating a large, late breakfast, and reading the newspaper.

And at once, as though feeling her eyes upon him, he looked up, saw her and smiled. She went through the doors and across the room to join him, regarding him anxiously, searching for bloodshot eyes, bad colour; but her eldest child, much to her relief, seemed to be in the best of health.

He pulled out a chair for her and she sat down.

"How was the party?"

"Great."

"The girls told me you'd all met up . . ."

"Yes, by the end it was a free-for-all; half the local inhabitants joined in, as far as I could see." He folded the newspaper. "You look as though you're planning a little outdoor exercise."

"Yes, I thought I'd go out for a walk."

"I'll come with you," said Tom.

"But . . ."

"But what? Don't you want me?"

"Yes, of course. It's just that I thought you'd have a million other things to do."

"Such as?"

"I can't think of one, but I'm sure there must be something."

"Neither can I." He got up. "Come on, let's go."

He wore a thick cardigan and did not seem to feel the need for a jacket. With no more ado, they went together out of the dining-room and out through the door. The wind had an edge to it like a knife, but the turf of the little pitch-and-putt course was green as velvet from the shower of rain which had fallen during the night, and all the flags on the greens blew straight and perky.

"Isn't it strange," said Tom as they set off at a spanking pace, heading for the right-of-way that led across the golf-links to the beach, "that the girl I marry should come from this part of the world, and we should all come back to stay in this hotel? Do you remember that holiday?"

"I shall never forget it. I shall always remember the rain."

"I don't remember the rain. I only remember trying to teach myself how to play golf." He stopped and took a stance and swung an imaginary club. "That was a good shot. A hole in one."

"I should have thought you'd have wanted to play with your father this morning."

"He asked me, but somehow it didn't seem quite the right thing to do on one's wedding morning. Anyway, if I had I should have missed out on this nice little walk with you."

He grinned down at her. He was fair like his mother, with the slightly curly hair that he had inherited from her. The shining commas of hair lay thick and close to his skull. Otherwise he resembled his father, except, in the discon-certing fashion of modern children, he had grown to be four inches taller than Roger, and was brawny to match.

She remembered the tough, peppery little boy, pitting himself against the complexities of golf, just as he had always flung himself head-first at any problem, not always with felicitous results. But he had never been discouraged and had finally got his quick temper under control; and some-how that little boy had turned into this shrewd, amiable young man who had finally got himself engaged, and today would be married to Virginia.

Virginia was, Laura often thought, a match for Tom: intelligent, capable, amusing and pretty to boot. If they had been less in love, she might have had reservations about two such positive people deciding to spend their lives together.

"There is not room," Laura's wise old grandmother had once said, "for more than one born leader in a family." But perhaps if the two born leaders loved each other sufficiently to take turns to stand aside, then it would be all right. She stole a glance at Tom, striding out beside her, and he caught this anxious glance and grinned reassuringly, and she thought, 'Yes, it will be all right.'

The path led over the dunes and down to the sand which was, at first, soft and dry, and then firm where the high tides had washed it flat. There was a line of seaweed and flotsam from passing ships. An old boot, a blue detergent bottle, a wrecked crate.

"Do you remember," said Tom, "reading *Ring of Bright Water* to me when I had that knee operation, and how we liked the idea of Gavin Maxwell making all his furniture out of old herring-boxes that had been washed up on the beach?" He stooped and picked up a ragged slat with a nail protruding from it. "Perhaps I should emulate him. Think of the money I'd save on three-piece suites. What could I turn this into?"

Laura considered it. "The leg of an elegant coffee-table, perhaps?" she suggested.

"Good idea." He leaned back, then flung the piece of wood far out to sea. They walked on.

*Ring of Bright Water* had been only one of many books that she had read aloud to Tom during the tedious weeks after the operation. His knee had been injured playing football; he had torn a ligament and a blood clot had formed, but the operation to clear this had been as delicate as a cartilage removal and he had lain on his back for six weeks while his mother played games with him, read to him, watched television or solved crosswords with him, anything to stop his getting bored. Both of them were devilled by the unspoken fear that Tom would never be able to play football again, and for Laura it had been a particularly anxious time and yet, looking back, she remembered it only with pleasure and gratitude. Pleasure at having him to herself, rediscovering with him all the books that she had loved at his age, and gratitude at being given time, like an unexpected present, really to get to know her son, to discover him as a person.

Tom, too, had been thinking about this time, for he suddenly said, "You read aloud so well. Some people are awful at it. You used to do different voices for different people. It made it all come real."

"Oh, Tom, it was about the only thing I could do."

"What do you mean?"

"Well, I was always so useless at anything physical, where you were meant to hit a ball. I could never play tennis and I was hopeless at skiing ... And when I came to watch school rugger matches everything always had to be explained to me, and I could never get the hang of the game."

"The great thing was you used to come and watch."

"Yes, but I always felt so inadequate. And whenever I tried to plan something really exciting, it always went wrong. I mean, that holiday we had here, it was meant to be all bathing and picnics and sand-castles, and all we did was to play 'racing demon' in the sun lounge and wait for the rain to stop."

"I liked that holiday."

"And that terrible time I took you three with the Richard family to Norway to ski. We got caught in a blizzard before we'd even got to the airport, and we missed the plane, and your father had to telegraph us enough money to spend the night in an hotel and wait for a flight the next day."

"That was an adventure. And it wasn't your fault."

"And the time I took you all to the Hebrides, and it was April and the boat hit the worst storm of the winter, and we got marooned on Tiree with a lot of hungry cattle. The awful things always happened when your father wasn't there. When he was with us everything went on oiled wheels. No snowstorms, no shipwrecks, and the sun always shone."

"I think you're underestimating yourself," said Tom.

They were alone on the beach now, away from everybody, out in a world of rushing air and flattened grass and blown sand. They came to a breakwater and Tom said, "Let's sit down for a bit," so they did, sheltered from the wind, and in the full benevolence of the sun. Suddenly it felt quite warm. The sun burned comfortably through Laura's coat and warmed her knees. It was companionable, just the two of them tucked into the shelter of the breakwater, with only the wind and the gulls for company.

After a little, Tom said, "You didn't really think I wanted a hockey-playing mother, did you?"

Laura's thoughts had already strayed from this line of conversation, and she was surprised to find that Tom still wanted to continue it.

"Not hockey ... but something, perhaps. Think what fun you're going to have with Virginia. You can do so much together. You both swim and play tennis, you'll probably find her beating you at golf one day. It makes life so much more ... I don't know ... complete, I suppose. It makes for friendship. And in a marriage that's almost as important as love."

275

"You never did anything sporty with Dad, and you don't seem to have managed too badly."

"No. But we raised a family together; perhaps that was enough."

"Only if you're pleased with the results."

"You wouldn't, by any chance, be fishing for a compliment?"

"No, I'm just trying to pay you one."

"I don't understand."

"Just that the results may not be all that outstanding, but the job you did certainly was."

"I still don't understand."

"You always treated us like people. I never appreciated this till I went to school and realised that not everybody was as lucky as me. And you never laughed at us."

"Was that so important?"

"More important than anything. We were allowed to preserve our dignity."

Laura frowned, determined to keep sentimentality at bay. "It's funny, growing older. You try to do all the right things, and you think it's going to last for ever, and suddenly it's all over. You are twenty-five and getting married today, and the girls are living in London and I scarcely see them..."

"But they come home. And when they do the three of you start gossiping and giggling just the way you've always done."

"Perhaps I should try to be more detached."

"Don't try to be anything. Just go on being nice you, and you'll end up the bonniest granny a baby ever had."

She began to laugh at the thought, then pulled back the cuff of her coat to look at her watch. "You know, we shouldn't dawdle. Time's getting on."

They got to their feet and climbed back over the breakwater and headed back for the distant hotel. Tom found for her a pair of tiny yellow shells, still joined so that they looked like a butterfly, and Laura put them in her glove for safety, and thought that when she got home, she would put them with her other small mementoes.

With the wind against them there was no breath to spare for conversation so they trudged in silence, each busy with his own thoughts. As they crossed the links they saw Roger coming down the fairway towards them. And all at once Laura was caught up in a gust of real excitement, the first she had felt all day. They were all converging, heading for the hotel, to change into their finery and to drive to the little church where Tom and Virginia were going to be married. The day that they had all looked forward to for so long was finally here, and although she loved her son and knew that she was losing him, she could not feel any regret. He was simply stepping on and out as they had always encouraged him to do, and she was filled with the deepest thankfulness at the way everything had turned out.

They reached the hotel porch at last, thankful to be out of the buffeting wind. They faced each other, surrounded by folded sun umbrellas and deck chairs. Laura said, "That was a lovely walk. The best. Thank you for coming."

"Thank you."

"I . . . I'll say goodbye now, Tom. I hate saying it in front of people. And darling," she took his hand, "you've been so clever to find Virginia. She's exactly right for you, and you're going to have a great time together."

He said, "Yes, I know. And I know why. It's because, basically, she's like you."

"Me?" The very idea was ridiculous. No two women had ever been more different. "Virginia like me?"

"Yes, you. You see, beneath the capability and the brightness, and the very pretty face, she's gentle and she's wise."

To hear her down-to-earth Tom come out with this brought a sudden lump to Laura's throat. Surely she was not going to cry? For a terrible second her eyes pricked and she could feel the tears rising, but she fought them back and the little crisis was over. She was able to smile and reach up to kiss him. "That was a nice thing to tell me, Tom. Goodbye."

"Goodbye, Mummy."

The baby name for her came naturally, although he had not used it for years. She let go of his hand and went, ahead of him, through the door and into the carpeted interior of the hotel.

Gentle and wise. The old-fashioned words filled her with warmth. Gentle and wise. Perhaps she hadn't done so badly, after all.

She headed for the staircase and went up, two at a time, to get changed for Tom's wedding.

# ❧ The Skates ❧

Jenny Peters, ten years old, opened the door of Mr Sims's ironmongery store and went inside. It was four o'clock in the afternoon, already dark and bitterly cold, but Mr Sims's shop was cosy with the smell of his paraffin heater, and all was adorned for Christmas. He had put a notice on his counter – *Useful And Acceptable Gifts For The Festive Season* – and, to prove his point, tied a red tinsel bow around the handle of a formidable claw hammer.

"Hello there, Jenny."

"Hello, Mr Sims."

"What can I do for you?"

She told him what she needed, not certain whether he would be able to help her. ". . . they have to be little lights, like the ones inside the fridge. And then clips. Like bulldog clips. To fasten them on to the edge of a box . . ."

Mr Sims considered the problem, gazing at Jenny over the top of his spectacles. "Do you want batteries?" he asked.

"No. I've got a long lead that plugs into the wall socket."

"Sounds like you're going to be electrocuting yourself."

"I won't do that."

"Well. Wait a moment . . ."

He disappeared. She took her purse out of her coat pocket and counted out the last few coins of her Christmas spending money. She hoped that there would be enough. If not, Mr Sims would probably let her have credit until next week's pocket money came in.

After a bit, he came back with the makings of exactly what she needed. He opened the boxes and put all the bits together. There was a little adaptor plug and a couple of yards of flex. The clips were meant for bigger lights but that didn't matter.

"That's perfect, Mr Sims. Thank you. How much is it going to cost?"

He smiled, reaching for a stout paper bag into which he put her purchases. "Cash down, you get ten per cent discount. That's, let's see . . ." He did a sum with a stubby pencil on the corner of the bag. "One pound eighty-five pence."

Relief. She had enough. She handed over two pounds and was solemnly given change. But Mr Sims could not contain his curiosity. "What's all this for, then?"

"It's Natasha's Christmas present. It's a secret."

"Say no more. Spending Christmas at home?"

"Yes. Granny's staying. Dad fetched her from the station last night."

"That's nice." He handed over the bag. "Too busy to go skating, are you?"

Jenny said, "Yes." And then, in truth, added, "I can't skate."

"Bet you never even tried."

"Yes, I did. I borrowed an old pair of Natasha's boots. But they were too big and I kept falling over."

"Just a knack," said Mr Sims. "Like riding a bicycle."

"Yes," said Jenny. "I suppose so." She took the bulky bag. "Thank you, Mr Sims, and have a lovely Christmas."

Outside, the cold hit her like a solid thing. A bit like walking into a deep-freeze. But it was not dark, because the street lights were on and the floodlights which Tommy Bright, who ran the Bramley Arms, had set up in the forecourt of his pub poured out like spotlights in a theatre over the flooded, frozen skating rink which the village green had become. For this gratuitous service he was rewarded by a packed bar every evening, and the constant ringing of his till.

The village lay in a bowl of countryside with a line of hills to the south. Houses, church, shops and pub were grouped around the green and a small river, hardly more than a stream, flowed through the middle of it. It was this river which had burst its banks. For most of November it had rained, and the beginning of December had brought the first snows. Old people said that they had never known such weather. The river had steadily risen and finally, unable to contain itself, overflowed and flooded the green. Then the temperature dropped abruptly, the night frosts were cruel, and all was frozen hard as iron.

A skating rink. The ice had held for a week and now it was Christmas Eve and, if the forecasts were to be believed, looked as though it was going to go on holding.

Standing outside Mr Sims's shop, Jenny paused to watch the carnival scene. The skaters, the sledges, the clumsy games of hockey. There were shrieks and shouts of revelry and whole families had turned out to enjoy the fun, pulling bundled babies on toboggans or skating hand-in-hand.

She looked for her sister Natasha and saw her almost at once, for she stood out in her bright pink tracksuit. Natasha skated the way she did everything, with consummate expertise and grace. She was tall and slender, with blonde hair and endless legs, and took any sort of physical activity in her easy stride. Captain of the junior tennis at school and in the gymnastic team as well, her great passion in life was dancing. She had been attending classes since she was five and had already won a number of medals and prizes. Her single-minded ambition was to be a ballerina.

Jenny, smaller, younger and a great deal more dumpy, trailed in this brilliant sister's wake. She went to dancing class as well, but never progressed further than the sailor's hornpipe, or some middle-European polkas. The trouble was, she had difficulty remembering which was her left foot and which her right. Games were little better, and when it came to leaping over the horse at gym, she nearly always ended up the same side that she had started off.

She did not like going to dancing class, but complied with the arrangement because it was about the only thing that the two sisters did together. Sometimes she dreamed about devoting her energies to something entirely different. Like learning the piano. There was a piano in the dining-room at home and the frustration of knowing that it stood there, filled with music which she was unable to release, was a constant reminder of her own inadequacies. But piano lessons were expensive. Much more costly than the communal dancing class, and she was too diffident to suggest them to her parents. Perhaps, for her birthday, she could ask for piano lessons. But her birthday wasn't until next summer. It was all very difficult.

"Jenny!" It was Natasha, sailing by, hand in hand with another girl. "Come on. Have another try."

Jenny waved but they had already gone, floating away to the far side of the ice. It looked so easy but she had discovered that it was the most impossible thing in the world. Wearing Natasha's old boots, she *had* tried. But every step was agony and her feet and legs had shot in all directions and, finally, she had fallen and hurt herself quite badly. But being hurt was not as painful as the knowledge that, yet again, she had made a fool of herself.

She sighed, turned, and set off for home. It was nice walking, with the Christmassy feeling all about her and people's windows bright with the lights of their trees, shining out into frozen gardens. Her own house had a Christmas tree, too, in the dining-room window, but the curtains of the sitting-room were drawn. Indoors, she opened the sitting-room door and put her head around the edge of it.

Mum and Dad and Granny were having tea by the fire, and Granny was knitting. They all looked up and smiled.

"Do you want a cup of tea, darling? Or shall I make you some hot chocolate?"

"No, thank you. I'm just going upstairs to my room."

Upstairs, she turned on the light and drew the curtains. It wasn't a very large room, but all her own. A good deal of it was taken up with her work table, which is where she did her homework and her drawing and set up her little sewing machine when she felt in the mood for making things. Now, however, it was littered with all the bits and pieces needed to make Natasha's present. Pots of paint and tubes of glue and bits of cotton wool and pipe cleaners and scraps of ribbon. The present stood shrouded under a dust-sheet. It had stayed hidden all the time Jenny was working on it, and she had enough respect for her mother to know that under no circumstances would she ever take so much as a single peep.

Now she lifted off the dust-sheet and stood staring at it, trying to see it with Natasha's critical eyes.

It was a miniature stage-set of a ballet. An empty wooden wine crate had given her the idea and her father had helped her adapt it so that she was left with a floor and three sides. Two of these sides she had painted green, but the backdrop was a reproduction of an old painting which she had found in a junkshop and which, with a bit of trimming, fitted exactly. A pastoral scene, wintry and bright, with farm animals about the place and a man in a red cloak pulling a sledge laden with logs.

The floor she had painted with glue and sprinkled with sawdust, and in the middle had fixed a round mirror, from an old handbag, to make a frozen lake.

There were trees as well, twigs of evergreen fixed into old cotton reels, and they sparkled frostily because she had sprinkled them with Christmas glitter. For the dancers she had made tiny people out of pipe cleaners and cotton wool, and dressed them in bright snippets of ribbon and scraps of white net. Making the dancers had taken ages because they were fiddly, with their tiny painted features and embroidered hair.

But it was done. Finished. Only the lights to fix. She opened the bag, and carefully assembled all the bits and pieces that Mr Sims had so kindly found for her. This took some time and necessitated a journey downstairs to look for a screwdriver. When all was finally accomplished, she fastened the lights with their clips on either side of the little theatre and then plugged the long flex into the socket of her bedside lamp. She pressed the switch and the little lights came on but scarcely showed, so she turned off the main light and, in the darkness, turned to see the full effect.

Better than she had ever expected. Perfect. So real you could imagine the tiny floodlit figures were about to spring into dance, twirling fouettés across the sawdust floor.

After a bit, she put everything away, covered the theatre with the dust-sheet, adjusted the expression on her face and went downstairs.

"All right, darling?" said her mother.

"Yes, all right," Jenny replied, at her most unconcerned, and went to cut herself a slice of cake.

The best of Christmas was that it was always the same. Carols after supper on Christmas Eve, with Granny playing the piano for all of them, and then bed, and hanging up stockings, and thinking that you would never go to sleep. And then, when you stopped trying, finding yourself awake again, and the clock pointing to half past seven and the stocking bulging at the end of the bed.

Christmas was the smell of newly peeled tangerines, and

bacon and eggs for breakfast. It was walking to church in the bitter, frosty air and singing 'Hark, the Herald Angels Sing', which was Jenny's favourite. And talking to people outside the church after the service, and rushing home to see to the turkey and light all the fires.

And then, when everything was ready, Dad said, "Ready, Steady, GO!" and that was when they were allowed to fall on the presents piled beneath the tree.

Natasha's present had posed something of a problem. How to wrap up a theatre? In the end, Jenny had made a sort of tea-cosy of holly paper, and put this over the theatre and carried it carefully downstairs. Then placed it on the sideboard where nobody would walk on it.

But, for the moment, she forgot about the theatre in the excitement of her own presents. A new lamp for her bicycle, a Shetland sweater in pinks and blues, and a pair of black patent shoes that she had been yearning for. From Natasha, a book. From her godmother, a china mug with her name in gold. And from Granny ... a large square parcel, wrapped in red and white striped paper. Sitting on the floor, surrounded by the detritus of ribbons and packages and cards, Jenny undid it. The paper fell away, disclosing a large white box. More tissue paper. Skating boots.

Beautiful, new, white skating boots, the blades shining steel, and exactly the right size. Jenny gazed at them with a mixture of delight, because they were so fantastic, and apprehension at the thought of what she was expected to do with them.

"Oh, *Granny*."

Granny was watching her. Jenny scrambled up off the floor to go and hug her. "They're ... they're *wonderful*."

Granny's eyes met her own. Granny's eyes were old but very bright. They never missed a trick. Granny said, "You can't possibly skate in boots that don't fit you. I bought them yesterday, because I couldn't bear to think of you missing all the fun."

"We'll go skating this afternoon," Natasha announced firmly. "You've *got* to give it another try."

"Yes," said Jenny meekly. And, at that moment, remembered the theatre, the only gift still unopened. "But now you've got to open your present from me."

The grown-ups sat back in some anticipation. In truth, they could scarcely wait to see what Jenny had been constructing in the secrecy of her bedroom over the last few weeks.

Crouching, Jenny put the plug into the hot-plate socket. "Now, Natasha, you've got to take the paper off the *moment* I turn on the switch, otherwise it might catch fire."

"Heavens," said Granny in some dismay. "Do you suppose it's a volcano?"

"*Now!*" said Jenny, and turned on the switch. Natasha whisked off the paper tea-cosy, and there it was. With the lights twinkling on all the sparkly bits of glitter, shining back from the mirror pond, gleaming on the satin-ribbon skirts of the miniature ballerinas.

For a satisfactory space of time there was total silence. Then Natasha said, "I don't believe it," and everybody started to exclaim.

"Oh, darling! It's the cleverest thing. The prettiest . . ."

"Never seen anything so enchanting . . ."

"Is that what you wanted the wine box for?"

They rose from their chairs, came to inspect, to stand back, to wonder and admire. No audience could have been more appreciative. As for Natasha, for once she seemed to be lost for words. Finally she turned to her sister and hugged her. ". . . I shall keep it, always and always."

"It's not a real ballet. I mean, it's not La Fille Mal Gardée, or anything like that."

"I like it better that way. My very own winter ballet. I simply love it. Oh, thank you, Jenny. Thank you."

By four o'clock, Christmas dinner was finished and finally cleared away. Over for another year. The crackers pulled, the nuts cracked. Jenny's parents and grandmother were in the sitting-room, enjoying coffee before taking a little necessary exercise in the outdoor air. Natasha had already gone, her skates in her hand.

"Come on, Jenny, I'm ready," she had called up the stairs.

"I'll be there in a moment."

"What are you doing?"

Jenny was sitting on her bed. "Just tidying up."

"Shall I wait?"

"No. I'll be there in a moment."

"Promise?"

"Yes. I promise. I'll come."

"All right, then. See you later!"

The door banged shut and she had gone, running down the path to the gate. Jenny was alone. She had been given skates and she wished she hadn't been, because she couldn't skate. It wasn't that she didn't want to, but she was frightened. Not so much of falling and hurting herself, but of making an idiot of herself; of other people laughing at her; of having to come home and admit the usual utter failure.

'I want to be like Natasha,' she thought. But knew that this was impossible, because she could never be like Natasha. 'I want to float over the ice, and have long blonde hair and long slender legs and have everybody admire me, and want to skate with me.'

But, *Poor old Jenny* they would say, as she hit the ice yet another time. *Bad luck. Have another go.*

She would have given her soul simply to stay where she was, to curl up on her bed and read the new book that Natasha had given her. But she had promised. She picked up the skates and went out of her room and down the stairs, slowly, one step at a time, as though she had only just learned how to walk.

They were talking in the sitting-room. She heard Granny's voice, quite clearly, through the closed door.

". . . such a talented child. The hours she must have spent constructing that little masterpiece. And the thought and invention that went into it."

"She's always been good with her hands. Creative." That was Dad. And they were talking about her. "Perhaps she should have been born a boy."

"Oh, really, John, what a thing to say!" Granny sounded quite irritated by him. "Why shouldn't girls be good with their hands?"

"It's funny . . ." Jenny's mother, now, sounding thoughtful, "that two daughters should be so different. Natasha finding everything so easy. And Jenny . . ." Her voice trailed to nothing.

"Natasha finds everything easy to do that she *wants* to do." Granny again, at her most brisk. "Jenny is not Natasha. She is a different child. I think that you should respect that, and treat her as such. After all, they're not a pair of identical twins. Why should Jenny have to dance, just because Natasha sees herself as a budding ballerina? Why should she even have to go to dancing classes? I think that you should let her talents lead her in her *own* direction."

"Now, what do you mean by that, Mamma?"

"I listened to her when we were singing carols last night. It seems to me that she has almost perfect pitch. I think she is musical. It is strange that her teachers at school have not already realised this. Have you ever thought of piano lessons?"

There was a long pause and then Jenny's father said, "No." He didn't say it crossly, but rather as though he had never thought of such a thing, and couldn't think why he hadn't.

"Dancing, Jenny will never do more than galumph about with a tambourine. Let her learn the piano, see how she does."

"You think she'd like that? You think she'd be good at it?"

"A child so talented could do anything she tried if she set her heart to it. She just needs confidence. I think, if you change your tack with her, she'll surprise us all."

The voices stopped. A silence fell. At any moment, her mother would start setting the empty coffee-cups on the tray. Not wishing to be discovered, Jenny tiptoed down the last of the stairs and let herself out through the front door, making no sound. Down the path, through the gate, out on to the road.

She paused.

*Have you ever thought of piano lessons? Let her learn the piano.*

No more dancing lessons. Just herself, on her own, making music.

*A child so talented could do anything she tried if she set her heart to it.*

If Granny thought she was as clever as that, perhaps she could. And she had gone to so much trouble and expense to buy Jenny the skating boots for Christmas. The least Jenny could do was to have another try.

The orange sun was dipping down over the rim of the hills. From afar, across the frosty stillness of Christmas afternoon, she could hear the laughter and the voices from the village green. She began to walk.

When she got there, she didn't look for Natasha. She knew what she had to do, and she wanted to do it on her own.

"Hello, Jenny. Happy Christmas."

It was a school-friend, with a sledge. Jenny borrowed the sledge to sit on. She took off her rubber boots and put on

289

the beautiful, new, white skating boots. They felt soft and supple and, when she laced them, hugged her ankles like old friends. She stood up on the frozen grass and took a step or two. No wobbles. She reached the ice. Remembered Natasha's instructions: 'Put your feet in third position, and push off.' A bit unsteady, but she kept her balance. Now. Third position. A big breath for courage. She could do anything if she set her heart to it. Push. All right. Now the other foot . . .

It worked. She was away. She wasn't falling or waving her arms about. One, two. One, two. She was skating.

"You're doing it! You've got it!" Natasha, all at once, materialised at her side. "No, don't look at me, keep concentrating. You mustn't fall over. Look, take my hand and we'll go together. Well done! You remembered what I told you to do. It's easy. The only reason you couldn't do it before was because of those stupid old boots . . ."

They were skating together. Two sisters, with hands clasped and the icy air burning their cheeks. Sailing over the ice. It was like having wings on your feet. The sun was gone but over in the east, like a pale eyelash, hung the crescent of a young new moon.

"The present you gave me was the best I had," Natasha told her. "What was your best present?"

But Jenny couldn't tell her. Partly because she hadn't the breath to talk, and partly because she hadn't had time to work it out for herself yet. She only knew that it had not come in a package wrapped in holly paper, and that it was something she was going to be able to keep for the rest of her life.

## AVAILABLE FROM
## HODDER AND STOUGHTON PAPERBACKS

### ROSAMUNDE PILCHER

| | | |
|---|---|---|
| ☐ 54021 4 | The Blue Bedroom | £5.99 |
| ☐ 52115 5 | Another View | £5.99 |
| ☐ 52119 8 | The Day of the Storm | £5.99 |
| ☐ 52118 X | The Empty House | £5.99 |
| ☐ 52117 1 | The End of Summer | £4.99 |
| ☐ 49181 7 | The Shell Seekers | £6.99 |
| ☐ 52116 3 | Sleeping Tiger | £5.99 |
| ☐ 52120 1 | Wild Mountain Thyme | £5.99 |
| ☐ 55613 7 | The Rosamunde Pilcher Collection Vol 1 | £6.99 |
| ☐ 55636 1 | The Rosamunde Pilcher Collection Vol 2 | £6.99 |
| ☐ 54287 X | September | £5.99 |
| ☐ 64685 3 | Coming Home | £6.99 |

# ROSAMUNDE PILCHER

# THE SHELL SEEKERS

Artist's daughter Penelope Keeling can look back on a full and varied life: a Bohemian childhood in London and Cornwall, an unhappy wartime marriage, and the one man she truly loved. She has brought up three children – and learned to accept each of them as they are.

Yet she is far too energetic and independent to settle sweetly into pensioned-off old-age. And when she discovers that her most treasured possession, her father's painting, *The Shell Seekers*, is now worth a small fortune, it is Penelope who must make the decisions that will determine whether her family can continue to survive as a family, or be split apart.

'A deeply satisfying story written with love and confidence'
    Maeve Binchy, in the *New York Times Book Review*

'A long, beguiling saga, typically English . . . splendid'
    *The Mail on Sunday*

HODDER

# ROSAMUNDE PILCHER

## SEPTEMBER

As spring comes to Scotland and the hills burst into life, a dance is planned for September. The invitations summon home the group of people Violet Aird has cared for most in her long life.

The oldest, strongest and wisest of them all, she sees Alexa, her vulnerable granddaughter, find love for the first time, while the decision to send her little grandson away to school is driving parents Edmund and Virginia even further apart. Far from them all is Pandora, the glamorous, exciting girl who ran away twenty years before. All will converge in Scotland this September.

'Wonderful, evocative and inviting'

*Woman and Home*

'Very special indeed'

*Books*

'Beautifully captures the magic of north-of-the-border country'

*Sunday Telegraph*

HODDER

# ROSAMUNDE PILCHER

## COMING HOME

'The novel has a gently sweet flavour, it continues to beguile because of Pilcher's warmth, sincerity and easy, undemanding prose'

*The Sunday Times*

'Compelling pages packed with convincing characters, vivid settings and weepy bits'

*Daily Mail*

'A great featherbed of a novel, all the right ingredients'
*Woman and Home*

'Especially good on atmosphere and a lonely teenager's bewilderment, Pilcher's storytelling skills are serene and beguiling'

*The Times*

'Much-needed balm to soothe the troubled mind'
*Sunday Express*

'A well-upholstered good read'

*Daily Mail*

'Classy, lavish entertainment . . . literate pleasure'
*Publishers Weekly*

HODDER